AN OXFORD FRAUD

An utterly gripping page-turner

FAITH MARTIN

writing as

MAXINE BARRY

Originally published as *Altered Images*

Revised edition published 2020
Joffe Books, London
www.joffebooks.com

First published in Great Britain 2001
as *Altered Images*

© Maxine Barry 2001, 2020

**Please join our mailing list for free Kindle books
and new releases.**

www.joffebooks.com

We love to hear from our readers! Please email any
feedback you have to: feedback@joffebooks.com

ISBN 978-1-78931-587-5

For my sister Marion,
the true artist of the family.

CHAPTER 1

It was early May, and almond and cherry trees competed with ancient wisteria and cheerful laburnums to spread colour and bees along the city of London's Belgravia pavements. A 1968 silver Aston Martin slowed as it approached the discreet entrance to the Greene Gallery. Steered down a narrow side alley, it halted beside a locked steel door, and Lorcan Greene got out, easing his six-foot-two-inch frame from the low bucket seat with a lithe ease that was almost feline.

As he strode briskly but easily to the side door, the afternoon sunshine lovingly touched the dark blond of his hair, turning it into the colour of ripe wheat. Inside, he sprinted lightly up a few steps and on to the main floor, where four big windows allowed in the bright, natural light. Large groups of extremely comfortable chairs littered the floor space, along with big flowering ferns. Five huge magnificent abstract canvases hung on the pure white walls, attracting the attention of passers-by.

The receptionist, Moira, who was infatuated with her boss, looked up, her eyes softening as she recognised him. 'Mr Greene. I didn't know you were coming in today,' she purred, surreptitiously patting the back of her chignon.

Lorcan strolled towards her, dressed in a slate-grey suit that could only have come from one of the best tailors in Savile Row. His shoes were hand-crafted, black Italian leather, his gold wristwatch Swiss. Hazel eyes swept over Moira, noting with approval her well-cut navy-blue suit, the neat hair and discreet pearl stud earrings. The Greene Gallery was known to be a class act, from its address to linen hand-towels in the public washrooms.

'I had a call from Basil Armitage this morning,' Lorcan explained, naming a very rich and well-known patron of the arts. 'He's coming in for a private viewing,' he checked his wristwatch, 'in about half an hour, so I think a selection of coffees and aperitifs is called for. All right?'

Moira readily agreed that that would present no problems, and Lorcan turned away, walking through several more hushed rooms, nodding amiably at the smartly uniformed security guards as he went. Each room was small, temperature-controlled, and had the finest art hung on its walls. As well as human watchdogs, each room was fitted with the latest security devices. Since Lorcan Greene had inherited the rather shabby, slightly run-down gallery from its previous owner, no single work of art had ever been stolen, and he aimed to keep it that way.

He noticed the Duchess of Avonsleigh in the Landscape Gallery avidly inspecting his newest acquisition — a small but charming Constable. It had a price tag of £1.3 million on it.

'Good afternoon, your grace,' he murmured quietly from the arched entrance. The elderly woman quickly turned and smiled at him, her wrinkled face lighting up flirtatiously. She quite liked square-jawed men who had a dashing dimple in the middle of their chins, and also rather admired his high cheekbones, strong, straight nose and fine white teeth. Ah, if only she'd been twenty . . . well . . . thirty years younger.

'Lorcan, how lovely to see you again. I was just admiring your latest find. How on earth did you manage to get it?' she asked curiously.

Lorcan, accepting the unspoken invitation to dally, stepped smoothly into the quiet room. 'Ah, now that would be telling,' he teased, his eyes twinkling. 'Persuasion is such a . . . personal thing, don't you think?'

The duchess adored being flirted with, but she was also a very astute businesswoman who ran her husband's vast estates with a hand of iron, and now she regarded Lorcan with a speculative gleam in her eye.

Like everyone else interested in the art world, she knew the story of Lorcan Greene's meteoric rise to fame and riches, for it was romantic and daring, and just the material that modern legends were made of.

He'd gone to work for old Samuel Goldberg as a sixteen-year-old school leaver with virtually no qualifications, no social standing, and no idea about art. Nobody understood what had prompted the old man to teach him everything he knew and, since the Goldberg Gallery had been no competition for the top London galleries, nobody had really paid much attention.

But that had quickly began to change, for contrary to all expectations, the young Lorcan Greene, son of an East End dustman and a barmaid, soaked up the old man's knowledge like a sponge. It took him less than four years to learn the business inside and out, until eventually Samuel entrusted him with the buying of original works, as well as classics.

Lorcan's choice of paintings shook the London art world to its foundations — mainly because they were so innovative, clever and uncannily spot on. He seemed almost psychic in his abilities to pick out the unknown artists who had 'it', the artists whose works would only rise in monetary terms. Consequently, it didn't take long for the art-buying public and professional speculators alike to realise that the Goldberg Gallery was now *the* place to buy modern art.

When Samuel Goldberg died, nobody was surprised either by the depth of Lorcan's mourning (for he'd come to love the old man like a grandfather) or by the fact that Samuel left him the entire gallery, lock, stock and Salvador Dalí.

Lorcan had wasted no time in spending some of his working capital on the gallery itself, renovating it inside and out. He'd hired new staff, embraced the technological age and within two years had succeeded in putting the gallery firmly on the map. So now nobody was surprised when hotly pursued pieces found their way on to the walls of the newly renamed 'Greene Gallery'.

The duchess was well aware of Lorcan's reputation as something of a shark at auctions, knowing just the right moment to enter into the bidding and, perhaps even more crucially, when to pull out. He was ruthless in the pursuit of professional private collectors who had pieces to sell, but always played fair, especially with the general public. She also knew that he'd made it a policy very early on always to explain to the unwary and uninitiated the true value of what they had. The result, of course, had been inevitable. In a world of unfair business practices, Lorcan Greene was one of the few art dealers people actively sought out when they were selling the odd family piece or two. So it was that the Greene Gallery often had first pickings of the new finds.

Such as the Constable the duchess was admiring now.

Not that Lorcan would ever admit to her that he'd acquired the painting by the simple expedient of answering a rather diffident letter from the widow of a merchant seaman, who'd sent him a photograph of the painting. Of course, he hadn't been able to tell much from that, but it had sent a curious tingle down his spine, telling him that it might just be worth the train trip.

And his hunches were seldom wrong.

'So, how did you come by it?' the duchess pressed again, but Lorcan merely shrugged his shoulders elegantly.

'Trade secret,' he whispered, then smoothly got down to business.

Not that he seemed to, of course. But he knew that she couldn't really afford the Constable, and she knew that he knew. But there was no embarrassment on either side, which said much for Lorcan's powers of discretion, tact and charm. Instead, very cleverly, he began to steer her towards a cheaper but utterly charming Cezanne, and thus became nearly a quarter of a million pounds richer.

* * *

With no classic sports car at his disposal, Detective Inspector Richard Braine of the Art Fraud Squad travelled by unmarked police car to Lorcan Greene's Belgravia apartment. For Lorcan had a second string to his bow, and one that was relatively well known to his acquaintances and those members of the public interested in art fraud. Namely, Lorcan was a celebrated fake-buster.

The police had first had dealings with him when an unwary faker had attempted to sell him a forged painting, supposedly by Hobbema, the artist famous for *The Avenue at Middelharnis*. It had been a very good forgery indeed, but it had taken Lorcan only a few minutes to spot it.

Richard had been the officer in charge and, with Lorcan's testimony, the forger got five years. Ever since then, whenever Richard needed an expert opinion it was to Lorcan Greene that he invariably came, and the two had become firm friends.

Greene's reputation as an expert in this field had quickly grown, and now everyone in the trade, whenever in doubt about the provenance or authenticity of a painting that their own experts couldn't agree on, came to Lorcan Greene. His fees were high but, so far, he'd never been proved wrong in his assessment of a work of art.

'Richard,' Lorcan smiled but glanced very discreetly at his watch as he opened the apartment door.

'You're just off out,' Richard Braine said apologetically. 'Who is it this time? Still the actress?'

Lorcan's short-lived affairs, Richard knew, were with women invariably of a type — independent, successful, wealthy and sophisticated.

Lorcan laughed. 'No, she's been lured to Hollywood. Come on in. I've got half an hour to spare.'

The flat was beautiful. The large living area was decorated in neutrals, but a single colourful Monet adorned one of the walls, transforming it. An open window offered a panoramic view of the city. Richard sat in a big black leather armchair, saying nothing as the art expert poured him, without asking, a fine malt whisky, just how he liked it.

During his time in the squad, the detective knew that he'd picked up more than his fair share of knowledge about art, but he also knew, without rancour, that his expertise was as nothing compared to that of the man he was here to see.

Lorcan possessed an instinctive, almost mystical sense of what was right and what was not. It couldn't be taught — only perfected. And it was probably what Samuel Goldberg had spotted in him all those years ago.

'So,' Lorcan said softly, sitting opposite his old friend and lazily swirling a deep-coloured burgundy in a large glass. 'What can I do for you this time?'

Lorcan had, of course, lost his cockney accent a long time ago. Now he not only dressed in style, lived-in style, ate, drank and partied in style, he *was* style. But Richard also knew him as a man who was warm and generous. Lorcan's parents, for example, now lived very happily in a villa in Portugal. He was, without doubt, the kind of man you could always turn to in times of need.

Lorcan raised an eyebrow in query, and Richard suddenly grinned. 'If I said Oxford to you, what would come immediately to mind?'

Unfazed, Lorcan shrugged slightly. 'Dreaming spires. Great university. Some great art. Apart from that . . .' he shrugged again, and took a sip of the wine.

'What do you know about the Ruskin?' Richard changed tactics slightly, and Lorcan's hazel eyes immediately sharpened with interest.

'The Ruskin School of Art,' Lorcan mused. 'Located on the High Street, not far from Magdalen Bridge. It's the university's Fine Art department. Its head is still, I believe, the very splendid and able Stephen Farthing.'

Richard nodded, and took a deep breath. 'I've arranged for you to have a visiting fellowship there for the rest of the summer term,' he stated boldly, and shot his friend a challenging look.

Lorcan's lips twisted. 'In Oxford, the summer term is called Trinity Term,' he corrected mildly.

Anybody else would have reacted angrily to such high-handedness, but Lorcan Greene was not like anybody else that Richard had ever known. He had a deep dislike for art fraudsters and, for a multi-millionaire, he was surprisingly helpful and generous to the police when it came to giving up his valuable time and energy.

'So what's up?' Lorcan asked simply.

Richard gazed silently into space for several moments and then began to talk in a slow, thoughtful voice. 'A few months ago we began to hear rumours that somebody, somewhere in Oxford is planning a big coup. We're not sure whether it's a theft or an attempt to sell a forgery. But, according to one of our more knowledgeable informers, we should take a special interest in the Ruskin. Specifically one of the students.'

Lorcan frowned, as his deep, well-modulated voice rose a scant octave. 'Ruskin undergraduates are more interested in pushing the boundaries of art than anything else. Besides, it would take an exceptional student indeed to be of use to a serious forger.'

'I know. I'm not so sure that Skeeter Smith, the inform-ant, isn't leading us around by the nose,' Richard mused. 'But on the chance that he's right, I want you to go down there. Just think of the cachet: a visiting fellowship to Oxford University, no less.'

Lorcan grunted, unimpressed. On the other hand, he *did* enjoy bringing down the parasites in the art world who preyed so readily on the unwary. 'All right,' he agreed, with an apparent reluctance that didn't fool the policeman for a minute. 'I'll do it.'

Selling the Constable to Sir Basil that morning had been a very satisfactory experience. But bringing an art forger — or art thief — to book, would be infinitely more satisfying still.

'You know,' he murmured softly, drinking the last of his exquisite wine with relish, 'I've always wanted to get to know Oxford better.'

CHAPTER 2

Raymond Verney unlocked the door to an empty, unfurnished flat in London's East End, and sighed deeply. He glanced at his watch, supposed glumly that the first members of the cast would straggle in shortly, and started pinning several sheets of paper on to the grubby walls.

He'd been hired by a publishing company holding a summer conference at St Bede's College, Oxford, to set up a murder-mystery weekend. Ray was a jack-of-all-trades, and hiring a cast of actors, writing their scenes, and concocting a believable murder mystery had taken him only a matter of a few weeks. It was, however, the hidden agenda that worried him.

Ray had, in his time, done many things that less liberal-minded people would have considered criminal. But nothing violent — a clever computer swindle or two, a property scam here and there. And since meeting up with a talented forger, the selling on of a dodgy painting or two. Ray knew people who knew people, and prided himself on being a creative kind of crook. He was a portly, amiable-looking man, with white hair thinning into a fringe just above his ears, leaving the top of his head shiny and bald. His eyes were a twinkling, easy-going blue. He spoke with a warmth and sincerity that fooled everyone — at first!

He'd never been to prison, though he'd come close once or twice, mainly because he preferred to be the anonymous middle man. But this time it was different. This job was like no other he'd ever tried to pull. And that's what was worrying him. That, plus the fact that he didn't trust his 'client'.

The man was cool, clever, and quite obsessed. He made Ray very nervous indeed. Especially since he insisted on being in at the kill, so to speak.

Ray sighed heavily and began to rehearse his welcome speech to the cast of actors due to arrive at any minute, plus an explanation of the murder-mystery weekend.

It was important to Ray that the weekend conference ran smoothly. Nobody must suspect that all wasn't as it should be. These actors, for instance, must have no idea that this particular gig would be different from any others they might have previously done.

To accomplish that, he had to act like a pro — as a proper producer, director and organiser — which would be easy enough for a man of Ray's talents. He'd even written the perfect plot to cover the real felony that was going to take place within St Bede's hallowed halls.

The conference itself, of course, was strictly legitimate, and the delegates would be encouraged to play Miss Marple or Sherlock Holmes to their hearts' content.

It was what was going on behind the scenes that worried Ray. For this time he was not going to be in the background — if something went wrong, it would be his head on the chopping block.

But the pay-off was so huge it was worth the risk. And the scam itself was so simple, so easy, that he wasn't seriously worried. This plan was one of Ray's best, right down to the finest detail.

And when he'd heard that the Art Fraud Squad had caught a sniff of something, he'd even fed that stool pigeon Skeeter Smith a false lead about the Ruskin School of Art. No, he'd left nothing to chance. Even so . . . he was worried.

He'd be glad when it was all over and he need have nothing more to do with his client ever again.

The door opened, making Ray jump. 'Er, is this the murder-mystery rehearsal?' a pretty blonde asked warily.

'That's right. I'm Ray Verney, the producer. And you are?'

'Julie Morris.'

'Right.' He ticked her off his list. 'You're playing one of the suspects. Not the killer or victim I'm afraid.'

And so it began. One by one the struggling, hard-up actors and actresses arrived. Tall, sandy-haired Gordon Fleming was cast as the policeman. Geraldine Edwards, a well-preserved redhead, was to play the wife of one of the murder victims. The oldest of the suspects, Norman Rix, was pleasantly greying and still handsome at fifty, while John Lore, a dark young man, was signed up as the first murder victim.

Some of the more experienced knew that weekend shows required living and working closely together, and everything went a lot more smoothly if you made friends. So by the time Annis Whittington walked in, the room was crowded, much warmer than it had been, and noisily filled with chat and gossip about 'the business'.

'I heard she only got the part because of her sister. You know, they wanted the name, but of course they couldn't afford the real thing. Still, the younger sister is nearly as pretty . . .'

Annis smiled at the two women who were talking about the latest English film to do well in America, and looked around. She quickly picked out Ray Verney.

'Hello, m'dear,' Ray beamed at her as she approached, ticking her name off his checklist. 'You must be Annis? Oh good — you're the killer.'

Annis laughed. 'Really?' She rubbed her hands together. 'I've always wanted to play a homicidal maniac!'

Ray quite liked actors — they were all so self-absorbed for one thing. All the better for him! Not one of them was

11

going to be much interested in what the producer got up to behind the scenes.

Ray's gaze lingered on her face as Annis smiled. Her flowing black hair was very appealing, and her eyes . . . Ray blinked in surprise. They were a strange, tawny, almost amber colour. Very striking. If he'd been a film producer, he would have been excited by those eyes. The woman certainly had . . . something.

'Who do I get to kill?' Annis asked, and several of the others looked up and grinned at her.

'Me, for one,' the actor playing the first murder victim spoke up, his eyes caressing as they ran over her. Annis glanced his way. From the way he smiled at her she guessed he was far too vain to be of any interest. She smiled politely.

'And your other victim hasn't arrived yet,' Ray noted with a slight scowl. 'Reeve Morgan.'

Annis frowned. She'd heard that name before somewhere. A faint prickle at the back of her neck told her that what she'd heard hadn't been flattering either. Reeve Morgan . . .

'Hello. I'm Julie.' A pretty blonde girl introduced herself. 'This is Gerry.'

'Hello. Annis Whittington. Have you ever done one of these things before?'

'I haven't, no.' Julie yawned and glanced at her watch. 'I thought we were supposed to get started at eight?'

Annis's own watch told her that it was already twenty past. She shrugged. 'We're missing one of our number. Reeve Morgan.'

'Reeve Morgan?' Gerry said sharply. 'Really? Too small potatoes for him I would have thought.'

'Oh?' Annis asked, raising one black eyebrow inquisitively. 'I thought his name sounded familiar . . .'

'He wrote a radio drama which was aired not so long ago.'

'That's right,' Julie said. 'I remember listening to it now.'

'It was good,' Gerry agreed. 'I suppose that's why the director cast him in the leading role.'

Annis's lips twisted. 'Very clever,' she said dryly. She herself had no talent in the screenwriting department, although she knew a lot of actors who dabbled in it. 'What's the betting he's recently written a murder-mystery screenplay?' she asked, looking at Gerry, who smiled at her knowingly. 'And what's the betting there's someone at this conference who's acquiring drama for television companies?'

'I've heard something else about him too,' Julie mused. 'Didn't someone say . . . ? I know! Isn't his father stinking rich?'

Annis smiled bitterly. The thought of rich, good-looking young men just waltzing through life, taking everything for granted, really got her goat.

Gerry coughed. It was a strange, choking-like cough, and Annis glanced at her in surprise.

'I daresay his father knows somebody in television, too,' Annis carried on. 'No doubt he's asked some old school friend of his to give his son's screenplay the once-over . . .'

Julie had begun to turn a distinct shade of red. That was odd for someone so very fair, and Annis glanced at her, puzzled. Then she became aware that everyone else had stopped speaking.

And then, slowly, Annis felt the colour ebb away from her face. Agonisingly, she glanced at Gerry, who gave an almost imperceptible nod and looked away.

Annis took a deep breath, and slowly turned around.

Standing right behind her was the most handsome man Annis had ever seen. He was about six feet tall, with dark brown hair which curled loosely. Everything about him screamed classical good looks — from the strong chin, to the straight, well-shaped nose, to the full but tightly moulded lips. His eyes were the deepest blue she'd ever seen. There was obviously some Celtic ancestry somewhere in his blood. Right now, those eyes were boring into her like lasers. He looked well-heeled. Successful. Too handsome for words. And angry.

And he had to be — could only be — Reeve Morgan.

And Annis knew with a sinking heart that he must have heard every derogatory word she'd been saying about him. She felt her chin angle up in mute challenge. Her tawny eyes flashed. She was damned if she was going to cringe with embarrassment or apologise. Even if she was in the wrong! She held out her hand. It was perfectly steady. 'Hello. You must be Reeve Morgan?' she asked coolly.

Reeve looked down at the hand she held out, and found himself taking it. Her grip was surprisingly firm.

When he'd walked in and heard himself being bad-mouthed, he'd found himself anticipating the black-haired woman's grovelling apology. But she looked about as embarrassed as an ice queen.

He looked into the level, unbelievably lovely eyes. They seemed to trap his breath somewhere between his lungs and his throat. Damn her, did she have to look so . . . amused?

'Yes. I'm Reeve Morgan,' he agreed, his voice cold and uncompromising. 'And you are . . . ?'

'Annis Whittington.'

'Annis,' he echoed grimly. And managed a smile — a simple flash of perfect white teeth. 'You obviously know my family background right down to my very rich father. By the way, he made his fortune in car parts.'

Annis forced herself not to blush. It was only because she was such a good actress that she managed it. 'How nice for you,' she said sweetly.

'And he did, as it happens, give me a loan to see me through my training. Anything else you'd like to know?' he asked grittily.

Annis's chin lifted yet another inch in defiance. As the rest of the cast held their breath, waiting for an explosion, Reeve wondered what those flashing tawny eyes would look like, sleepy and sated after a night of passionate lovemaking . . . He felt his body stir, and firmly held it in check.

Annis ignored the voice at the back of her mind that insisted she owed him an apology. Instead she asked coolly,

'Yes. Just one thing. Do you have a screenplay you're hoping to sell at this murder weekend?'

And suddenly it was Reeve's turn to use every ounce of his acting skill; to keep the tell-tale shocked reaction off his face. Because she had him, fair and square. He *was* hoping to sell a screenplay he'd written to one of the literary agents at the conference. Not that he'd ever admit it now. He'd rather undergo torture than admit anything to this tawny-eyed virago!

He allowed himself a single, cool, mockingly superior smile. Then, with some effort, dragged himself away. He left Annis standing there, fuming, and walked towards Ray Verney. As he did so, he could feel her eyes boring into his back.

What a sharp-tongued, evil-minded . . . beautiful, interesting woman . . .

CHAPTER 3

Second-year student Frederica Delacroix pushed open one of the two heavy wooden doors of the Ruskin School of Art and found herself in a tiny space with eggshell-blue walls and two other doors facing her, giving way to a black-and-white tiled hall. She paused in the entrance foyer as she noticed that a new exhibit had gone up: the work of a photographer.

She sprinted up the concrete stairs to the second floor and glanced into the studio to see whether anybody was about. Nobody was. It was only nine-thirty in the morning, and most of her fellow artists were late risers. She carried on up to the top floor, where her small workspace, shared with three others, waited for her.

Frederica uncovered her easel and, with a rubber band, gathered her tightly curled, long auburn hair off her face and into a rather becoming ponytail. She reached for her smock, which smelt of linseed oil, as her deep velvet brown eyes assessed her work in progress. She looked even taller than her five feet eight, possibly because she had that particular kind of slender build that made her seem willowy. At only twenty, she carried herself with the confidence of a much older woman, but a smattering of freckles ran across the bridge of her nose like impudent childish memories. Men found the combination irresistible. Not that she ever noticed male appreciation.

From the age of five, her ambition had been to break through the male-dominated world of painting to become a respected, noted artist. She therefore had little time or inclination to pursue such feminine things as trendy hairstyles, fashionable clothes, make-up or men. It would have annoyed many women to see how she wore the old canvas smock as if it were a designer original. Her skin, the fair, creamy pale colour of camellias, didn't need cosmetics. Her hair, a Titian cascade of rich auburn which had never felt a hairdresser's scissors, would have made an advertising mogul drool.

But Frederica had eyes only for her latest canvas.

It was a depiction of a semi-detached house on a council estate, poverty-stricken and lived-in. The bumper of an old car was in the foreground. A satellite dish was on the wall of the neighbouring house. A cat slept on the roof of the porch. Nearing completion, even a novice could tell that it was extremely well-painted. The cat was black and white, and Frederica was just in the process of giving it whiskers. It was so real that anyone looking at the painting could almost hear it purr out loud. The liquidity of the bones, the upturned chin, were so . . . feline. It was an hour before Frederica finally stepped back, looking at her work, wondering if it really was good or if she was only fooling herself. She removed the smock, glancing at her watch as she did so.

It was Friday, and she had no tutorials until Monday, so she left, trotting lightly back down the stairs. In the Hall, a first-year student stopped, his eyes lighting up. Tim Gregson was good-looking — and he knew it. All dark hair, grey eyes and flashing grin. 'Hello there, gorgeous.'

Frederica gave him a good-humoured if slightly jaded smile.

'Fancy coming with me to check out that new jazz club?' he asked, leaning as close to her as he could get without being obvious about it.

Frederica took a hasty step back. 'No thanks. Busy.' She quickly cast about for something to take his mind off his libido. 'How are Prelims going?' she asked, and watched his face tighten in apprehension.

The three-year Bachelor of Fine Arts course at the Ruskin was divided into distinct stages — the first year being the hardest, for it was then that every student had to pass exams in no fewer than six disciplines: painting, drawing, print-making, sculpture, human anatomy and art history. In the second year, students chose one or two areas to concentrate on. The third year was then taken up with building a body of work for the Final Degree Show.

Tim Gregson gulped as he contemplated exams. 'Oh, all right, I think. It's the drawing I'm worried about. Sculpture is more my line.'

Frederica nodded, not without sympathy, and managed to slip away. If she'd been paying more attention to the noticeboard, she would have noted the imminent arrival of a visiting fellow — the eminent art expert and gallery owner Lorcan Greene. But she didn't see it, however, and instead strolled back to St Bede's.

Situated just off St Giles', St Bede's was a large college, with three big student residences. As she made her way to her pleasant room in Walton, overlooking the Fellows' Garden with its impressive silver birches, she began to smile. Life was looking good. She was on her way. She had all but waltzed through her Prelims, and had no doubt about her choice of future discipline. Her tutor was in complete agreement with her: Frederica Delacroix had been born to paint. She was one of those students tutors lived for — an obvious, stunning talent.

Frederica packed a small overnight case, and as it was a fine day, she decided to walk to the train station. Her home was a small village in Gloucestershire on the edge of the Cotswolds, and it was prime landscape-painting country. The train was on time and the journey was relatively short.

When she alighted, carrying her case with carefree ease, it was barely one o'clock.

As she walked up a narrow lane frothing with cow parsley, she noticed with pleasure that the swallows had arrived. Rainbow House, the Delacroix family home for centuries, was on the very outskirts of Cross Keys, and was a sturdy, square, no-nonsense country gentleman's residence; her heart lifted when she turned the last bend in the narrow country lane and saw it. Her mother, a keen gardener, kept the colourful walled garden in immaculate condition.

She walked through the gate that led to the west side of the house, glancing up at the dormer windows on the second floor as she did so. She coveted that corner room — dual aspect, meaning it got both morning and afternoon sunlight. It would make a perfect artist's studio. Now that her father was finally convinced she was going to be a painter, it wouldn't take much to persuade him to convert the room for her.

'Frederica! Darling! I didn't know you were coming home for the weekend!' The voice came from a big clump of beautifully scented white peonies. Closer inspection revealed Donna Delacroix, Frederica's mother, on her hands and knees, pulling up some recalcitrant groundsel.

'I did tell you,' Frederica said mildly with a fond smile. Her mother's memory had nothing on a sieve!

'Oh, yes, I suppose you did.' Donna stood and hugged her daughter. 'Do you want some lunch?'

'Ooh, yes please,' Frederica said, following her mother into the cool, terracotta-tiled farmhouse kitchen. She ran up to her room to unpack and freshen up, and when she came back down, the kettle was boiling merrily.

Donna was a small, neat, utterly English country lady. She worked in a charity shop two days a week, was a member of her local Women's Institute and took pride in her home and garden — opening both to the public in the summer to raise money for charity.

Her mother rushed off after lunch to join one of her friends in a baking marathon for the forthcoming village fete, so Frederica had the whole afternoon to herself, spending some of it in the small but well-stocked library and the rest of it walking in the bluebell woods at the furthest boundary of her father's small plot of land. When she returned, the church clock was just striking five. Surprisingly, her father's car was already parked in the driveway. He was a solicitor, and was rarely home at such a respectable hour.

James Delacroix was sitting in his favourite chair, smoking his pipe, when Frederica whirled into his study.

'Freddy!' He regarded his only child with affection, expecting, and receiving, an embrace and a kiss on the cheek.

'Dad.' Frederica stood back, her head cocked to one side. 'You're home early.'

James coughed. 'Er . . . yes. Your mother is out, isn't she?'

Frederica suspected that he already knew the answer. She smiled. 'Yes, she is.'

James grunted, looked at his pipe, looked at his daughter, coughed again, and stuck the pipe in his mouth. 'How's school?' he mumbled around it.

He always insisted on referring to her studies at Oxford as 'being at school'. He'd never really approved of her choice of career, but when she'd won a place at the prestigious Ruskin, he'd become resigned to his fate of having an artist for a daughter. Not that Frederica could blame him for having doubts. Despite being only tenuously related to the great nineteenth-century French artist Eugène Delacroix, several members of her family had, in the past, tried their hands at painting — with only one or two having met with even modest success.

In the Victorian era, an ancestor had begun collecting paintings, and his descendants had caught the bug, the result being that Rainbow House now possessed some very fine paintings, as well as some mediocre ones and some that made Frederica cringe with embarrassment! In addition, scattered among these paintings were Delacroix family originals, most of which were quite dreadful.

So when his only daughter had announced, at the age of five, that she was going to be a famous artist, it was hardly surprising that James Delacroix had hoped she'd grow out of it. But she hadn't. Now, with her tutor's recent endorsements still echoing in his ears, James Delacroix was hoping that Freddy's artistic expertise could come in downright useful.

'Dad . . .' Frederica said cautiously. 'Is something wrong?' She knew that sheepish look on his face only too well.

James sighed. 'Come with me,' he said, leading her to the blue salon, which appeared much as it always had: good, solid country furniture, fine but faded velvet curtains, and the usual Rainbow House mix of paintings — the good, the bad and the ugly. Frederica immediately noticed the gap on the wall and quickly pointed it out.

James blushed, making Frederica stare at him in amazement. 'Dad?' she said, her voice sounding sharper than she'd intended.

James sighed. 'It's the Forbes-Wright.'

Frederica's eyes widened. Forbes-Wright was a local artist, who had died in 1882. He'd recently begun to become quite collectable — quite rightly, in her opinion. The painting was of the old mill house, right here in Cross Keys village. A pretty little painting, complete with a pair of inquisitive swans and some exquisitely painted willow trees.

'I've told your mother it's being cleaned. We've got the Society of Art Appreciation coming this August,' James Delacroix mumbled unhappily. 'But it isn't.' As his daughter turned to look at him questioningly, he added helpfully, 'Being cleaned, I mean. I sold it.' He said the last three words in a rush, as if expecting a storm.

Frederica was too surprised to be angry. It was an unspoken rule that the family works of art were never, ever sold! James blushed again. 'I had to do it, Freddy. It was the kitchen roof. So much expense, all at once. I had no choice.'

Last winter, due to a leaking roof, the kitchen had required a completely new ceiling. No doubt it had been expensive.

Frederica shrugged, a little sadly. She'd been fond of the painting. 'Never mind, Dad,' she said softly. 'It obviously couldn't be helped.' Then she turned sharply. 'Wait a minute . . . You told Mum that it was being cleaned?'

James nodded.

'But, when she learns the truth . . . ?'

'She'll hit the roof,' James supplied, and it was no understatement.

Donna was not at all artistically minded, but was very, very protective of the Delacroixs' reputation as collectors.

'But she'll find out!' Frederica gasped, dismayed. 'Who did you sell it to?'

'A man called Horace King. He's a recluse, lives up in Cumbria. He's rumoured to have a vast collection, but nobody's ever seen it. He won't even admit he's got the Forbes-Wright. So there's no reason for your mother ever to know. Is there?' James smiled in enquiry.

Frederica stared at the blank space on the wall, then at her father's anxious eyes. 'But don't you think she might begin to wonder when it doesn't come back from the cleaners?'

James stared down at his feet, at his scuffed leather shoes, and coughed. 'Well, Freddy . . .' he began, looking at his daughter pleadingly, 'I rather hoped you might do a copy of it for me.'

CHAPTER 4

Frederica gaped at her father, her jaw falling open. 'What?' she squeaked. 'You want me to do what . . . ?'

Her father flushed at the sight of her incredulous face and hung his head. 'Really, Freddy, it's not as if we'd be doing something illegal, is it? We're only going to have a reproduction made to hang on our own walls, for personal viewing. And, naturally, we won't be claiming the Forbes-Wright to be authentic.'

Frederica shot him a grim look. 'But, Dad, I can't produce a copy just like that!'

'Can't you?' her father asked innocently. 'I thought your tutor said that you could paint. I mean *really* paint.'

Frederica, seeing the stubborn look on her father's usually placid face, took a deep breath. 'Dad, it's not a question of *can* I do it, it's a question of *should* I do it,' she told him firmly. 'And the answer has to be no.'

'But, Freddy,' James wheedled, 'so long as we don't intend to sell the painting on then where's the harm?'

Frederica shook her head. 'And it's not as if I can just get a canvas and start painting *The Old Mill and Swans*,' she pointed out prosaically. 'I'd need good photographs of it . . .'

'Ah, I've already thought about that.' James walked to a bureau and extracted several true-to-size photographs of the Forbes-Wright painting. 'I had photographs taken when we changed insurance companies. Remember?' he prompted.

'Yes, but—'

'And there's this.' James reached for a large coffee-table book. In it was yet another picture of *The Old Mill and Swans* by Forbes-Wright, together with a neatly printed history of the painting. Forbes-Wright, who'd lived in Gloucestershire all his life, had painted the picture at the age of twenty-eight. He was a fast painter, with a charming freestyle brushstroke that was quite distinctive.

That would make it easier to capture, wouldn't it? If she could just get the movement right . . . Frederica shook her head vigorously.

'Dad, it's not possible. I would need a canvas of the same age, for a start. And modern paints just wouldn't be the same. You're asking the impossible!' But it was such a fantastic idea. The thought of even trying was . . . seductive.

'If you think it's too much for you . . .' James said, with a casual shrug. His daughter's dark eyes flashed. Then she smiled, and wagged an admonishing finger at him.

'Oh no you don't. You go and try your reverse psychology on someone else. I'm not doing it! Besides,' she carried on, 'a good oil painting can take anything from six months to two years to dry completely. So supposing that I did make a perfect copy, not even I could wave a magic wand and dry it out in time.'

James smiled slyly. 'Your mother wouldn't know it was wet though, would she? I mean, it'd be dry to the touch within a fortnight. She's not going to investigate it more thoroughly than that — why would she?'

Did he never give up? 'NO!' she said firmly.

James Delacroix sighed. 'So it looks as if I'm going to have to face the music after all. Your mother will kill me,' he added pathetically.

But Frederica wasn't fooled. By the time she took the train back to Oxford on Monday morning, James still hadn't admitted his sins to his wife. But if he thought his daughter would change her mind, he had another think coming!

* * *

When Frederica's tutor finally left for the Ashmolean Museum print room, she quickly descended to the library beside the admin offices, which consisted of just six rows of grey metal shelves. She easily found a book on Tom Keating, the famous art forger, and was leaning against the wall, deeply into it, when she heard vague murmurings from the office. It sounded as though quite a crowd was gathering. But she ignored the buzz of conversation and concentrated on the fascinating world of art forgery. Keating had been a prince among forgers, and one of his tips was to paint at the same speed as the original artist. He'd also gone to extraordinary lengths to eliminate all personal habits when working, thus leaving no tell-tale signs for experts to identify.

It was nearly noon by the time she put the book thoughtfully away and returned to her own workspace, barely acknowledging the distracted greetings of her fellow students.

As she approached her own little cubbyhole, she felt a small trickle of excitement climb up her spine. Keating had made it all seem so feasible. Her latest canvas was finished, so the timing couldn't be better — she could at least attempt it, couldn't she? After all, what kind of daughter wouldn't at least try to help her father? And if she couldn't manage it . . . No! It was crazy.

Frederica was staring blankly at her painting when she became aware of a sudden shadow falling over her shoulder. She spun round, expecting to see a fellow student and instead came face to face with . . . *him*!

For a second, all she could think . . . all she could feel . . . was an overwhelming male presence. Then her dazzled brain began to take in specifics. He was tall, a veritable blonde

Adonis of a man. He seemed to dominate the room with his powerful aura, leaving him in a vacuum where nothing could reach him. Except . . . her?

Frederica blinked, totally stunned. She was not used to men affecting her like this. So far, she'd never had a lover — not so much from lack of opportunity, or even out of conscious choice, but because she'd never met a man who made her heart beat even just a little bit faster. Now, suddenly, her heart was *hammering*! She snatched a breath, but the air didn't seem to reach her lungs. She put a hand out against the wall to steady herself.

Lorcan Greene saw the young student go suddenly pale, and noticed her sway slightly. Alarmed, he quickly reached out a hand to steady her. As his hand curled around the top of her arm, eyes the colour of bitter chocolate looked up at him. He felt a curious numbness shoot from his fingers, travel up his arm and lodge in his chest. Then, in an instant it was gone. And in its place was warmth. A growing, persistent tide of warmth, flooding over him.

He looked at her closely, studying her as he would a fine painting. He noticed her hair first, and was reminded of a canvas by Titian — a mass of tightly curled ringlets cascading to her shoulders. If it hadn't been caught up in a ponytail on the top of her head, he was sure that it would fall to the middle of her back. He wanted to run his hands through it, and the very thought made his fingers twitch.

Quickly he withdrew his hand from her arm. She was slender as a reed beneath that smock, he gauged, and had a complexion of peaches and cream. A beautiful and very young English rose, he thought a trifle grimly. For she was much, *much* too young for him. He smiled, more at himself and his foolish thoughts than at her. 'Hello,' he said quietly.

He saw her eyes widen. They had the darkest, most velvety depths and he had to force himself to look away from her, moving behind her to stare at the finished canvas. He sighed softly. 'Ah, a painter, I see,' he murmured. 'I've been in the company of printmakers, sculptors and photographers all morning. I'm glad to meet someone at last who shares my own particular passion.'

Frederica blinked again. 'What . . . ?' she mumbled. 'Passion?'

His voice was a curious mixture of rough and smooth. She managed to drag in another breath, and her head slowly began to clear. Although she was no expert on men's tailoring, she realised that the lightweight cream jacket he was wearing over a dark-green shirt was expensive. He was well-groomed and smelt of expensive cologne. Everything about him screamed masculinity. Neither a country gentleman like her father, nor an arty bohemian like her fellow students. He was . . . different. And so utterly, utterly potent. Once again, air was hard to come by. She cleared her throat. Eclectic student body or not, if this man was a student, she was Bo Peep. He looked somewhere in his thirties, and probably ate girls like her for breakfast.

'Painting,' he said.

Frederica blinked yet again. 'Sorry?'

'You have a passion for painting, I see,' Lorcan repeated himself patiently. The beautiful young student had obviously been so deeply in thought that she was having trouble concentrating. He wondered what she'd been thinking about so intently. Some boyfriend, he supposed. And, surprisingly, the thought gave him a small, sharp twist of pain.

'That is your canvas, isn't it?' he asked, nodding to the painting behind her. Better not to linger on visions of a long-haired Lothario running his dirty fingers through that glorious cascade of hair.

Lorcan gave himself a mental shake. She was far too young for him, and it was clearly ridiculous for him to be feeling jealous.

Frederica, too, pulled herself together. 'Oh, yes. *Post-Millennium Home*.' She cast her eyes over the canvas, a twinge of doubt making her frown. Was it really any good?

Lorcan moved closer, his eyes moving over the canvas, every inch the art expert now. Modern acrylic paints, of course. Good size canvas. Good balance of colour. Perfect perception. It really was very well done. Surprisingly good, in fact. Although he'd come to the Ruskin to keep his eyes peeled on behalf of his good friend Inspector Braine, he hadn't realistically expected to find this amount of talent among the students.

He'd been prepared for all the modern approaches, of course, like the sculptor who made such intriguing use of plastic bags. What he hadn't expected, though, was to come across a painting like this one. This was no chocolate-box decoration. His eyes sharpened on the detail — the trees were superbly done. The cat was good too. The composition spot on. 'Why have you put the car bumper in? And the satellite dish?' he murmured.

Frederica hadn't a clue who he was. She only knew that he'd stopped her heart at first sight. And his closeness was generating in her a sexual arousal no other man had ever stirred in her before. She knew he was totally, utterly out of her league. And when he turned those stunning eyes on her again, she had enormous difficulty in concentrating on his words.

After only one quick glance, he'd gone straight to the heart of her painting. A tutor then, obviously someone new. There was no way she could have failed to notice him walking around.

'Oh, that,' she said, her voice coming out in a slightly husky croak. She swallowed, noticing the way his eyes darted to her mouth. 'It seems to me that the post-millennium needs as honest an eye to paint it as any other period in our history. So I've included cars, milk bottles, dustbins, telephone poles, road signs and various other articles of modern life. But I still paint truth. Because this is a home. Not just a house. Real people live in it. And somebody feeds the cat,' she said finally, with a rather defiant smile.

Lorcan understood at once what she meant. Her approach was different — clear and honest — and he felt a different tingle beginning to sweep through his bloodstream now. This had nothing to do with her exquisite hair and to-die-for eyes — this was purely professional. Lorcan knew when he stumbled upon fresh, raw talent. So far, the Greene Gallery had never sponsored an artist exclusively. Perhaps it was time to start doing so . . . ?

Frederica found her breath catching as he bent closer to the painting. Somehow, for some reason, his opinion of it mattered to her more than anything else in the world.

'And you can paint,' he muttered to himself.

Frederica, blushing with pleasure at his endorsement, set about uncovering her other finished canvases — a dirty double-decker bus unloading its passengers and a grey and grim local primary school with a series of cheerful traffic cones in front of it. Lorcan realised she'd captured the essence of pop art, together with a unique ability to paint reality in a classical style. The mix shouldn't have worked, but it did. Through her canvases, he found himself living in modern Britain. But the talent of the artist was from a different, much earlier century. 'Yes,' he repeated, gratified, 'you can definitely paint.'

Nervously, she uncovered one canvas that was as close to abstract as she'd ever come — a massive red combine, harvesting a field of over-ripe wheat. White blotches of seagulls streaked across the sky while green hedges wilted in the dry August heat. When she'd painted that canvas during last year's heatwave, the countryside had been suffering from a bad drought. She could almost taste the dust now, as she had then. Although he hadn't seen the original scene, Lorcan could taste the dust too. 'Is this for sale?' he found himself asking.

Frederica shook her head. 'Not until after my Final Degree Show. My tutor wants me to include it.'

'I'm not surprised.' Lorcan said, and reached into his inside jacket pocket. He drew out a small, plain white card, and watched as she reached for it gingerly. Her fingers brushed against his as she took it, and a giddying rush of desire shot through her, turning her pale skin even paler, and causing the smattering of freckles to stand out in stark relief across the bridge of her nose.

Lorcan found himself staring at them. Freckles, for pity's sake. She was still a schoolgirl! And then his eyes fell to her T-shirt, and he could make out the mature curve of her breast.

Frederica took the card. GREENE GALLERY. She knew it at once — everyone in the art world knew that it was one of the top London galleries, with a growing reputation. In the bottom right-hand corner was a phone number. In the middle of the card was a single name, in bold black letters: LORCAN GREENE.

Frederica blinked and looked up at him. 'You're Lorcan Greene?' she gasped.

Lorcan smiled. 'You didn't you see the announcement of my arrival on the noticeboard?'

She shook her head. Then she remembered the noise from the office earlier, and realised that it must have been the welcome reception for him.

'I'm here for the rest of the term, and the summer vacation,' he explained. 'On a visiting fellowship.'

'Oh,' she said flatly. What else could she say? Just looking at him made her feel tongue-tied. This man bought and sold Van Goghs. He hopped on planes and flew to New York, Paris, Rome, the way she caught the number seven bus to and from St Bede's. He dated famous actresses. He was in the papers regularly, giving evidence at . . . Frederica paled even further.

Art fraud cases.

This man was a notorious catcher of forgers! 'You're the one who detects big-time forgeries,' she said, with just a tinge of panic in her voice.

Lorcan looked down at her, biting back an unexpected feeling of regret. He couldn't be mistaking the signals — that shortness of breath, the flushed cheeks, those melting brown eyes. Lorcan was too much a man not to know when a woman wanted him.

But he was not in Oxford for romance. And definitely not with someone so young. But hell, she was making it difficult!

He smiled, a shade more arrogantly than he'd meant to, and reminded himself why he was there. 'That's right,' he said, his voice rich with confidence. 'I catch the fakers.'

Frederica found herself reacting to that voice, to that face, to that male dominance, in a purely feminine way.

So he was the scourge of crooked artists, was he? She fought back a wild, intoxicating desire to laugh.

For, as those eyes looked at her, and as she felt her body throb to some strange and powerful force that he seemed to be exuding, she suddenly realised that she was going to copy her father's painting after all.

And, what's more, she was going to do it right under this man's arrogant nose.

CHAPTER 5

Annis pushed open the door to the empty flat, glad to see that nearly all of the others had already arrived and were good-naturedly camped out in the middle of the floor, chatting like old friends.

A mocking, sapphire-blue gaze turned her way as she approached, and Annis could feel it taking in every inch of her — from the top of her loosely flowing black hair down to the tips of her trainers.

Ray had decided to forsake the first rehearsal in favour of a get-to-know-you session. Luckily, after giving each other a few fulminating and wary looks, Annis and Reeve had settled down, and for this Ray was very grateful. Warring actors were not exactly his idea of keeping a low profile during the conference.

'Right then,' Ray began briskly, handing around photocopies of the basic details of the conference. 'You can see that St Bede's is quite a small building, as Oxford colleges go, and on the map . . .' Everyone turned a page to look at the diagram. ' . . . the locations of key rooms are clearly marked. You'll notice that a lot of the action takes place in Hall. I've been told that the dining hall in St Bede's is quite something. But we'll also have scenes in the chapel, the JCR — that's the

Junior Common Room where the students hang out — and various other sites.'

There was a murmur of approval. All actors liked authentic surroundings. It aided a performance.

'Now, as to the actual murder mystery itself,' Ray continued, 'Annis is our murderer.'

Annis gave a wide grin, and acknowledged the catcalls. 'She is at the conference in order to steal a very valuable painting from the college,' Ray said casually, enjoying the sense of irony as he casually tossed out this snippet of information. Briefly he wondered what these people would say if he told them that that really was what was going to happen but he shrugged the thought aside. 'The college principal, Lord St John James, has agreed to the actual removal of one of St Bede's paintings which hangs in the dining hall.'

'That's great,' John Lore spoke up. 'It'll really help the atmosphere along.'

Reeve nodded. 'I agree. The more authentic touches we can include, the better it'll be.'

Each and every one of the group was determined to give a good performance. Of course, Annis thought sourly, there were always exceptions, and she shot Reeve a look. If he let the others down because he was concentrating too hard on selling his damned script, she'd . . . she'd . . . kill him! Rather appropriate, she thought, smothering a smile, for Annis the murderer!

'John here,' Ray continued, 'is determined to get a piece of the action. So Annis bumps him off. This she does in the Hall. The diners all come in to find him dead, artistically arranged and bleeding, on the main table.'

John grinned. 'I'll be the best corpse since Banquo,' he promised modestly. There were more catcalls and whistles. When they'd settled down, Ray continued to move them along. 'The most popular theory you'll come up with is that John saw who stole the missing painting. But he didn't. It'll later be proved that he couldn't have.'

'Oh good,' Julie Morris piped up. 'I love red herrings.'

'Enter our young policeman,' Ray said, pointing to Gordon, who raised a hand in greeting. 'He'll lead everyone through the questioning of the suspects. It will emerge that you, Norman,' he pointed to the oldest member of the team, 'used to be on the force, but left under a cloud.'

'Is there any other way to leave?' Norman Rix asked.

'Reeve here announces that he's discovered the identity of the killer but needs proof.'

'Dicey,' Geraldine Edwards murmured, her lips smiling knowingly around the cigarette she was smoking.

'Some of us like to live dangerously,' Reeve shot back at her, grinning at the still-attractive older redhead. Annis looked away in disgust. He was just the sort of man who would take advantage of an older woman. She could imagine him reassuring Gerry what an attractive woman she still was . . . She flushed, wondering why she was being such a bitch. Ever since her divorce, she had a rather worrying tendency to think the worst of everyone. Well, not everyone, she admitted to herself fairly. Just good-looking actors.

Philip, her husband of three years, had left her when a famous American actress from a popular comedy show had come to London. Their affair had been brief but well-publicised, and as well as getting a divorce from Annis, Philip had gone on to bag a very well-paid part in an American afternoon soap. She shook her unpleasant thoughts away and concentrated on their director as he swept the story along.

'And Reeve is subsequently seen talking very forcefully with Norman here. Afterwards, again in the Hall, Reeve is fatally and very dramatically poisoned.'

Reeve's hand shot to his throat. With a very clever trick of temporarily cutting off his air supply, his face suddenly became an alarming shade of purple. *'Aagggh* . . .' He gave a gurgling, strangulated cry that literally raised the hairs on the back of everyone's neck. He sounded like a soul in torment as he slowly slumped forward, giving a final convulsive twitch that both shocked and worried his audience, and then lay perfectly still. They couldn't even see his chest rising and falling as he breathed. Everyone burst into spontaneous applause, even, reluctantly, Annis. It had been a good performance after all.

Reeve straightened up, his healthy colour returning, and took a half-bow. Since he was sitting cross-legged on the floor it wasn't easy, but he managed it.

'Do I get to kill him too?' Annis asked, ever so sweetly, as the applause died away. She saw his dark-blue eyes slew across in her direction, and watched his lips twitch.

'You do,' Ray confirmed. 'By poisoning his wine. But not before Gerry here also takes a sip. However, she doesn't die, because you haven't yet slipped in the arsenic. You're to pass your hand over his wine cup after she's already had a taste of it. That's one of the clues. If you turn to the second page, you'll find the basic plot written out for you, and a list of all the clues that must be included. I think it's best if you stick with your real first names, to avoid any slip-ups.'

Once again there was a turning of pages and general silence as the cast read the script. Among the other clues for the delegates to pick up on, one was the way that Annis reacted to the news that Norman was an ex-cop, and another was the diamond pendant she was wearing. This diamond, she noted with interest, was what she was meant to use later on to cut the painting free from its glass case. Very clever. She was also to hide the painting under a pew in St Bede's chapel, she noticed, and during the Sunday morning service there, she was to be seen making a point of sitting in a pew far from the radiators. This, she surmised, was for the benefit of the hidden painting, so that it wouldn't dry out or be damaged by the chapel's heating system.

'And what do the rest of us do?' Gerry asked. 'Make ourselves as suspicious as possible, I suppose?'

'Of course,' Ray confirmed. 'Gerry, you play John's suspicious wife. Julie, you're his mistress. You cause a very public scene, Gerry, when you discover your husband's infidelity.'

'So I'm to be the leading contender?' Gerry asked, obviously enjoying the thought.

'You are suspect number one for a while,' Ray confirmed. 'But Reeve also has a big argument with John — he's angry that John has demoted him because of professional jealousy. Then it's discovered that Julie is pregnant, and that John was pushing her to have an abortion.'

'Am I a Prince Charming or what?' John Lore asked wryly.

'So, is everybody clear on the basics?' Ray asked. 'We'll get down to individual scenes later.'

All the actors agreed they were happy with the plot. It looked like a really good weekend for all concerned.

'I have the timetable here,' Ray said. 'I want you all to memorise it.'

Annis accepted her copy and shifted a little to get more comfortable. Reeve looked up as she tucked her legs more firmly under her. He grinned at her, and she shot him a don't-you-dare look. She wouldn't put it past him to make some sort of jeering comment. After their rocky start the night before last, they'd lapsed into a wary sort of truce. But the gleam in his dark-blue eyes didn't bode well for the peace treaty lasting. She forced herself to look away from those gleaming, pearly white teeth, the flashing, devilishly attractive eyes, the crisp dark hair, and concentrated on the timetable. As a professional, she knew the importance of learning her lines.

The schedule appeared to give them quite a lot of free time, and Annis could almost hear her fellow actors giving a silent hurrah, but she failed to notice the way Reeve's eyes kept straying to her bent head.

She really did have an intriguing profile, he thought. Hers was a strong, interesting sort of face, a face that went beyond mere beauty. A pity she seemed so determined to take pot-shots at him — no man liked being the object of such open scorn. Not that it worried him so much . . . He sighed, caught Gerry Edwards giving him a wry, knowing smile, her full mouth curling around her cigarette, and he quickly turned his attention back to the schedule.

* * *

John Lore sighed. 'I suppose I have to make sure I'm not seen all the next day?' he murmured, sounding aggrieved. After all, you couldn't have a 'corpse' walking around.

'Poor baby,' Annis said softly, grinning at him as he shot her a quick, thoughtful look. It was the kind of look that promised a heavy pass at her later, but Annis wasn't worried about John — she knew she could handle him.

Reeve shifted uncomfortably on the floor. He hoped John and Annis weren't going to become an item. Short-term relationships were so messy, he thought sourly. And wondered, annoyed, why he was feeling so jealous. Annis just caught the sarcastic look Reeve sent her and John Lore, and fought the childish impulse to stick her tongue out at him. Really, the man was a pain in the derriere. What was it to him if she did flirt with John? It was none of his damned business, that was for sure! She turned back to the job in hand. The last day of the conference looked as busy and action-packed as any of them!

'Phew,' Norman Rix said, speaking for them all, as he finally put the schedule aside. 'You have dialogue for all this?'

Ray nodded. 'Yes, I have. But please feel free to ad lib. Just don't overdo it.'

'Are you listening, Reeve?' Annis couldn't resist asking. 'No over-acting.'

Gerry coughed to hide her laughter. Gordon, the closest to Reeve in age, gave him a commiserating look. Annis Whittington really seemed to have it in for him for some reason.

Reeve bit back a savage grin. What was it with the woman? She seemed absolutely hell-bent on picking a fight. 'Oh, I'll do my best,' he drawled. 'I wouldn't, after all, want to provide too much contrast to any weaker performances.' Then, lest any of the other members of the cast take offence, he added pointedly, 'After all, the murderer, not the victim, is supposed to be the star of the show.'

Annis felt herself go pale as the insult hit home. As if she wasn't capable of giving just as good a performance as he was! 'Oh don't worry, Reeve,' she purred. 'I'll make sure you don't have to worry about that!' Her eyes flashed a silent addition; something along the lines of *I'm going to act you under the floorboards, pal.*

Ray coughed. 'Now come on, you two,' he said, and Annis felt herself flush. It was the first time one of her directors had ever had to tell her off, even mildly, for unprofessional behaviour. She felt like reaching out and kicking Reeve Morgan on the shin. Hard!

The rest of the night was taken up with questions and answers, until everyone was satisfied that they had every facet of the murder mystery down pat. It was nearing midnight when they finally broke up. Annis paused on the middle of the stairs to slip her sweater over her head and smiled a goodnight to Julie, who dashed past her.

Reeve was waiting in the darkness at the bottom of the stairs, and when he saw her he stepped in front of her.

Annis gasped. 'Damn it, Reeve, you scared me. Do you have to lurk about in the dark like that?'

Reeve scowled. 'Well, excuse me for breathing!' Would he ever do anything right in this woman's eyes? He somehow doubted it. 'Look, why don't we go for a drink somewhere?' he asked, following her out on to the lamplit streets. 'Ray's right. We should try to get along.'

'It's late,' Annis said discouragingly.

'I know a small club just around the corner. It's private — members only. We can get a good glass of Bordeaux there.'

Annis grimaced and planted her hands on her hips. 'Now why doesn't that surprise me? Daddy's club is it?' And who the hell could afford a Bordeaux, good or indifferent? Not struggling actresses that was for sure.

Reeve drew in a long, calming breath. 'Look, lady, why don't you just drop the attitude for a while, huh? It's wearing thin,' he gritted.

And Annis knew that he was right. But the sight of all that powerful male beauty was making her unusually reckless.

'What's the matter, Reeve? You like to dish it out but don't like to take it, is that it?' she shot back.

Now why, she thought exasperatedly, had she said that?

Reeve's eyes flashed. His hands clenched spasmodically by his sides as he took a half-step towards her. The little . . . All right. She wanted him to handle it. His pleasure! 'Suit yourself,' he said, and shrugged one shoulder. 'I thought we should bury the hatchet, but if you want to keep it childish and petty . . .' He reached for her suddenly, dragging her into his arms before she knew what had hit her. She felt herself cannon against a wall of solid, warm muscle, her nose picking up the fresh pine scent of his aftershave.

Annis gave a startled shriek, but then his lips were on hers, the harsh heat of them causing her heart to give a convulsive leap. Her insides contracted in a short, sharp, molten-hot flood of desire . . .

And then he thrust her from him.

She blinked. 'What the hell was that supposed to prove?' she squeaked, too breathless to shout as she had intended.

Reeve shook his head. What had he meant to prove? Somehow, in the last few seconds, he'd forgotten. Not that he'd ever admit as much to her! 'Well, I'm supposed to be the enemy, aren't I, Annis?' he drawled mockingly. 'I just thought I'd let you know what you were taking on.' And with that, he turned and left her.

Literally walked away from her.

The louse!

* * *

Frederica didn't usually leave Oxford during the week, but her latest canvas was finished, she already had four good pieces for her Finals Show, and nobody was going to jump on her if she went home midweek. This didn't stop her feeling guilty, though, as she walked up the narrow country lane towards home.

Frederica loved the countryside in May. It was, without doubt, the best time to be in England. But as she turned up the familiar drive of Rainbow House, she acknowledged to herself that she wouldn't be here at all if wasn't for her father.

And Lorcan Greene. Her steps faltered as she thought, once more, about that man. Since his advent into her life four days ago, he'd become a permanent fixture in her mind.

Her tutors and the Ruskin master were all delighted to have him around, of course; of that there could be no doubt. And her fellow students, too, were avid in their attendance of his lectures. She'd never known a lecture be so well attended as the one he'd given in the Drawing Studio yesterday.

And she had been the most fascinated of all. His subject was the trial of an art forger who'd tried to sell the Greene Gallery a fake. Lorcan had slides of both the original and the fake, and Frederica was sure she wasn't the only one in the room who hadn't been able to tell them apart. Even the tutors had looked uneasy. But it wasn't until Lorcan began to explain how he'd uncovered the fraud that the real genius of the man began to appear. Whereas before his aura of power and knowledge had been unmistakable, now it suddenly became overwhelming. Within minutes, it became clear to everyone that he was one of the greatest experts of fine art anywhere in the world.

Not that Frederica herself had required any additional proof. From the moment she'd set eyes on him, she'd known he was a man like no other. It embarrassed her now, as she thought back to their first meeting, the way she'd gaped at him like a moonstruck calf. It made her cringe to think how it must have amused him — for it was hopeless to think that a man as astute as he would not have noticed.

She pushed open the gate angrily and marched up the wallflower and forget-me-not strewn path, trying to thrust the thought of Lorcan Greene far away. But the damned man just wouldn't go. He lingered in the back of her mind, looking down at her, dressed in his expensive suit, his green gaze washing knowingly over her. Taking in every little sign of her infatuation. It was enough to make her want to spit.

Everyone was out, so she headed straight for the kettle, a cup of tea, and hopefully a return to sanity. As she made a drink, she told herself not to be so hard on herself. A man like Lorcan was bound to have women falling for him like ninepins. Besides, he'd probably never even given her a second thought.

During his lecture he'd been quite upfront and honest about why, as a businessman, he hated fakers. But he'd also spoken with sincere passion about the immorality of forging the works of other, greater geniuses.

It had made Frederica feel absurdly guilty. Even now, she could remember standing at the back of the room, her insides churning when his green eyes swept over her as he spoke. And yet, it was not as if he was looking at her particularly — although she felt her guilt must be written in large letters on her forehead. No, he'd seemed to be talking to the entire student body and watching each of them with sharp, all-seeing eyes, almost as if he was looking for something, some sign in particular.

She sighed as she drank the last of her tea, and sent up a silent 'sorry' to Forbes-Wright, the talented artist. She hoped, wherever he was, that he really didn't mind that she was going to copy his painting. Then she shook her head at herself. It was no good feeling guilty. She'd made up her mind to try painting a copy of *The Old Mill and Swans*, so she'd best get on with it.

And it was all Lorcan Greene's fault. She'd returned to Oxford determined to forget her father's outrageous plea, and if Lorcan hadn't been there, sweeping her off her feet and being so damned arrogant and challenging, she wouldn't be here at Rainbow House now, about to raid the family attic for a 150-year-old canvas.

She climbed the stairs to the top floor, pausing to admire a Jackson Pollock on the landing, one of her father's few 'lucky acquisitions', before forcing her feet onward and upward.

The attic at Rainbow House was probably unique in that all the accumulated 'rubbish' was art-related, so it didn't take her long to find what she was looking for. She already knew that one of her ancestors, a particularly talentless lady called Ariadne Delacroix, had painted several truly awful paintings. With a tape measure in hand and hope in her heart, Frederica inspected the canvases for her ancestor's signature.

She coughed in the dust, and cursed her father under her breath, but eventually found what she was looking for. What's more, one of Ariadne's efforts, dated around the same time as *The Old Mill and Swans*, was exactly the same size as the Forbes-Wright original. Although she could have cut down a bigger canvas to size, of course, Frederica was determined to take no chances. She was going to do this thing properly. And an expert like Lorcan might be able to tell if a canvas had recently been made smaller. She hadn't read about Keating's meticulous attention to detail for nothing.

She lugged the painting downstairs and propped it up in the kitchen, careful to wash her dirty hands in the sink before subjecting the canvas to microscopic scrutiny. Canvases came in all sizes and types. There were the linen ones made from flax, which she favoured at the Ruskin. She would always degrease those, use a pumice stone on them, then add other layers of primer herself. Mounting and stretching was another time-consuming business too. Non-artists were always surprised by the amount of work that had to be done before an artist even picked up a paintbrush. But she wouldn't have to worry about any of that with this canvas, of course. It was perfect as it was: the right age, size and type. It was just what Forbes-Wright would have used for his original painting of the old mill.

She'd have to be careful how she cleaned Ariadne's picture off, though. Not even a minute trace of it must be left. She quickly wrapped the canvas in an old sheet from under the stairs, and, not wanting to give her father the satisfaction of knowing what she'd done, washed up her cup and put it away, leaving no trace of her visit behind her.

She was by now used to lugging ungainly equipment about, so the journey back on the train presented her with no difficulties.

Once back in Oxford, she took the canvas straight to her workspace at the Ruskin and paid another visit to the tiny library. Although she knew well enough how she herself would set about cleaning the canvas for repainting, what she really needed to know was how Forbes-Wright would have cleaned a canvas in his day. She wasn't sure if even Lorcan Greene would be able to tell whether or not modern chemicals had seeped into a canvas, but she was taking no chances.

Without quite knowing why, or how, it had become utterly important to her that she create a forgery that the great Lorcan Greene could not detect. It was as if, on some primitive level, he'd challenged her so outrageously that she was determined to beat him, come what may. She was also uncomfortably aware, on some soul-deep level, that the challenge he'd issued had nothing to do with painting, and everything to do with the way her heart beat faster whenever he was around. But since there was nothing she could do about being attracted to him — all right, hopelessly, devastatingly attracted to him — there *was* something she could do about competing with him on his home ground . . . art. And, more specifically, the forging of art.

And so she spent the rest of the afternoon learning how a Victorian would have set about preparing a canvas. And first thing the next morning, she began the task with vim and relish, humming softly under her breath as she worked. There was something about helping her father out of a jam, and putting one over on the superior Lorcan Greene at the same time, that made her feel downright cheerful!

* * *

Lorcan awoke that morning pleasantly aware of the sunshine outside. It was Friday, and he was in Oxford.

As his friend DI Richard Braine had predicted, he'd found somewhere to lay his head — renting a spacious, two-storey house on Five Mile Drive, a cherry-tree-lined avenue in prestigious North Oxford.

He shaved and dressed in a pair of cream slacks, a hand-tooled leather belt that an ex-girlfriend had brought him back from Spain and, in deference to the heat haze building up outside, a dazzlingly white, cool silk shirt. He was the epitome of an elegant, classically good-looking Englishman about to enjoy a summer's day.

As he drove his faithful Aston Martin down the Banbury Road towards the centre of town, he fully intended to check out the botanical gardens. So when he found himself making his way to the Ruskin instead, he smiled ruefully, acknowledged his subconscious whim, and let himself into the cool hall. On the second floor he quickly realised that the school didn't really start to come alive until well after ten. It was now only nine-fifteen. Suddenly he heard a noise above him. It sounded as if someone had dropped something heavy. Vaguely curious, he sprinted lightly up the stairs and walked quietly across the paint-daubed floor.

A glimpse of curly auburn hair, glowing like fire in a stray misty beam of sunlight, told him the identity of the student long before he reached her workspace, and he felt his footsteps faltering. Although he was loath to admit it, even to himself, he didn't really want to see or talk to Frederica Delacroix.

He tried telling himself that his reluctance was merely precautionary. A wise man's decision to distance himself from the temptation of forbidden fruit. But the simple fact was that Frederica had been haunting his dreams ever since their first meeting on Monday. Those freckles of hers had featured in many restless nights' twisting and turning.

So, reluctantly, and yet with a growing sense of pleasure that he couldn't deny was somewhat dangerous, he found himself once more, walking silently up behind her, watching her work. He felt a bit like a teenager with a crush, getting an unexpected and forbidden glimpse of the object of his desire. Ridiculous. But heady.

She was dressed in the ubiquitous dirty smock, and her hands were filthy. Not surprising, when he realised what she was doing: cleaning a canvas. Even half-erased, the disappearing painting had obviously been hideous and amateurish in the extreme. There was no way it could have been one of her own efforts. He stepped a bit closer, looking at the beetle in one corner. As ill-painted as it was, he could see that the artist had been influenced by a certain style.

He frowned. If he had to make a guess, he'd say the painting had been done by a Victorian trying to ape his or her betters.

Lorcan was about to make a discreet noise and advertise his presence, when suddenly he realised that she wasn't using a common stripping agent. In fact, she was using such an old-fashioned mixture that it was taking her much longer, and required much more elbow grease, than it should have done.

What the hell . . . ? Every suspicious cell in his body began to tingle. Why was a modern artist using such a laborious and old-fashioned way to remove paint? And why, if it came to that, was she removing it at all?

Frederica's movements gradually slowed. She'd been aware of a chill down the back of her neck for some time, but had been too busy to take any notice. Now she could feel a tightness in her breast that was making her nipples tingle. When, she thought desperately, and with a leap of unstoppable excitement, had she felt that before? With a sharp upward movement of her chin, she shot a rapid glance over her shoulder.

And speared him with her brown eyes.

Lorcan took a sharp breath, caught by surprise at the sudden confrontation with those velvety depths. 'Hello again,' he said smoothly, and forced himself to smile.

Frederica licked lips gone suddenly dry. 'Hello, Mr Greene. I wanted to tell you how much I . . . er . . . I enjoyed your lecture the other day.'

'Please, call me Lorcan,' he corrected her briskly. The 'Mr Greene' had made him feel about a hundred years old. 'And I'm glad I didn't bore you.' His eyes swept to the canvas again. Suddenly, he was sure that his lecture about art forgery hadn't bored her at all. Far from it, in fact.

He felt an unaccountable sinking feeling deep inside him. He knew he should be elated. Richard had asked him to keep his eyes open for something unusual, especially among the students. And here he was, his excellent instincts screaming at him that he'd stumbled on to something, and all he could feel was . . . dismay.

'Oh no, it was really, really interesting,' Frederica said hastily, wishing she could stop herself from gushing. She must sound like a right ninny.

Lorcan nodded at the canvas. 'Not one of yours, I trust?' he teased craftily.

Frederica laughed. 'Oh no. No . . . er . . . a friend of mine had an aunt who hated it. Said I could have it . . . to reuse the canvas, I mean,' she stuttered, blushing, wishing a hole would open up and swallow her.

She's not a very good liar, Lorcan thought, with a mixture of savagery and relief. Savagery, because he hated being taken for a fool — especially by this woman. And relief because . . . well . . . because it showed that she wasn't a habitual liar. Which was something, at least. 'I see,' he murmured. 'But surely you're not so hard-up that you have to scrounge old canvases?'

Frederica drew in a shaky breath. A nervous voice at the back of her head piped up with some sound, if obvious, advice: *Don't panic!* But he didn't believe her, she knew that. And as she looked at his openly mocking smile, she knew she had better do something to salvage the situation. And quick!

She tilted her head back and laughed. 'Don't you believe it! We can't all be millionaires you know,' she said, with just a little bit of a snap. 'Despite what impressions you might have formed, we only get a small allowance from the Ruskin. We get a materials bursary from our own college, too, but that hardly covers the cost of paint. Believe me, the chance of a canvas for nothing isn't something to be sniffed at.'

Now that, Lorcan acknowledged, had the unmistakable ring of truth about it. But it was also a little too pat. He knew when he was being played with. And although he'd been dreaming of playing games with this beautiful young lady all night long, this wasn't exactly what he'd had in mind.

'I see. Well, in that case let me contribute by taking you out to dinner tomorrow night,' he said smoothly, not missing the sudden mix of dismay and pleasure that flared in her dark, velvety eyes. 'If you don't have to spend those precious pennies on anything as mundane as food, you can treat yourself to another tube or two of cadmium yellow.'

Although his voice was teasing and his smile light, Frederica sensed the hidden gleam of a predator behind the facade. He definitely had the eyes of a tiger — all smoky green, dangerous indolence.

A warning voice was screaming from the back of Frederica's mind, telling her to run. To head for cover. To say no. To make some excuse — any excuse — not to spend time alone with him. She had nothing to wear, for instance. She was washing her hair . . . anything. It was almost overwhelming, this sense she had of being way out of her depth.

But another, even more persistent voice told her not to be such a chicken. Men of the world were a danger all women had to face sometime or other. And shy virgins had better learn to sink or swim along with all the others.

'Thank you, I'd love to,' she heard a voice say.

Her voice!

Lorcan smiled. 'Great. I'll pick you up about seven then. Where?'

'I'm at St Bede's. In the Woodstock Road.'

'I'll find it,' he promised, gave her one last, long, thoughtful look, then was gone.

Frederica let her breath out in a whoosh. Wow! She leaned weakly against the wall. She supposed she should be flattered. Lorcan Greene could have his pick of beautiful women, but he'd invited *her* out to dinner. A hitherto unheard and rather wild voice began to stir inside her,

47

wondering what it would actually be like to take him as her lover. Her first lover. It would certainly be an experience.

But she quickly quashed that incredible thought. Prepared to do battle with Lorcan Greene when it came to the world of art, she might be. But on the intimate battle-ground that was the bedroom? Forget it!

Frederica would have been even more panic-stricken if she'd realised that Lorcan, at that very moment, was heading for the admin office, determined to find out all he could about the background of one Frederica Delacroix. And he was bound to learn that she was hardly the poverty-stricken student she pretended to be — indeed, that the Delacroixs were renowned art collectors themselves. If he did discover everything about her Frederica would have reason to be flat-out terrified.

But she didn't know any of that.

And as for the predatory gleam that leaped into Lorcan's eyes as he contemplated his forthcoming date with Frederica Delacroix . . . ? Well, it would have been enough to make even the most seasoned of women think twice.

CHAPTER 6

'You should let yourself go a bit more,' Reeve said, his voice rich with persuasion. He leaned across the table and reached for Annis's hand, rubbing his thumb caressingly over the tops of her knuckles. 'A woman like you shouldn't be so standoffish.'

Annis smiled softly. 'Oh? I wasn't aware that I was.'

Reeve shrugged. 'You shouldn't be so shy, then. Let yourself have some fun for a change.' His voice dropped a suggestive octave. 'You might like it.'

Annis laughed, a cool, silvery, tinkling laugh that carried well. 'And what exactly did you have in mind? As if I couldn't guess.'

'Now, now,' Reeve wagged a finger at her. 'Don't go all prudish on me. You know what they say about all work and no play . . .' He lifted her hand, about to kiss it . . .

'OK that's perfect,' Ray said, his bald head gleaming in the overhead lighting. The rest of the cast gave them a small ripple of applause. Annis quickly snatched her hand away and moved back from the trestle table. The unfurnished flat had now been fitted with rudimentary tables, chairs and a few props. Rehearsals were well under way.

'Of course, this scene takes place long before Reeve announces he knows who killed John,' Ray explained. 'He's a bit of a Casanova. Reeve, you can flirt with some of the conference-going ladies to add authenticity to your character.'

'That shouldn't be much of a hardship,' Annis muttered under her breath. But Reeve obviously had good hearing, for he shot her a sharp look from under his dark brows. His lips, though, couldn't help but twitch. Could she, by any stretch of the imagination, be jealous?

Ray gave them both a wary look. Never had he seen sexual tension shimmer so obviously between two people.

Reeve said something to Gerry, who laughed huskily, then whispered something to Julie, who blushed.

Annis scowled. Older redheads and very-nearly schoolgirls. The man certainly had a wide repertoire. Just as she was thinking this, Reeve swivelled round on the rickety chair and caught her in mid-scowl.

He grinned. Yep, no doubt about it: Miss Annis Whittington was positively green with jealousy. Annis didn't remove the scowl. She'd been fairly and squarely caught out, and in cases like this, attack was always the best form of defence. 'Why are you grinning like a very bad impression of a Cheshire Cat?' she hissed at him. 'I don't see that in the scene.'

Reeve allowed himself a small sigh and a shrug. 'You really are uptight, aren't you?' he said loudly.

Annis started. 'What? Who the hell . . . ?' She saw him tap the script knowingly, and blushed, realising what he'd done. It was a line from the scene they were rehearsing.

Annis's face suddenly softened. 'It's not that, Reeve, precious,' she purred, reading her own lines with perfect timing, determined not to be outdone.

Ray nodded in approval. If nothing else, their personal feud would keep them distracted. Of them all, Ray had come to see Annis and Reeve as the most astute. If anyone realised that something odd was going on, it would be these two.

The cast worked solidly for an hour, then were given an hour and a half off for lunch. As they all trooped outside, Norman Rix glanced up the busy road. 'There's a cafe just round the corner I know, serves great fish and chips. Cheap too. Who's up for it?' Naturally, everyone was.

Annis felt a hand curl around her arm, and stopped dead in the middle of the street. She tilted her head sharply, knowing full well who it was that had hold of her. Nobody else would dare manhandle her except Reeve Morgan.

'Don't tell me you're not on a permanent diet,' he drawled, watching her flashing eyes warily. 'My flat's just a short bus ride away. I've got some fresh crayfish and salad on offer.'

Annis's eyes narrowed. 'After what happened the other night, what on earth makes you think I want to go back to your flat?' she snapped.

Reeve smiled grimly. 'What's the matter? Lost your nerve?'

Annis's eyes narrowed, the orange flecks shining like little embers. 'Don't flatter yourself! Better men than you have tried to make me nervous. And failed.'

'So, you prefer greasy fish and fattening chips to fresh crayfish?' he teased. The sun was bathing his dark curls with a golden lining, and something about the way he stood there made her feel suddenly weak at the knees. Annis felt herself breathing hard, perched on the edge of rage and desire. What was it about this man that could tie her up in knots? It couldn't be his looks alone. Annis had met men whose good looks could peel the paper off the walls. And she could hardly accuse him of using excess amounts of charm on her! So what . . .

'Look, don't bust a gasket,' Reeve said drolly. 'If you don't want to eat, you don't . . .'

'Oh all right!' Annis sighed, then broke out into a sprint as they saw a double-decker pull in and Reeve shouted that it was their bus. They just made it, and lurched their way on to one of the downstairs seats.

'Good grief, I'm out of shape,' Annis panted. 'I'd better start doing dance classes again.' Reeve, she noticed wryly, was breathing normally. The sight of his calm, unruffled composure when she knew her own face must be pink with exertion did nothing much to improve her temper. Nor did his flat. It was in a leafy little cul-de-sac with a pleasant view over a group of horse chestnut trees and a handkerchief-sized park. It had all the hallmarks of being professionally decorated, and she thought with a pang of her own tiny bedsit.

She sighed and followed him into his kitchen. She watched him walk to a fridge that was as tall as he was and extract crayfish, already marinating in a glass dish and ready to eat. His hands were deft and knowing as he assembled different salad leaves and mixed a lemon vinaigrette. Next, he chopped cold bacon, tomatoes, avocado and cucumber into a basin, before carrying it to the table.

By the time he'd warmed crusty rolls in the oven, set the table and opened a bottle of expensive-looking white wine, her stomach was rumbling, and she was forced to admit, albeit grudgingly, that he was at least domesticated. Some men couldn't look after themselves if their lives depended on it, her ex-husband having been just such a man. She couldn't imagine Reeve Morgan going about in a dirty shirt because he didn't have a little woman waiting at home to do his laundry.

She sat down, reaching for one of the stiff green linen napkins Reeve had put out. She accepted her glass of wine and took a tentative sip. Properly cooled, dry, tangy and delicious. She thought of the others, drinking lukewarm cafe tea, and felt a tiny twinge of guilt.

'To the murder-mystery weekend,' Reeve said, raising his glass. Annis clinked her own glass to his.

'May nobody guess whodunit.'

'You would hope that,' Reeve teased. 'You being the killer!'

Annis couldn't help but smile. 'You know, sometimes you can be . . . all right,' she said grudgingly.

Reeve shot a stunned look at her, then burst out laughing. He couldn't help it. She looked so disgruntled. In his mirth, he nearly choked on his wine. Finally, eyes streaming, he managed to shake his head. 'I'll bet that was positively painful!'

Annis smiled, again grudgingly. 'OK, OK,' she held her hand up. 'No need to make a meal out of it.'

Reeve coughed and leaned back in his chair. He was wearing a simple white T-shirt that strained across his well-formed biceps and hard, contoured chest. The sight of all that lounging male indolence made Annis want to stroke him like she would a cat.

'Truce?' he asked quietly.

Annis dragged her mind away from thoughts of stroking him and managed a shrug. 'Sure, why not?' she said, with something less than grace. 'It's not as if we're going to have to put up with each other for too long. Even I can put up with you for a little while.'

Reeve's lips twisted. 'Gee, thanks,' he drawled. But the thought of how soon the murder-mystery weekend would come and go made him feel oddly depressed.

He watched her eat with pleasure. She seemed to enjoy the food so much that he found a tender feeling beginning to glow just below the region of his heart. Which was patently ridiculous.

'So, what have you got lined up after this murder-mystery gig?' he asked, absently brushing crumbs off his thighs, unaware that Annis was following the brushing motion of his hands with a mouth gone suddenly dry. He was wearing tight-fitting jeans along with the T-shirt, and she could almost imagine the firm, warm feeling of his flesh . . .

She blinked mid-chew, realising that he was gazing at her with a slightly quizzical look in his eyes. 'Huh? Oh . . . um . . .' She swallowed her food hastily. 'I'm not sure. I've got one or two commercials lined up. Voiceovers mostly. But my hands might get famous.'

Reeve looked puzzled for a moment, then nodded. 'Oh. A hand cream commercial?'

Annis nodded and regarded her hands thoughtfully. Reeve did too, and understood at once how she had got the role. Her hands were pale and exquisitely shaped. He had a sudden vivid picture of them on his chest, the long slender fingers running through his dark chest hairs, her fingertips moving slowly down over the rest of his body . . .

'What about you?' Annis asked, and Reeve dragged his mind away from her hands to concentrate on her face. Her eyes really were a tawny blaze of colour, he thought, wondering how it was that no director had yet realised their potential. In a close-up, the camera swinging in towards her face, those eyes looking straight at you out of your television screen . . . it would be enough to curl the toes of the entire male population of Great Britain.

'Oh, well, I've got an audition for that new soap,' he said, and Annis felt herself chill by several degrees.

'Isn't that the soap that's being directed by Gale Evers?' she asked. When a woman grabbed a top job like directing a glitzy new soap, it was news. What was also news was that Reeve Morgan and Gale Evers were rumoured to be . . . if not an item exactly . . . then more than just passing buddies.

Reeve, unaware of the sudden danger, nodded. 'That's right. The part I'm reading for is a cockney villain, in love with a character who's blind. She's a good, salt-of-the-earth type who's having nothing to do with him. But I don't suppose that'll last for long,' he finished, grinning.

Annis managed a tight smile. 'No, I suppose not. Just so long as the ratings say it's a popular storyline.'

She pushed her plate away, her appetite suddenly gone. She knew she shouldn't begrudge another actor moving up the ladder, but she did, dammit! She supposed she was old-fashioned, but she didn't like the idea of a man using a woman to get ahead in life. It stuck in her throat.

Like his damned crayfish was doing. She picked up her glass of wine and walked with it through to the living room, leaving him without so much as a word. Reeve watched her go, his face a picture of surprise.

Dammit, now what had he said? She was like mercury — as changeable as a barometer in the Caribbean during the hurricane season. He stacked the dishes in the sink and wandered back into the living room with his own glass. She was standing at the window, looking out over the towering horse chestnut trees, her face pensive. He could see the tension in her shoulder blades.

He watched her, unsure what to say next. It was a new sensation to him — usually when he was around women, he knew exactly what to say and do.

'We should be getting back,' he murmured at last, noticing the way her hair swung just to the top of her arms as she turned and glanced at him. Her face, he noticed with something approaching despair, was tight and pinched. 'Annis, what on earth is the matter? You've got more prickles than a hedgehog.'

Annis shrugged. 'There's nothing the matter,' she said loftily. Insincerely. 'Besides, why should it bother you if there were?'

Reeve grunted. 'True.' And yet, it did matter. And he had the nasty feeling that what she thought was going to matter to him more and more as time went on.

'I just hope you don't do anything stupid at the audition for the soap, that's all,' Annis said flatly. 'But then, men like you don't make mistakes, do they? I'm sure you'll be perfect.' And she was sure too.

Reeve blinked, surprised by the unfairness of her attack. Then he understood. 'You think Gale will give me the part just because we're supposed to be sleeping together, don't you?' he asked bitterly.

Annis's tawny eyes darkened and she shook her head. 'It's none of my business,' she said, her voice unusually meek. For suddenly she realised that it wasn't her business. What Reeve Morgan did with his life was nothing to do with her. But it should be, a forlorn little voice piped up from somewhere deep inside her. Annis paled as she was forced to listen to what she was telling herself. Oh dammit, no! The last thing she needed to do was fall in love with Reeve Morgan.

'No, you're quite right,' Reeve said heavily. 'It isn't anyone's business but our own.'

In truth, he and Gale were not lovers.

Gale was, in fact, gay — but she didn't mind that others thought they were involved. He'd have to tell her to make it clear from now on that they were just friends.

And when Reeve listened to what he was telling himself, he wondered how it was possible for a woman to become the most important thing in his life practically overnight.

He stared at Annis's pinched and unhappy face and shook his head.

Face it, Reeve, he thought grimly. You're in trouble.

Annis turned away. 'We'd better go,' she said flatly.

It was hard to say which of them felt the more miserable as they made their way back to rehearsals.

CHAPTER 7

Frederica dumped her packages on to the bed and sighed. She couldn't believe she'd just blown two months' allowance on a single outfit. She went to the bathroom at the end of the corridor, and further indulged herself by adding the expensive bath oil her father had bought for her birthday. When she was finished she smelt of freesias and utterly feminine. Back in her room, a glance at her watch told her it was still way too early to get ready, so she pulled out her books.

As well as the Final Degree Show, every Fine Art student had to submit an extended essay in Hilary Term of their last year, and although she was only just finishing her second year, Frederica was already planning for both. But after an hour she gave it up — studying was just too difficult when her concentration had gone out of the window. All she could think about was that tonight she was going out with him. It still seemed too incredible to be real.

She got her hairbrush and sat down in front of a small mirror, thinking about her first date with the sophisticated, wealthy, devastatingly good-looking male called Lorcan Greene. What on earth did she think she was doing? Just why had she accepted his dinner invitation? Come to that, why had he given it? When she thought of all the women he must know, worldly wise, beautiful and sophisticated, she felt distinctly gauche by comparison.

She met her dark brown eyes in the mirror and stuck her tongue out at her reflection. With the summer under way, her freckles were making their presence known, and with her hair loose like this, she looked about fourteen. Perhaps she should just plait it into two pigtails and have done with it.

But she knew there was no point in trying to belittle this evening in her own mind. The plain and simple fact was . . . she was excited. On tenterhooks. Wildly, massively happy at the thought of seeing him again.

She turned on her stool and lifted her hair off the back of her neck, piling it up on her head, then let it cascade over her shoulders and down her back. Better or worse?

She thought of Lorcan — that elegant height he carried off so easily. That cool blonde handsomeness that was so much a part of him. That aura of power and knowledge. A man like that deserved a woman who was prepared to make the effort for him. And then she felt angry. Damn it, why should she primp and preen in front of a mirror? He was only a man after all. But she so wanted to look good!

Grimly, she reached for the expensive cosmetic case her mother had given her, which she seldom used. First she put on a base cream, then a very fine coating of powder. Next she added the barest touch of glittering golden eyeshadow, and a clever mascara that was guaranteed not to clot, rub off or be sticky. And when she looked at the result, she had to admit it was quite startling. Her deep, velvety eyes had always been one of her most striking features, but highlighted with gold, and framed by such thick dark lashes, they looked positively amazing. Pleased with her experiments so far, she added a dark bronze lipstick, then added lip gloss. The result was to highlight her deep cupid's bow, and give her mouth a moist, mysterious look. Frederica stared at her freckles. Should she conceal them after all? She shook her head crossly. Enough was enough!

Hair. She forced her mind back to the auburn tresses. Up or down? She settled for a softer chignon, which let little tendrils and wisps curl over her forehead, cheeks and neck. Then she walked over to a carrier bag and extracted a length of black velvet ribbon, which she wound artfully around her hair, tying it in a bow on the back of her neck and letting the long V-cut ends trail to a point just at the nape of her neck. Black strappy sandals that criss-crossed her ankles and fastened with a buckle at the back were teamed with a floaty black skirt. It was surprisingly full, and floated to just below her knees. Tiny gold bells had been cunningly added to the scalloped hem. They tinkled musically whenever she moved. The blouse was black silk, and completed the outfit perfectly.

Finally, with the time nearing seven-thirty, Frederica walked to her tiny wardrobe and opened the door, looking at herself in the full-length mirror. Gone was the paint-besmirched, ponytailed Fine Art student. In her place was a Romany princess, with mysterious dark eyes and a provocative mouth.

'What the hell am I doing?' she heard her own voice, breathless and shaken, echo around the room. 'I can't go out to dinner with Lorcan Greene dressed like this!'

But she didn't have time to change. And something inside her didn't want to. The woman in the mirror was the kind of woman Lorcan Greene would take to dinner. And isn't that what she'd wanted to be, from the very first moment she'd set eyes on him? She turned away, reaching for a bottle of Allure by Chanel, yet another gift from her ever-hopeful mother. She dabbed it behind her ears and on her wrists, then left her room, her heart thumping. She passed several students on the way out, men and women she'd known for the past year, and every single one of them watched her go out of sight, a stunned look in their eyes. She heard one boy, a medical student, say to his slack-jawed friend, 'Now that's what I call a hot date.' And they both laughed.

But, instead of cheering her up and bolstering her self-confidence, their words echoed ominously in her head as she walked towards the lodge. What if Lorcan Greene, too, took one look at her and immediately thought that she was 'hot'?

In theory, she was a modern woman in charge of her life and destiny. But inside, she felt cold and just a little frightened. In fact, she almost turned back. But then he stepped through the open lodge gates, saw her, and stopped dead. He was dressed in richly tailored twill trousers with a deep wine-red shirt. The evening sun was colouring his wheat-gold hair a fairer shade, and as she approached, the hazel eyes seemed to fix her in a state of unreality.

She found herself walking towards him helplessly, like a metal filing drawn to a magnet. The birdsong around her seemed softer, the air thicker, the beat of her heart more insistent. Lorcan watched her approach, hardly able to believe his eyes. Always before, he'd seen Frederica Delacroix at the Ruskin, in her persona of artist. The 'fake-buster' in him saw her as a potential con artist. But now he was seeing the woman. And what he saw took his breath away.

'Hello,' she said nervously. 'I'm not late, am I?'

Lorcan shook his head and held out his hand. 'The car's just outside,' he said simply, and led her to a glamorous silver Aston Martin. She felt absurdly privileged as he opened the door for her, a solicitous hand cupped under her elbow, before shutting the door carefully behind her. As he got in lithely beside her, she was suddenly aware of the smallness of the sports car, how near to the ground it was, how powerful it sounded. As he put the car into gear, his hand brushed against her leg, and a powerful current of shivering electricity shot up her thigh, lodging itself somewhere deep inside her, making her face flame.

'I thought we'd go to The Trout Inn at Wolvercote,' he named a local pub-cum-restaurant, well-thought-of and well frequented in Oxford circles. She nodded, but the fact was she hadn't even given their possible destination a single thought. She wound down a window, aware that her face was still flaming, and didn't give a thought, either, to the effects of the wind streaming into the car on her much-worried-over hairstyle.

Lorcan found it difficult to concentrate on driving with the breeze wafting tiny plumes of Titian hair about her face like that. Luckily the drive was short, and soon they were angling over the hump-backed bridge that preceded the inn.

He'd booked an outdoor table, and as they were led to it, the sound of the weir on the river filled the air with the pagan roar of rushing water. They sat at the table, tucked away in a little bower of fragrant honeysuckle and pastel-pink clematis. 'Would you care for a drink, sir?' the waiter murmured discreetly.

'Thank you,' Lorcan said casually. 'Scotch and water for me and . . .' he looked at Frederica, whose mind went promptly blank. He saw the brief look of consternation cross her face and added smoothly, 'A glass of Pinot Grigio for Miss Delacroix.'

Frederica found that her white wine, when it came, was delicious. Dry but refreshing, somehow just right. But then, she thought with a touch of asperity, what else could she have expected from a man like this? The words 'suave' and 'charming' in the dictionary probably had his picture beside them.

'I was never a student myself,' Lorcan surprised her by saying, 'so it's easy for me to forget how different your lifestyles must be. If you don't like the drink, I can easily get you something else.'

Frederica shook her head and reached for her glass defensively. 'No! This is . . . perfect.'

He can read me like a book, Frederica thought despairingly. Which, considering she was in the process of forging a Forbes-Wright, didn't bode too well for her immediate future.

Lorcan's smile was a touch knowing as he watched her sip, but he quickly became fascinated by her moist, trembling lips. He imagined himself kissing them, anticipating the slight clinging of the lipstick, the taste of the woman beneath.

Frederica quickly looked away. The river flowing past them was filled with trout, and when the waiter brought a basket of bread rolls, she began to feed them, almost without thinking.

The sun was lowering behind the screen of trees, casting the Trout Inn in an early twilight glow. A waiter came and lit the candles, but she was unaware of the way the candle-light transformed her face, catching the dancing lights in her hair, darkening her eyes to a mysterious midnight, and complementing the downy peach bloom on her cheeks. Lorcan, however, was only too aware of it, and found himself dragging in a suddenly much-needed breath. This was getting out of hand.

So far, all the forgers he'd helped put behind bars had been men. The thought of persecuting a young, beautiful girl was distinctly unappealing — which was why he'd decided to use tonight to scare her off. 'So,' he said, 'tell me about yourself.' He crossed his legs casually and gave her a smile that curled her toes. 'I understand your family has quite a reputation as collectors,' he added pointedly.

Frederica tensed visibly. 'Oh?' She swallowed a sudden dryness in her throat. 'How did you . . . ?'

'I'd heard of your family,' he said, with perfect truth-fulness. When researching her, the name 'Rainbow House' struck a chord. A friend of his had visited the place one summer, years ago. It had had some remarkable paintings, he'd told Lorcan — both extremely good and extremely bad.

'Oh,' Frederica said. 'Yes, well, the family have been collecting bits and pieces for centuries,' she admitted, shrugging modestly. 'Dad's best find was a Pollock.'

She reached for her drink and sipped it again, desperately searching for another topic. 'How are you finding Oxford?' she asked brightly, fixing a smile on her face. It was so bright it hurt her cheeks.

The waiter arrived with the menu just then, saving him from answering. Lorcan opted for a stuffed artichoke starter, and the inn's speciality for his main course — fresh baked trout. Frederica chose a cheese soufflé and the lamb. When they were once more alone, Lorcan smiled at her across the candlelight, having thought of a nice little rejoinder to her question. 'I'm beginning to find Oxford very interesting indeed,' he drawled dangerously. 'There's so much going on. Most of it under the surface.'

Was it his imagination, or did she look suddenly guilty then? 'Oh, yes I suppose that's fair,' Frederica said gamely. 'But you shouldn't neglect the obvious either. The museums, for instance, are world class.'

'I'm sure.' His green eyes looked wickedly amused. 'But whenever I go into any museum I can't stop myself from looking for fakes,' he added, so silkily that she almost forgot to laugh. She felt her colour fade, rush back, and her hand shake. Then she remembered to laugh — as if he'd just told the best joke in the world.

'Oh, I'm sure there aren't any in the Ashmolean,' she managed to choke.

This time there was no mistaking her unease. Dammit, he was right. Whatever Braine had sniffed out going on down here in Oxford, she was in it right up to her pretty swan-like neck. He wanted to reach across the table and shake her for being so stupid. But he restrained himself.

'So, tell me about . . . er . . . your travels,' Frederica said hastily.

'For a Fine Art student you seem determined to steer the talk away from art.' He couldn't resist the dig.

Frederica managed a sickly smile. 'Oh well . . . who wants to talk shop all the time?'

The waiter's arrival with their first course rescued her, while Lorcan set himself out to be deliberately charming.

He told her tales of Florence, and Venice in the rain; he talked about the perils of gallery ownership, and made her laugh with a tale about a visit to a Royal Garden Party, and the trouble the Ambassador of Spain had got into with one of the corgis. By the time the main course arrived, she was smiling and relaxing, and beginning to enjoy herself at last.

Lorcan supposed that it was now he should pounce. Ask her a very pointed question about the old-fashioned way she'd been cleaning the canvas, for instance. He was sure that she'd be unable to think of an excuse, and her face would pale, and those amazing pansy eyes of hers would flood with fear and anger. But he didn't want to see those lovely eyes filled with either of those emotions, he realised grimly. Damn it, he didn't want her to be mixed up in anything illegal at all. He was beginning to wish that Detective Inspector Richard Braine had gone to somebody else with his knotty little Oxford problem. He looked at her for a long time through the flickering candlelight, then he half-nodded.

Frederica had the strangest feeling he'd just come to some sort of an important conclusion, but how she knew this, she couldn't have said. She was developing instincts where this man was concerned, and the realisation of it was both alarming and exhilarating. 'When you've finished your course here,' he said softly, caressing his wine glass in a way that made her jealous, 'I'd like to buy some of your canvases. The harvest scene, for one. Will you let me?'

Frederica felt her breath catch. Would she let him? Being exhibited at the Greene Gallery would make her reputation overnight! Her face lit up.

Lorcan once again felt his breath catch. In the candle-light, her eyes glowed, and those lovely, ridiculous freckles marching across her nose just begged to be kissed, one by one . . .

'Oh, Lorcan — do you really think . . . ? Am I really good enough?'

He dragged his thoughts away from freckles and turned his attention back to the artist in front of him. 'Yes,' he said simply. 'You're good enough. All you have to do is stay true to yourself and your work. And, of course,' he added casually, 'keep out of trouble. An artist, more than any other, lives and dies by his or her reputation.'

Just then, the server came over with the dessert menu came and, cursing the bad timing, Lorcan selected the cheese platter, while Frederica, in a suddenly buoyant mood, opted for the far more opulent raspberry meringue. When they were alone again, Lorcan leaned forward, determined to give her a way out. 'You know, unlike most artists, you really have a bright future ahead of you. It won't just be me who'll want your work.'

Frederica nodded happily. 'Thank you.'

Lorcan sighed. Had she taken the hint? He hoped so. Because, even for her, he could do no more. If Richard arrested her . . . then it would be the finish of her.

They lingered over their coffee and discussed her work and bright future as the last rays of the sun set behind Port Meadow. Lorcan drove them silently back towards the centre of town, but parked before they got to St Bede's. He turned, and found her eyes, which had been misty with happiness, suddenly wary. Once again it struck him how inexperienced she seemed. How innocent. It made him feel like a prize villain. And also like a man who'd stumbled upon buried treasure.

'I thought we'd walk back to college,' he said softly. 'That is, if you don't mind a moonlit stroll?'

Frederica swallowed hard. *Mind* . . . ? The moon was full as they walked down the cherry-tree-lined pavements. Behind them, St Antony's College clock struck ten. Ahead of them, lit up with orange lights, the towers, crenelated walls and fabled 'dreaming spires' of Oxford shimmered in the evening heat. A single blackbird, fooled by the artificial light, sang mellifluously from the branches overhead.

Lorcan reached for her hand and Frederica's heart leaped. She could hardly feel the pavement beneath her feet as they headed back to St Bede's. They said little as they strolled together, and she was once again beginning to tense up, he noticed, as she led him to the main door of her residence.

'Well . . .' She turned, not about to ask him in. 'I . . . would you like to . . .'

Lorcan reached up and put a finger against her lips. 'I won't come in,' he murmured softly. 'Frederica, think about what I said tonight. You have a bright future — provided you don't do anything to jeopardise it.'

Frederica stiffened, for the first time really hearing the stark warning in his voice. What . . . ? How . . . ? And then his head was lowering. She had one brief instant to think 'He's going to kiss me!' and then he *was* kissing her.

She swayed at the first contact of his lips on hers — warm, firm, gentle, and . . . oh so wonderful. Lorcan felt his arms slip around her waist. Felt himself pulling her to him. Some last vestige of self-protection warned him to stop, to push her away, but it was already too late. He felt her lips part pliantly beneath his. Heard her moan a soft, sighing sound of pleasure, and his own groaned answer.

Frederica felt her legs turn to water, and was glad when he held her tighter to him. Her head was literally spinning. She could sense every atom of their twin beings flowing together — their breath merging, their scents, their senses, everything becoming a single entity. Her eyes closed as she felt his hands splay open against her back, his fingers warm against her spine.

And then he was moving back from her, slowly, oh so slowly, but leaving her. Their lips lingered, moving millimetre by millimetre, until they eventually parted with a soft sigh of loss.

Lorcan took a ragged breath and a step back. He felt staggered. Shocked. Utterly shaken. He saw her open her eyes — those dark, velvety, midnight eyes, and shook his head.

It was madness. The whole thing was madness. He couldn't be falling in love. Not now! Not with this woman of all women!

'Frederica,' he said softly. 'Goodnight.' And goodbye, he added silently, with a pain as sharp as any he'd ever felt before. For he was, in that instant, utterly determined that he wouldn't be seeing her again.

CHAPTER 8

Reeve hopped off the bus and made his way towards the rehearsal room, ignoring the many admiring female glances thrown his way. Dressed in his form-fitting cycling gear, his arm and leg muscles rippled as he moved. But he was thinking about his phone call to Gale Evers and his frown made him look moody and dangerous.

Gale had been typically noncommittal about his chances of getting a part in the soap, but had gone on to wish him luck and then promptly invited him to a high-profile television awards ceremony later on that week.

He'd accepted gladly, but now found himself, annoyingly, worrying about how a certain young woman might react to the news when it became known. But not even for the deliciously sweet-and-sour Ms Whittington was he willing to back off. He needed to raise his profile in any way he could — by foul means or fair!

But as he approached the block of flats and saw Annis herself mount the steps to the hall, he broke out into a run with all the fluid ease of a leopard. This time, women positively gaped! 'Hey, Annis. Wait!'

Annis, in the act of pushing open the doors, jumped and looked around. The city was busy. Since most of the actors all had regular day jobs, rehearsals were always held at night, and the rush-hour traffic pounded the streets and pavements with weary commuters, but she had no trouble picking him out of the crowd. She watched him running towards her, the skin-tight clothing clinging to his muscular form, dark curly hair flopping attractively above his forehead, and felt desire start deep and low inside her.

Since her divorce she had been 'off' men. Right off. The only male her bed had seen in almost a year was Fletcher, her ancient teddy bear. Now, suddenly, her hormones were reminding her of what she was missing. She forced back her unwelcome primordial urges with a monumental effort, and by the time he'd reached her she was wearing what she hoped was a neutral smile.

To Reeve it was more like the grin of a she-wolf before she sat down to dinner — the dinner being him, of course — but he was getting used to that by now. 'I thought I'd missed you,' Reeve said, leaning against the wall, looking down at her with sparkling eyes.

'You ran all that way to tell me that?' she asked, one eyebrow raised provocatively. 'And in this weather too.'

May was turning out to be a scorchingly hot month. And standing this close to him, aware of the small beads of sweat on his forehead and having to fight the urge to lick them off, was doing nothing to cool her down at all.

Reeve opened his mouth, realised he had no possible comeback and promptly closed it again. He smiled and shook his head wearily. 'Annis, Annis, Annis,' he said sorrowfully. 'What do I have to do to make you give me a chance? Get down on my knees and beg?'

Annis swallowed hard. A vivid picture of him kneeling down before her, dark-blue eyes looking up at her, his lips just a scant inch away from her bare navel . . . She blinked away the fantasy quickly.

'Well, it would be a start. But not out here, I think,' she drawled, and pushed the door leading into the cool hallway.

Several people who lived in the block of flats arrived back from work and made to brush by them, and Annis was relieved to be able to stop and chat. Funny how being forced to be polite in public could take your mind off less pressing matters. Like having a dangerously attractive man literally breathing down your neck. She could feel Reeve's warm breath on her skin, he was standing so closely behind her.

She paused beside a young mother with a baby in a pram. The baby was gorgeous — but the mother's eyes were all for Reeve, who winked at her as they moved past. Annis pretended not to notice.

As they walked up the second flight of stairs to the empty third-floor flat, they saw that the door was already ajar.

'The others are early birds,' Annis said, glancing at her watch. 'I thought we'd be the first to arrive for a change.'

Reeve smiled knowingly. 'Getting excited?'

Now that their weekend gig was fast approaching, Annis had to admit that she was. She was currently working as a receptionist at a fairly nice hotel, but nothing could match the buzz she got when performing. Even in front of only fifty or so people.

Acting was something that was simply in her blood. The chance to recreate a little fantasy, a little glamour, a little romance, to explore human emotion, to find the limits of her talent and stretch it just a little further.

As they walked to the door and pushed it fully open, they were surprised to see the place deserted, although they could hear voices coming from what must be a bedroom. The cast usually stuck to the big living room only.

'Do you suppose Ray is laying down the law to someone?' she whispered, a little bit worried.

'Possibly,' he conceded. Reeve too knew the pitfalls of falling foul of producers and directors. 'I don't recognise the voice, though. Let's hope it's nothing serious. Nobody wants trouble, least of all me. In my time I've taken more flak than the Dambusters.'

Annis grinned. But he was right — it didn't sound like one of the members of the cast being told off. The stranger's voice was more deeply pitched than any of the actors in the upcoming murder-mystery weekend, and even through the closed door she could hear an unmistakable hint of upper-class superiority.

'Look, I've told you . . . and it's . . . working out fine. Just leave me alone to . . . and you'll have it, just . . .' Ray's voice rose and fell, obviously agitated. It had the effect of making only some of the words audible, giving them maddening bits and pieces of the conversation.

'I wonder what's going on?' Annis said, curious, and took a tentative step further into the room.

Reeve, less inclined to pry, simply shrugged. He had other things on his mind — like finding out some more titbits from Annis Whittington's life story.

'Have you ever been to Oxford before?' he asked casually, content merely to stare at her. She had the kind of side profile that would look absolutely superb on a cameo brooch, all character and soft curves and intriguing, cool beauty. It was only when she turned full-face that one got that tawny spitfire effect!

'What? Oh, no, I haven't,' she turned towards him, then back to the closed door again, as once more the stranger's voice rumbled warningly.

'That's all very well . . . but . . . paying you good money . . . painting . . . I must have it!'

Reeve scowled, a nasty thought suddenly impinging on him. 'I wonder if it's the man who pays the piper in there? I hope it doesn't mean the murder mystery's off. Or, worse, they're going to try and foist a cut in wages on us.'

'Don't even think that!' Annis wailed. Loudly. And suddenly everything went silent. Then, cautiously, the door opened and Ray stuck his head out. His bald dome was glistening, and his eyes looked distinctly nervous.

'Oh, hello, you two,' he muttered, coming out and shutting the door firmly behind him. 'You're early. Why don't you go down to the off-licence and bring some beer back? It's going to be a long, thirsty night's work.' He reached into his wallet for a couple of ten-pound notes and Reeve moved across the room to take them.

'Sure, Ray, whatever you say,' he agreed casually. But he didn't like the look in the man's eye. Not a bit. He all but dragged Annis out of the room.

'Let go of me,' she hissed, snatching her arm out of his hand once they were out into the stairwell. She cast a final, puzzled glance behind her as Reeve shut the door of the flat.

'You know what curiosity did to the cat, don't you?' he asked her drolly. He had the feeling that, whatever Ray's problem was, they didn't want to get caught up in it. Reeve began to wonder about their producer. Good ol' Ray.

'But don't you want to know what that was all about?' she asked in frustration.

'No. And neither do you,' Reeve said, with just enough bite in his voice to surprise her. 'If Ray's having money trouble, the last thing he needs is for us to get in the way. Just think about your pay cheque and what happened to the cat, and then you won't be so nosy.' He stopped in the middle of the busy pavement to give her nose a pinch. Annis brushed his hand away, putting her sudden breathlessness down to the stifling city heat.

'Clown!' she scowled. But she was smiling as she followed him into the off-licence and carried one of the six-packs he handed over to her without complaint. By the time they had returned, Ray's mysterious visitor had gone and the rest of the cast had arrived. They fell on the beer like desert travellers spotting an oasis.

If Ray cast the two of them an odd, anxious look, Annis didn't notice. But Reeve, though he gave no sign of it, definitely did. He made a decision to keep a close eye on Annis during their weekend in Oxford; it wouldn't do for her to get too curious again. Then he quickly forgot his unease as they knuckled down to work, running through every scene.

'Right then, I think that went well,' Ray said when they'd finished. 'Now, accommodation. I've booked rooms for everyone in a small lodging house in Headington. It's in the suburbs, but only ten minutes' bus ride from the centre of town.'

John Lore and Norman Rix exchanged knowing looks. 'I can see it now,' John said. 'No hot water, but plenty of cockroaches and a landlady whose speciality is liver and onions.'

'Oh don't,' Julie shuddered, while Reeve coughed apologetically.

'There's no need to book me in, Ray,' he said with pseudo-regret. 'I've got a friend in Oxford who's off to the Caribbean next week. He's asked me to house-sit. I know, it's a rotten job, but someone's gotta do it. I can't have the swimming pool, hot tub, Japanese garden and king-sized bed feeling all alone, can I?'

There were riotous catcalls at this announcement, and on that happy note the rehearsals broke up.

Annis was not surprised to find him waiting for her in the hall this time. When he fell into step companionably beside her, she tried to tell herself that it meant nothing. That she felt nothing. It didn't do any good, but she tried telling herself so anyway.

'This place of my friend's,' Reeve began casually as they stepped outside into the warm, dark night. 'It's got two en suite rooms. If you want, you can have the other.'

Annis stopped dead in her tracks. She looked at him, or rather stared at him, her breasts heaving as she fought back a wave of anger. And desire. Oh yes . . . definitely desire.

'Well that was quick work, even for you,' she finally managed to say.

Reeve sighed heavily. 'I said it has two en suite rooms, Annis,' he reminded her, his voice heavy with irony. 'As in one for you and one for me?'

Annis snorted. 'Huh. And you're seriously trying to tell me that during the wee small hours of the night you won't come tiptoeing into my room? Getting lost on your way to the bathroom, perhaps?'

Reeve smiled at her savagely. 'And of course, you'd really object if I did, isn't that right, Annis?' he challenged her.

She remembered her earlier, very vivid fantasies about him, and flushed angrily. Because he was right, damn him! From the very first moment he'd mentioned having a house to himself during their Oxford break, she had been wondering if he'd ask her. She took a deep breath that seemed to originate from somewhere in her shoes.

'Reeve,' she said sweetly, 'you can take your offer of accommodation and—'

'Ah-ah-ah,' he interrupted her. 'No bad language please. Remember you're a lady.'

Annis nodded. 'You're right. And when a lady's been propositioned by a self-satisfied jerk, there's only one thing left for her to do.'

She swung her arm like a cricketer about to bowl a blinder, and carefully angled her open palm with the smooth plane of his right cheek. Unfortunately he was a little too quick for her and ducked at the optimum moment.

Annis found herself swiping air, spinning around and staggering to regain her balance.

Then she heard his rich deep laughter as, once again, he left her alone, gaping and rattled, on the city's pavement.

CHAPTER 9

Frederica awoke, stretched, yawned extravagantly, and lay grinning up at the ceiling. It was four days since her date with Lorcan Greene, and still she couldn't seem to get the smile to leave her face. The ride in the silver sports car — surely the best stand-in for a knight's white steed? — the romantic inn, with its rushing trout-filled stream, candlelight and delicious liqueurs. Then the stroll back through Oxford's moonlight streets. And the man . . .

The man who was everything any woman could ever dream of: rich, handsome, cultured, clever, witty and charming. A man who shared her passion for art. A man who wanted to buy her work. A man who could teach her everything she could ever want to know — from how to make love, to speaking Italian, from appreciating good wine, to making love, from teaching her how to drive, to how to make love.

Frederica sighed and got dressed, then made her way to breakfast in Hall, smiling at the scouts who served the toast and marmalade, smiling at her fellow students, smiling even at the painted portrait of a previous principal, centuries dead. Life was looking good.

She'd telephoned her father the day before to ask him to look out the diaries of one of their ancestors, Francis

Delacroix, a competent biographer of the artists of his day, and to tell him she'd changed her mind about the painting, and that she would help her old dad out after all. The relief in his voice was palpable.

As she tucked into her cornflakes, she dragged her mind from Lorcan Greene back to her current project. The old canvas was now clean and nearly dry and she was ready to begin. And having Lorcan hovering in the background gave an added piquancy. It was the feeling of beating him, without hurting him, that was so thrilling. He was so much more than she was. Older, more experienced, more confident. And while that delighted her in some strange, utterly feminine way, it also made her ache to put just a slight dent in that armour of his.

She was due at one of his lectures on Friday, and kept imagining the way their eyes would meet across the crowded studio. Could almost see his hazel eyes becoming smoky as she smiled at him.

Pulling herself together, she finished her toast and walked to the lodge to collect her mail, surprised to find that the diaries had already arrived for her via special delivery. Back in her room, she lay on the bed and reached for the top copy.

The diaries vividly conjured up the mind and mood of an early Victorian gentleman, but it was when she got to the technicalities of life as an artist that she began to get really excited. Nearly two hours later, she was still making copious notes, and was relieved to discover that she had cleaned the canvas exactly as she should have done.

'So you won't be able to tell from the age and state of the canvas that it's a fake, Lorcan darling,' she murmured, her voice lingering caressingly over his name and tinged with triumph.

The imaginary game she was playing with him was intoxicating. Should she let him view the finished painting when it was hung up back in Rainbow House, just to see whether he spotted it as a forgery? No. Too dangerous. And yet . . .

She read on, forgetting lunch, and then suddenly sat up with a lurch, hardly daring to believe what she was reading. Paints. Her good old great-great-great grandfather was going into details about paints, and she could have kissed him for his pernickety attention to detail. She'd never expected to be given, on a plate as it were, the recipe for mid-nineteenth-century oil paints.

As she stared at the faded blue ink on the diary page, she recognised the name of a shop Francis Delacroix had mentioned, one of Oxford's oldest speciality artist's shops. She'd heard of it, but had never been there. She quickly reached for her copy of the university prospectus, turning to the map on the back. She memorised the shop's location and snapped the prospectus shut with a grin. This was such an unbelievable stroke of luck she could hardly believe it. Of course, the shop wouldn't sell Victorian-style paints ready-made. But now she had the recipe, she would only need to do some experimenting to get the mixes right. The trick was always in the mixing. She'd just have to keep at it until she was confident she'd got it right.

But during her research, she'd discovered that there was another Forbes-Wright picture right here in Oxford, in a college not far from her own. That would give her a better idea of how the man himself preferred to apply his paints.

Smiling and humming to herself, Frederica left her room and walked out into the bright May sunshine.

She'd have to ask the bursar if she could 'stay up' for another month. Like all Oxford colleges, St Bede's did a lot of conference trade in the summer, and she didn't want to get thrown out until her canvas was finished. Working at home would be impossible — her mother was so nosy.

She walked to St Giles' and hailed a taxi.

* * *

Lorcan cruised down the Woodstock Road, keeping his eyes firmly averted from the entrance to St Bede's. He'd been out that morning to a country house sale and had bought a simple little painting, unsigned, of an apple orchard. He had a few good ideas about its provenance, and its style was of the Newlyn School. So when he pulled to a stop at the junction of St Giles' his mind was, for once, a long way from Frederica Delacroix. When he saw her getting into a taxi, his hands tightened ominously on the steering wheel. The sensation of soft lips clinging to his rose into his mind, making his heart thump and his loins tingle. And before he knew it, he found himself following the taxi out of the centre of the city.

As it led him to the old suburb of Holywell, he felt faintly ridiculous — like a weary gumshoe tracking a femme fatale to a hideout. But when she got out in front of a rickety shop named 'The Painters' Emporium', he nevertheless parked out of sight and made his way back to it. There, a dirty coat of arms informed him that the shop had been established in 1799. And it looked it.

Through the grimy windows, he could see that the interior was stacked high with plain easels and donkeys — those with a built-in seat and painter's box; jam jars full of brushes; and a large array of artists' palettes.

What was she doing here, in an out-of-the-way, old-fashioned speciality shop? In his heart, he knew there could only be one answer. He paced restlessly, getting angrier and angrier. With her. With himself. And, alarmingly, with Detective Inspector Richard Braine of the Art Fraud Squad.

He told himself that he'd forgotten that Friday-night kiss.

He told himself that this feeling he got whenever he was near her meant nothing more than the arousal any man would feel when close to a beautiful young woman. He told himself he should go back to London and forget that he'd ever seen her face. But still he waited. Like a kestrel, hovering, awaiting a glimpse of a field mouse, chained to a predatory nature and unable to prevent himself from closing in for the kill.

CHAPTER 10

Inside the shop, Frederica waited for the ancient proprietor to come back from the depths of the cellar, where he'd gone in search of one of her rarer requests, and idly inspected some brushes. There was everything an artist could want, from the expensive kolinsky sable-hair brush which tapered to such a beautiful dark point, to polecat, goat, camel, ox and hog's hair. Frederica could have spent over a thousand pounds here on brushes alone. When she sold her first painting to Lorcan, she promised herself, she was going to spend every last penny on setting up a really good, well-equipped studio.

The proprietor, eighty if he was a day and as bright as a button, returned. Frederica had all but fallen in love with him the moment she'd stepped inside.

'Here we are, miss. Mind you, the solution is so very old . . .' he trailed off anxiously, staring doubtfully at the ancient, brown-stained bottle in his hand. Could he really sell it to her, in all good conscience? He only had it at all because he was too old and too lazy to clear out the cellars.

But the beautiful young lady only smiled at him. 'No, no, that's fine. That's just what I want, in fact.'

Finally satisfied that she had all she needed, Frederica paid the man, wincing at the sum, and determined to ask her father for a bigger allowance next year. After this, he owed her big time! When she left the shop, her bag of precious goodies hugged close to her chest, she now had the ingredients to copy Forbes-Wright's paints right down to the finest detail.

She was so excited by this prospect that as she hailed and climbed into another taxi, she didn't even see the golden-haired figure that watched her go then entered the art shop she'd just left. The old man inside looked up, surprised by the tinkling of the doorbell.

The man who walked in instantly had the old owner smiling. A gentleman! He served so few of those nowadays. 'Good afternoon, sir,' he welcomed. 'Unseasonably warm for the time of the year.'

Lorcan smiled and nodded. 'It certainly is.'

In the octogenarian he instinctively recognised a dying breed — a true shopkeeper. Moreover, one who knew his art from his elbow. He would have to be careful if he was to get the information he needed. 'I'm a visiting fellow at the Ruskin,' he established his credentials right away, pleased to see the old man stiffen and look even more alertly impressed than before. 'You've been here for some time, I see by the crest outside?'

The old man's face radiated with pride. 'Indeed we have, sir. My family first opened the doors back in 1799. In our time we've sold paints to all the greats.'

Lorcan nodded. 'I can well believe it.' The shop was impressive. 'I suppose you get quite a few of my students in,' he enquired craftily.

The old man sighed. 'Not as many as once before, sir, I'm sorry to say. Still . . .' He brightened. 'These things are like fashion trends. We'll be popular once again someday, no doubt.'

Lorcan nodded. 'I'll be sure to mention your shop in my lecture on Friday,' he promised, and meant it.

The old man's face lit up at such good news, his eyes twinkling. 'Will you, sir? Well, now, thank you very much.'

Lorcan smiled. 'One other thing I've noticed about Oxford,' he smiled, leaning a little closer to the proprietor, 'is how many pretty girls there are here.'

The old man beamed. 'Ah yes indeed. I met my Muriel here, having tea in the Raleigh Hotel.' He sighed heavily.

Lorcan, feeling like all kinds of a heel, nodded, but carried on relentlessly. 'That beautiful red-headed lady who was going out just as I was coming in, for instance. If I wasn't a tutor, I'd have been inclined to ask her to tea at the Raleigh.'

Knowing instinctively that the old man wouldn't approve of an Oxford don acting like an Oxford student, he kept his voice purposely respectful — but with just a tinge of we're-all-men-together in his voice.

'Ah yes. A very beautiful young lady, and a real artist.'

'Really? How can you tell?' he asked, looking intrigued.

The old man's chest swelled with pride. 'Well, sir, from the things she asked for,' he replied innocently. 'Real paints, not these modern mixes.' And, before he knew what was what, he found himself listing all the young lady's incredible purchases.

Lorcan listened and smiled, and felt a cold hard fist forming in his stomach. Frederica Delacroix had just bought everything she might need if she was going to try to forge a painting of the 1860 period.

'You're right,' he said at last, his voice curiously lifeless now. 'That's the shopping list of an old-fashioned painter. But I would have thought such items like that were obsolete now.'

'Ah yes, sir, but this is a speciality shop, sir. I have things in the cellar that were around in Stubbs's day,' the old man said, and Lorcan didn't have any difficulty in believing him.

When he walked miserably back to his car, he carried a big bag of expensive paint-cleaning materials in one hand. The gallery's restorer could always do with them, and after the bonus the old man had given him, he hadn't wanted to leave without spending a fair chunk of money by way of recompense.

He got into the Aston Martin and drove slowly through the town. As he approached Carfax, at the bottom of the High Street, he saw her. Just for a moment, bobbing along with the crowds of shoppers and tourists. Her auburn hair was loose, and swung around the dusky orange of her blouse. She was smiling, but as he was obliged to turn up the High Street — Oxford's one-way system was a killer — he didn't get to look at her for more than a second.

He drove home, feeling oddly deprived. And still furiously angry. Had she listened to nothing that he'd said on Friday night about keeping her reputation spotless? Damn the woman, couldn't she take a hint? He slammed into the house on Five Mile Drive, went straight to the kitchen and poured himself a large glass of rich burgundy. He took it into the living room, where he sat down on the sofa, trying to force himself to relax. He spread one arm across the back of the sofa and drank the wine morosely, hardly tasting it.

'Damn it, Frederica,' he said softly, staring at the ceiling. 'I'd have made you famous. I'd have exhibited every canvas you ever painted.' He'd have done more, so much more than that . . . He shook his head. No. That was dangerous. So incredibly dangerous. Besides, all of that was over now. The dream, barely begun, was shattered for ever. He reached for the phone and angrily dialled a familiar number.

Detective Inspector Richard Braine of the Art Fraud Squad answered on the sixth ring. 'Hello, Richard?' Lorcan said grimly. 'I've got news for you. Yes. A nibble. A definite nibble. Yes, one of the students.' He paused, listened, took a deep breath and another mouthful of wine.

'Frederica Delacroix,' he said, his voice as dead as the feeling in his heart.

CHAPTER 11

Annis and the rest of the gang stepped off the train at Oxford's station and stood, pooling their luggage around them on the platform.

'Hardly a teeming metropolis, is it?' Gordon, the play's 'policeman', said wryly.

'You're out in the boonies now, dear,' Gerry drawled cheerfully, her red hair newly coloured and cut.

'Well I for one am glad to be out of London for a little while,' the ever-enthusiastic Julie said. 'Just fancy — Oxford. I wonder where the dreaming spires are?'

John laughed. 'They're not a theme park, Jules. They'll be scattered about all over the place, I expect.' Everyone collected their luggage and set off, groaning, up the stairs. No moving escalators for Oxford, it seemed.

'I'd forgotten,' Norman puffed, 'the delights of provincial . . . tours.' Annis offered to carry one of his bags for him, and got a very sad look in return. They decided to share the cost of two taxis to their digs, and quickly piled in, chattering like magpies.

Annis craned her neck for her first glimpse of the university city and the colleges with their crenelated Cotswold stone walls. They'd arrived during the exams season, when students on their way to examination schools were required to wear 'subfusc' — the black undergraduate gown — and caps. Tutors and fellows, on their way to the Sheldonian Theatre for a special ceremony, could be seen walking down the streets, dressed in ceremonial robes that were everything from scarlet to royal purple, emerald to azure, yellow to pink. Some gowns even had ermine lapels and were lined with silk.

Julie, her mouth open wide in astonishment as the taxi narrowly avoided knocking one magnificently capped, white-haired fellow off his rather ancient bicycle, gave him a wave as she caught his eye.

'This town is amazing,' Gordon spoke for them all as they passed the Randolph Hotel, the Memorial, and the facades of Balliol and St John's Colleges on their right, and the Taylor Institution Library, Blackfriars and St Cross on their left. Then they were approaching the Banbury Road, with the out-of-place modern glass and concrete building that was the part of the Engineering department, before heading for the hilly suburb of Headington. The big white building of the John Radcliffe Hospital dominated the skyline, but then they were twisting down side streets, finally pulling up outside a house that had obviously been converted from two semis.

The troupe of actors looked at the unprepossessing building with a mutual feeling of gloom. Pooling their change, they paid off the drivers and stood in silence on the pavement outside the lodging house. The garden was choked with weeds and the front door was slightly warped, its once cheerful sky-blue paint peeling badly.

'Welcome to Bleak House,' Gerry drawled as John knocked on the door. There was a muffled noise and then suddenly Mrs Clemence stood there in all her glory.

She was a scrawny sparrow of a woman, with a thin neck and unsympathetic brown eyes. She wore a dirty flowered apron and was smoking with gusto. 'You're the actors then?' she hazarded around the vile-smelling puffs.

Annis's stomach heaved uneasily as she imagined this woman standing over the stove, cooking their food.

Norman Rix smiled. 'Indeed we are, madam,' he said.

Mrs Clemence shot him a suspicious look. 'Righto. I've got your rooms all ready for you. Doubles, all of 'em.'

The house was full, which meant, Annis thought, that the amount of accommodation available in this city must be appallingly small.

Annis's mood nose-dived as she entered the room that she and Julie were to share. The two young women gazed around in acute dismay. 'Oh no,' Julie wailed. 'She's got to be kidding! Ten days of *this*!' But, Annis grimly suspected, Mrs Clemence wasn't.

The roof sloped in two places, which meant they'd have to spend their time permanently stooped if they didn't want to keep banging their heads. The beds were of the steel-framed, folding variety, the kind taken on camping holidays. The reason for this, it was plain to see, was that proper single beds simply wouldn't have fitted in. There was one wardrobe, which had about enough room to hang two dresses, and a set of drawers that had been placed precariously on the deep windowsill, blocking out the light, that being the only place it would fit in. The walls were damp.

'Do you think the boys would do a swap with us?' Julie asked hopefully.

Annis, much more conversant with the current state of male gallantry, snorted inelegantly. 'Fat chance.'

She walked to one of the beds, banged her head on the ceiling, sat down, shot up as the bed wobbled and threatened to collapse under her, banged her head on the ceiling again, and duck-walked back to the door. 'This is impossible,' she snarled. She slung her unopened suitcase on to the floor, her elbow banging into Julie's rib as she did so. The younger actress yelped; Annis apologised and backed out. 'Look, you unpack first,' Annis offered, summoning up the last dregs of her patience. 'There isn't room for both of us in here at the same time. I'll go downstairs for a cup of tea and then come up and do my own unpacking.'

But there was to be no tea. Mrs Clemence, it seemed, had a strict kitchen-exclusion rule when it came to her boarders. Annis suspected that the landlady simply didn't want her paying guests to see the state of her kitchen. Even though the kitchen door was closed, the rank smell of stale grease wafted up through the rest of the house.

As she turned to leave, her landlady reminded her that hot water was scarce, and she had her regular boarders to think of, so to be sure to tell the others not to have a bath too often. The sitting room was a study in clashing colours — salmon pink walls and dark red carpet. The sofa and chairs were horsehair and itched like hell.

By now, Annis had come to the conclusion that this was no accident. Mrs Clemence obviously didn't like having people under her feet all day long, and nobody in their right mind would want to sit on her furniture for more than a minute. In despair, Annis wandered out into the garden — or rather, weed and nettle patch. There wasn't even a plastic garden chair to sit on. 'Oh, this is ridiculous!' she cried, and marched to the gate.

She knew Reeve had driven up to Oxford last night, and had overheard him talking to Gordon and Norman about the bizarre address of his friend's house. What the hell was the name of that street? Something really odd. Squitchey Lane? Yes, that was it. She found a bus stop at the end of the cul-de-sac and, asking the bus driver's advice, got off at a stop that would take her to within walking distance of it.

* * *

Reeve stepped under the needle-sharp power shower and sang happily as he washed his dark curly hair, gargling under the spray and soaping himself all over with Vince's luxurious shower gel. When he was finished, he wrapped a voluminous fluffy towel around his waist and padded down the spiral staircase, across a deep-piled carpet and into the conservatory. There he stretched out on a sun lounger and sipped the long cool glass of lemonade he'd made up earlier, chinking the ice cubes thoughtfully.

May was in one of its sweltering moods, and he had all the windows open, as well as the French doors, to allow a pleasant breeze to stir the wonderfully fragrant orange blossom that was growing along one glass wall. The house was modest in proportion, but Vince had decked it out like a single man's dream. The bed in the master bedroom was king-sized and dressed in black satin sheets. In the en suite bathroom next to it was a sunken bath with gold taps, surrounded by mirrors. The ground floor was carpeted in expensive white Axminster, the couches deep cream leather, the tables smoky glass. It was air-conditioned throughout. The built-in stereo and sound system came with more hidden speakers than MI5 owned. All in all, Reeve was sure he could put up with it for the next week or so.

They'd come to Oxford early because Ray had wanted them to get a feel for the city. The cast had also been given chunky dossiers about the way publishing companies worked, the idea being that they were to absorb as much about the industry as possible, so that the delegates wouldn't be able to distinguish the actors from the real members of their profession — or at least not until things really got going.

Leaning back on the lounger, Reeve opened one curious eye as, outside the open windows, he heard a loud crack.

Annis, who'd just trodden on a dry twig, instantly froze. She'd found Squitchey Lane easily, and a few enquiries of the neighbours had quickly pointed her in the direction of Vince Margetti's house. It was set in grounds of blossoming rhododendrons and azaleas, bubbling carp ponds and velvety green lawns. She'd crept into the garden and been staring at the house with a mixture of rage, envy and indecision, when she'd seen a naked figure walk past the window.

Or naked from the waist up, at least. His dark curly hair was still clearly wet from a shower, and his bronzed chest had been mute testimony to the sunbathing he'd already managed to get in. As she'd followed his progress through the house, sneaking from rhododendron bush to rhododendron bush, she eventually saw him emerge into the conservatory, a white towel wrapped around his waist, bare shins and calves still glistening with water.

Annis's breath caught as she watched him stretch out on the brightly patterned sun lounger, the towel falling perilously open as he moved. She caught a brief glimpse of hard, muscled thigh, the merest dark shadow of hair and . . . then he was lying down. Sipping a glass of something long and maddeningly cool, he looked like a Roman emperor about to have someone peel him a grape — while *she* couldn't even get access to a kitchen! It was then that she had stood on a fallen twig.

Inside, Reeve got up and walked slowly to the entrance to the doorway, looking out. Vince had had the house outfitted with a state-of-the-art security system, but it was switched off at the moment.

Something had definitely made a noise out there in the garden. Reeve shrugged. Probably a cat. He turned, and then caught a movement out of the corner of his eye. A flash of dark hair swinging around a shoulder.

He gazed at a rhododendron bush full of hot-pink flowers, and detected a rounded rump. Blue jeans and female. There was only one woman he knew who had such a deliciously rounded derriere as that.

Annis froze, head down, and waited. It would be too much if he found her skulking about in here. Now that she had actually arrived, there was no damned way she was going to ask if his offer of a room was still available. She'd perish before she'd ask him for a favour now. She told herself firmly that her room back at Mrs Clemence's wasn't *all* that bad.

She held her breath. Had he gone yet?

Reeve grinned, long and slow. Then he turned and went back to his sun lounger and icy drink.

* * *

'Look who's dropped in!' Gerry drawled.

It was six-thirty in the evening, and they were all sitting out in the garden, John and Gordon having cleared a space in the stinging nettles that afternoon. Everyone looked up as the gate creaked — there wasn't anything in the boarding house that didn't — and everyone gave a slow hand clap as Reeve walked up the uneven path, tripping over a broken paving stone.

'How the other half live!' He greeted them with a wide smile, his sapphire-blue eyes twinkling with amusement. Annis, who'd seen for herself just how he was living, bared her teeth in a ferocious smile.

'So, what do you think of our esteemed landlady's abode?' Norman, wincing as a stray nettle attacked his ankle, spread a fulsome arm towards the house. Reeve looked at the grey concrete oblong and was reminded of a prison.

He grimaced. 'Oh, very "des res".'

'Hope nobody wants a shower,' Julie called out gaily as she came through the door. 'There's no hot water. And there's a spider in the overflow. It keeps hiding in ambush, waiting to crawl out whenever you turn on the taps — so watch out!'

Annis, who loathed spiders, shuddered visibly.

'Oh joy,' Gerry drawled, and lit yet another cigarette.

Annis, who didn't much care for passive smoking, moved a little further away from her. The ten days in Oxford, which had initially looked like being such a pleasant working holiday, were fast taking on all the appeal of an endurance test.

Reeve nudged John over and sat down on the blanket beside them, wincing at the stone that bit into his backside. 'Wouldn't it be better inside?' he asked.

'No!' the chorus of voices was unanimous and emphatic, and Reeve grinned. He couldn't help it. No wonder Annis had come calling on him this afternoon. One look at this place was enough for any sane, sensible person to realise that they wouldn't want to stay in it. If they had a choice, that is.

'So, who's had a chance to read the "publishing company" blurb?' he asked, deeming it prudent not to mention his own bachelor's-fantasy digs.

'Oh shut up,' Gordon growled. 'We'll do it tomorrow.'

'Are we going to look around the college tomorrow?' Julie asked. 'St Bede's, I mean? You know, get a feel for the place.'

'Can we just go in and wander around?' John asked.

'I think so,' Reeve replied. 'They're fairly public places. St Bede's has pretty gardens, apparently. The silver birches are quite famous — like Christ Church's deer, and Worcester's lake and tame squirrels.'

'Who's been a good boy and done all his homework then?' Annis drawled, wanting to hit him and kiss him all at once. She was particularly irritated by the way he was lounging on the blanket, oozing male hormones like a . . . like a sultan surrounded by his seraglio!

She'd had to buy a warm can of coke from a shop on the way back, and she was damned sure it hadn't tasted as good as whatever it was he'd been drinking in that glamorous house! Suddenly she felt thirsty again.

By mutual consent, they retired to a pub, where Julie, pumped artfully by Reeve, described the horrors of her room, the rickety beds, the killer ceiling and the dire state of the kitchen. Afterwards, they took a bus to a green and pleasant park, and as dusk fell, wandered off in groups — Gerry and Norman to talk about 'the old days'; Julie, John and Gordon to plot about ways of foiling Mrs Clemence's no-kitchen rule.

Annis let Reeve lead her to a pretty bridge over the River Cherwell. There she leaned on the white-painted railings under the willow branches and stared down into the placid water.

She could feel him beside her like a burst of energy. When he leaned on the iron railing beside her, she watched the way the summer's breeze toyed with the silken strands of hair on his forearms. A wonderful aroma arose from his warm skin — expensive toiletries and clean, intoxicating maleness. The combination made her knees wobble in sudden weakness.

'So, the digs are a bit of a nightmare then?' he enquired innocently, looking out over the river, biting back a grin as he remembered her skulking in the shrubbery.

'Reeve,' she said sweetly, 'do you want to get pushed into the river?'

'Annis,' he said equally sweetly, 'would you like the spare room at my place?'

Annis longed to say no. Literally itched to throw his offer back in his face. But the memory of Mrs Clemence was too strong. And the memory of him walking about in only a towel was even stronger.

'Reeve,' she said softly, 'I thought you were never going to ask!'

CHAPTER 12

Lorcan spotted one of the Ruskin secretaries, just on her way into the office, and hailed her. 'Hello. I'm looking for one of the students. Frederica Delacroix? She's not here. I don't suppose you know where I could find her?'

Even as he asked, he mentally winced. Was she wondering why he wanted to know? Was his own male weakness carved on his face, obvious for anybody to see?

But the secretary merely shrugged. 'I don't know, Mr Greene. You could try Queen's Lane Coffee House — that's the favourite student hangout at the moment.'

Lorcan thanked her and made his way there. Richard, he knew, was checking up on her at his end, but he doubted that he'd find anything.

Although the Art Fraud Squad had a huge source of information at their fingertips, his gut instinct told him that Frederica had only recently fallen in with whatever gang was behind this Oxford job. For one thing, she was still too young for this to be anything but her first forgery job. No, the more he was around her the more sure he was that she was a kid who'd just got in over her head. Not a hardened criminal. He couldn't believe she was crooked.

Couldn't, or didn't want to, a voice mocked him from deep inside his head. Grimly, he shook the thought off. He had enough to cope with without contemplating the ridiculous thought that, at his age, he might be falling in love with a woman barely out of her teens!

At the coffee house he found a third-year printmaker who told him that Frederica had gone home for the weekend.

With Frederica out of the way . . . He returned to the Ruskin, relieved to find that the third floor contained only an absorbed sculptor and a few first-year students chattering about the evil-mindedness of exam-setters.

Frederica's workspace was empty. Casting a quick glance around, he walked to a covered canvas set up on her easel and lifted the sheet off. He recognised the canvas as the one she'd been preparing the previous week — now clean and dry, he could see it definitely didn't have the look of a modern weave.

He leaned forward, picking out faint lines already marking the piece. There was . . . yes . . . a building of some kind, perhaps a barn? And the beginnings of . . . water? Trees in the background, a large expanse of sky . . . ?

What the hell had she used? Manoeuvring the canvas near a window, he peered closely at the faint lines and realised what she'd done. She'd used charcoal at first, drawing in a freehand that looked shockingly competent. Then . . . yes. His heart thumping, he realised she'd gone over that with a fine brush charged with raw umber and much diluted with turps. He knew what her next move would be, as surely as he knew his own name. When it was dry, she would brush off the loose charcoal. Once painted, the tell-tale lines would disappear and not even an expert like himself would ever guess they'd been there.

It was remarkably cunning. 'Oh, Frederica,' he murmured sadly, a resigned smile twisting his lips. 'Well, at least you're good, my girl. Very good. But not, my darling, good enough to fool me.' He put the canvas back, covering it in precisely the same way as he'd found it, and left the Ruskin again, this time heading straight for his car.

The village of Cross Keys was a tiny place, and at the village pub he was easily directed to Rainbow House. As he parked in front of the pleasing farmhouse, he realised that he hadn't yet thought of an excuse for the visit. As he got out, his feet crunching on the gravel, a sun hat popped up from behind a rose tree. 'Hello, can I help you?'

Lorcan turned at the woman's voice, seeing an older version of Frederica step out of the rose garden and walk towards him.

'Hello, you must be Frederica's sister,' Lorcan smiled.

Donna Delacroix blushed happily. 'Her mother, actually,' she said modestly.

Lorcan looked surprised. 'Oh. I'm so sorry.' He held out his hand. 'I'm Lorcan Greene, one of . . .'

'The gallery owner?' Donna breathed, an excited look in her eyes.

'Yes. I'm a visiting fellow at the Ruskin at the moment. I wondered if—'

'Freddy never told me!' Donna interrupted, and Lorcan began to relax, realising an excuse was not going to be needed.

'Well, please, come inside. You'll want to see the collection of course?' she asked.

Lorcan could see that as far as this woman was concerned, anybody coming to Rainbow House had to be coming to see the paintings. He smiled and simply let himself be carried along on the tide of her enthusiasm. Now all he had to do was . . . what? Always before he had worked to a certain pattern — logic, reason, a smattering of instinct. Now he was just blundering about blindly, acting on impulse. And he knew why of course. Or rather, he knew who had got him into this state.

He'd woken that morning with one, single thought, a single command in his head — and nothing was going to shift it. *I need to see Frederica.*

The big flagstone kitchen was blissfully cool, and in a moment he had a glass of iced tea in his hands and was being shepherded into a library, where a man snoozed contentedly on a leather-buttoned armchair.

'James!' Donna hissed, waking her husband and introducing him to 'Frederica's teacher', Lorcan Greene. Lorcan bit back a grin at the description. So far, it was the other way round. Frederica had been teaching him a thing or two! Like the fact that he was vulnerable when it came to dark velvet eyes and freckles.

With her husband in reluctant tow, Donna began the journey through the house's many rooms and various artworks. After an hour and a half they were back in the kitchen. 'Well, that was simply . . . incredible,' Lorcan said. Never had he been shown so many good and bad paintings hanging side by side.

'I'm surprised Frederica didn't tell us you were coming,' James Delacroix said, helping himself to a piece of fruit cake while his wife's back was momentarily turned.

'Oh, I was just passing through on the way back from an auction,' Lorcan lied smoothly. 'And since I met Frederica a few weeks ago and offered to buy some of her work . . .'

Donna shot Lorcan a glance of utter astonishment. Even James paused in the act of transferring the cake to his mouth.

'You want to buy Frederica's work?' he asked, hardly able to believe his ears.

'Of course,' Lorcan said, genuinely puzzled. 'Didn't she tell you?'

James shot his wife a 'help me' look, to which Donna responded with a rather unconvincing laugh.

'Oh, she probably wanted to surprise us. She's very . . . er . . . very spontaneous isn't she, James?'

James, thinking that his daughter was more likely punishing him for getting her into this copying business, coughed and looked away.

'She's gone for a walk by the river,' Donna added hastily. 'It's such a nice day . . .' She trailed off suggestively, and Lorcan instantly took the hint.

'Hmm. I think I could do with stretching my legs a little.'

Donna directed him to the public footpath that led past the river and mill race, and watched him go, an excited look in her eyes. Could it be possible that the Delacroix family, at long last, had produced a real artist? Then Donna's excitement turned in another direction altogether. Lorcan Greene, she'd read in a woman's magazine recently, was one of Britain's most eligible bachelors.

* * *

Frederica stood on the riverbank, more or less where Forbes-Wright must have placed his original easel when he sat down to paint *The Old Mill and Swans*. Of course, the mill house had long since been renovated but the basic structure was the same. The pollarded willows in Forbes-Wright's painting had been left to grow unchecked, and on this occasion there were no swans on the mill pond — they were too busy sitting on eggs, but still, this was the original scene which . . .

'Your nose is turning red.'

Frederica yelped and twirled around, hardly able to believe her eyes. Lorcan Greene, dressed in casual grey slacks and a shirt open halfway down his chest, stood behind her. The summer breeze was ruffling his sleeves, making the material billow out from his shoulders, giving her a glimpse of lightly tanned skin. She blinked.

'You need sunscreen,' he added. 'Fair people like us can scorch easily in the sun. Come on, let's head for the shade.'

He held out his hand and she took it. It felt like the most natural thing in the world for both of them. Lorcan led her to a crumbling wall, overhung by a massive red horse chestnut tree, alight with buzzing honeybees and singing birds. He stretched out on the cool grass, slipping off his shoes, and, after a moment's hesitation, Frederica did the same. He leaned back on one elbow and picked a blade of grass, twirling it and looking at her with an oddly helpless look in his hazel eyes that set her heart racing.

The fact was, when he'd seen her standing there on the riverbank, dressed in an almost translucent white summer dress, her hair flowing free down her back, he'd been gripped by a sense of destiny that had all but paralysed him. Even this particular spot seemed magical — completely hidden from human eyes by the wall and the shade of the tree.

Knowing that he was about to make a momentous decision, Lorcan slowly tossed away the blade of grass.

Frederica watched the small green blade twirl away, and when she looked back he was already reaching for her. She swayed forward, turning into his embrace, until she was lying in his lap, her arms looped around his neck. His mouth lowered to meet hers and she felt their lips touch. He seemed hesitant at first, almost reluctant. Almost as if he didn't want to kiss her. Then they were clinging together.

Her hand wandered to the nape of his neck, running through the wheat-coloured locks of hair, warmed by the sun. She could smell the slight scent of his lemony, cool aftershave, the warmth of the dappled sunlight on her bare legs, the burning touch of his fingers on the tops of her arms and the small of her back. And then his hand was moving, from her arm to her ribcage, and up, up and around, to curl around her breast. This was the point where she tensed up. Where she pushed her groping suitor away. At least, in the past that's what had always happened. The touch of a male hand on her breast had always felt like a trespass before. An unwanted liberty. But now . . . now . . .

She gasped, feeling her nipple harden and pulsate in the palm of his hand. The late May day had become too warm to wear a bra, and the thin silky material of the dress was no barrier at all to the questing strength of his fingers.

Lorcan raised his head and took a shaky breath. He looked down into trusting eyes as beautiful as ebony velvet. 'This is . . . impossible,' he said, his voice sounding husky and thick, and for the first time in a long time, bearing the faintest nuances of a cockney accent.

Frederica blinked. His eyes, she thought, were the colour of a Turner seascape — not greeny-blue, not grey or hazel, but a combination of all three. Like a warm, inviting sea.

'It's impossible,' he repeated again.

'Why?' she asked simply.

Lorcan couldn't think of an answer. He knew there was one somewhere, but right at that moment, when he needed it the most, he couldn't think of it. A ray of sunlight filtering through the trees turned a lock of hair curled around his wrist into a flaming auburn manacle. All he had to do to be free was to pull away from her. But his limbs felt like lead.

She reached up, her hand cupping the hard, flat plane of his cheek. She rubbed a thumb across his lips, felt the small sigh of his breath, and then a molten heat began to flood through her, turning her bones liquid and her body into a sensual, warm, waiting receptacle.

Lorcan shut his eyes, but it didn't help. The touch of her thumb on his lips became a torment. The scent wafting from her hair reminded him of violets. She felt light as air in his arms, but somehow she was dragging him down, down, down . . .

They lay sprawled on the grass now, one of his legs between hers, his hands on either side of her head. They kissed, parted, kissed, parted and kissed again, each touch of the lips becoming more urgent, more needy, more passionate.

His fingers found and unbuttoned the plain buttons of her dress. His hand slipped inside, and she cried out, her back arching off the grass as skin touched skin, palm to breast, the sheer intimacy of it taking her breath away.

Lorcan moaned, finally surrendering to the inevitable. Ever since he'd met her, he'd been fighting a losing battle against attraction. A battle against his own desire. A battle where logic fought emotion — and emotion, smug in the knowledge of its superiority, now emerged the clear victor.

He sighed somewhere deep inside him, knowing that he was now entering uncharted territory. No woman had ever affected him like this. And it had to mean . . .

He moved his lips down over her pale, arched throat, down to the tender spot on her sternum, then across to one hot, pink, pulsating nipple. Frederica cried out, opening her eyes to a giddying kaleidoscope of blue sky, pink blossom and wheat-coloured hair. She closed her eyes again as his lips left her tender breast, but then she was sitting up, and he was smothering her neck, her throat, her shoulders with kisses, pushing the dress back off her arms, the material falling down to her waist. Her skin was pale as milk as he lay her back against the grass.

He took a few deep breaths and opened his eyes, but the sight of her, half-naked and innocent, eyes as dark and knowing as Eve, had him closing them again. He knew, dimly, that he was on the edge of a precipice. That if he fell, he might never be able to climb back to where he'd been before. For an instant, a fierce primordial anger began to rise from deep inside him.

But then, Frederica reached up and pulled him back to her, sighing with pleasure at the feel of his firmly muscled thigh against hers. Her hands brushed against the hardness of his loins, and she felt him stiffen and tense. She saw his jaw clench, saw the eyes snap open and spark.

So much power! She had never realised before how much power women had over men. And, in that instant of eye-clashing, soul-exchanging intensity, Lorcan was lost. Frederica watched him unbuttoning his belt and stiffened, waiting for some sensation of denial or panic to start building up in her.

But it didn't come. It was as if all those boys she'd rejected suddenly made sense. In the past she had never really understood why she'd clung on to her virginity for so long, but now she knew. It wasn't because she was frigid, or immature, or downright prim. It was because none of them had been *him*. The man for whom she'd been waiting all her life.

Now she reached out, helping him to push the slacks down, and when she finally saw him, proud and hard, she swallowed back sudden tears of tenderness. 'Lorcan,' she whispered, about to warn him. He was used to women who were his equal when it came to lovemaking. Not . . . But his lips were on hers again, and when she felt his hand move up her thigh, pushing aside the dress, finding the plain white cotton of her briefs, she felt her legs fall apart, welcoming him.

She gasped as he pulled the panties down over her knees and tossed them to one side. Lorcan groaned, his body as tense as violin wire. He moved over her, her knees like silken pillars as they moved against the sides of his buttocks. 'Lorcan,' she tried to warn him again, but then she felt the very tip of him pressing against her, and she gasped, tensing for just one instant before melting, melting . . . And then, with one fluid, sure, dominating thrust, he was inside her, filling her, causing just one instant of shocked pain before a sensation of fulfilment and pleasure took its place, blocking out that memory forever.

Lorcan's eyes shot open. 'Frederica . . . ?' he whispered, realising, in one heart-stopping, earth-shattering moment, the precious quality of the gift she'd given him. A gift he'd never even suspected might be his for the taking.

She sighed, opening her velvet eyes and smiling up at him. 'Make love to me, Lorcan,' she commanded him softly.

And so he did.

Gently. Carefully. Skilfully bringing her to the brink of desire again and again with slow, deep, powerful thrusts, until her head was thrashing from side to side in the grass and her fingernails raked down his back in frustrated ecstasy. The spiralling sensation of tight, undreamed-of pleasure exploded inside her, and she called out his name, sending a pair of thrushes flying from the tree in alarm.

Her back arched, her bare heels dug convulsively into the ground, and her head fell back against the grass as she trembled in the violent aftermath of climax. Lorcan watched her with a confused tenderness that she was too oblivious to notice. And then, just when she thought it was all over, it began again.

* * *

Back at Rainbow House, James got a telephone call from George Makin, an old friend of his from college days who was now the senior partner of a large firm of solicitors.

'So,' George said, after they'd caught up, 'who's the big villain you're working for now?'

'Big villain? Around here? You must be joking,' James laughed.

'Oh.' George, a big, amiable man, sounded suddenly uncomfortable. 'But I thought . . .' There was a long silence, and then, 'I say, James, old chap — you haven't by any chance been doing anything . . . odd . . . with that collection of paintings of yours?'

James bolted upright in his chair. 'No!' He cleared his throat. 'No, why do you ask?'

Now George's embarrassment was palpable, even over the telephone. 'Oh, nothing much. It's just . . . a clerk over at the Fletcher chambers told me . . . well, that someone in the Art Fraud Squad had been nosing around. Something about an ongoing investigation in Oxford. Your name was mentioned. Naturally, I thought . . . well, that you were acting for some dodgy dealer or something.'

James Delacroix licked lips gone suddenly dry. 'No, can't say I know anything about it. But there's nothing wrong here, I can assure you.'

'I can't tell you how glad I am to hear to it,' his old friend laughed. They chatted about a class reunion for a while, and then hung up, George cheerfully, James worried.

For a long while he sat and stared at the carpet in front of him. Nobody could know that he'd asked Freddy to copy the Forbes-Wright for him, could they? So what interest could the Art Fraud Squad have in them, for pity's sake! It wasn't as if Rainbow House ever sold paintings, they only bought them.

No, they were all right, him and Freddy. They must be. Weren't they?

CHAPTER 13

The small gaggle of interested actors approached the set of massive gates and stepped through the entrance to St Bede's, finding themselves in a small flagstoned quad.

'Wow, I feel like I've just stepped into a church or something,' Julie whispered in awe, looking round at the mellow ivy-covered walls and rows of large sash windows.

On their left was indeed a large building with a beautiful round stained-glass window. A student, slouched against a wall, suddenly came to life. 'Hello. Are you the people who are doing the murder-mystery weekend?' he asked jovially.

'That's us, dear heart,' Norman Rix couldn't help teasing.

'Er . . . right. I'm Barry — the principal asked me to show you around.'

Nods and murmurs of greeting were exchanged.

'Well this is the lodge, as you can see, where we pick up our mail. Over there is the chapel, built in the Middle Ages.'

'Can we go inside?' Annis asked, thinking of the Sunday morning scene, when she had to make a fuss about sitting in a pew far away from the radiators.

'Of course. It's always open,' Barry said, and led the way inside, the cast shivering in the sudden coldness. But the high-beamed ceiling was magnificent, and Annis began to fully appreciate how much this magnificent backdrop would help the play.

Reeve watched Annis pick up a hymnal, and wondered if she'd been disappointed to get three uninterrupted nights' sleep. It had been sheer murder for him to lie there, night after night, knowing she was just a door away. But he'd managed it. He was going to force her to make the first move even if it killed him. And from the way his body ached whenever he was near her, it probably would!

'We have three houses, all named after literary figures,' Barry said. 'Fellows that live in have rooms scattered throughout the college.'

'Interesting,' Reeve murmured, and Annis shot him a fulminating look. The rat. She'd been living at Squitchey Lane for three days now. Why hadn't he come to her room?

Perhaps she wasn't good enough for him. Wasn't famous enough. Didn't have enough power to help his career along. Perhaps struggling actresses didn't appeal to him . . . ?

She turned away from him sharply and Reeve would have smiled if he hadn't noticed the gleam of pain in her eyes. He felt his heart lurch. Dammit, what was wrong now?

'This is the dining hall. We refer to it simply as Hall.'

All the cast looked with interest at the newest of the college's buildings. 'Most of our best scenes take place in there,' Julie said. 'Can we have a look?'

Hall was simply breathtaking. As soon as they stepped into it, looking around at the long tables, the rows of tall windows, the imposing portraits of past principals and the High Table raised on a small dais with the impressively carved and velvet-backed principal's chair, they got a real sense of 'theatre'.

'I can just see them, dressed in ruffs and silks, in Queen Elizabeth the First's day,' John said.

'That's a good painting,' Reeve murmured, moving to a large gilt-framed portrait hanging between two big windows. 'Who is it?' He pointed at the bewigged, imposing-looking man.

'That's Principal Alfred Gore, painted by William Hogarth,' Barry offered.

'The murder scenes will really go down well in here,' Annis said, and everyone agreed. It would, indeed, be high drama.

'Where's the JCR?' Reeve asked, remembering they had to do several scenes in there.

'That's in Webster house. Through here is the main garden.' The lawns underfoot were centuries old, and it felt as if they were walking on carpet. A pond full of koi carp brushed shoulders with a croquet lawn. Walton house was spread out to their left, and to their right was a mellow red-brick building, faded to a rich rose colour. The place was steeped in academia, drowsy with ancient learning, heavy with old-world charm and beauty.

'I could stay here for ever,' Annis murmured. 'Except, of course, I couldn't. After a week of this I'd be climbing the walls. It's so quiet.'

'Yeah, but it makes a great backdrop for a murder mystery,' Julie said, reliving her scenes in her head.

'There aren't many students around,' John mused, as they headed towards the library.

'A lot of them have gone home by now,' Barry confirmed. 'Only those sitting exams are still up.' As he spoke, a beautiful red-headed girl pushed open one of the big glass doors of the library and came walking down the steps.

'Hey, Frederica, hang about,' Barry called, and the young woman paused, swinging her head around, exposing huge shining dark eyes. She smiled as she recognised the Physics student who had rooms next door but one to her own.

'Hello, Barry. How were finals?'

'Bloody,' Barry said gloomily. 'What are you doing still up, anyway?'

Frederica grinned. 'I seduced the bursar into letting me stay on an extra few weeks.' She glanced curiously at the group of people with Barry, and he introduced them.

'This is a group of actors who're going to be performing a murder-mystery weekend at a conference coming in soon. Everybody, this is Frederica, a Fine Art student. Frederica, do you know anything about a painter called . . . er . . .'

'William Hogarth,' Reeve supplied helpfully.

Annis watched the auburn-haired girl glance at Reeve curiously. 'Hogarth was one of the greats,' she said sweetly, as if surprised that everybody didn't know of him. 'One of his paintings, *The Graham Children*, is in the Tate. What about him?'

'One of his paintings is in Hall,' Barry said.

Frederica nodded. 'I know. He painted Alfred Gore.'

'Who was he?' Reeve prompted, grinning as Annis shot him a foul look.

Why was he making eyes at every woman but her, damn him!

Frederica smiled, but although the actor was as handsome as Byron, she hardly noticed. Annis, sensing this, both relaxed and became intrigued. If this girl was unaffected by Reeve, she must have one hell of a boyfriend.

'Alfred Gore was an ex-slave trader turned abolitionist. His appointment as principal here caused quite a stir, and the portrait is rather famous because of it. In fact, it's one of our best.'

Reeve whistled. 'I'm surprised it's just hanging on the wall like that.' Frederica blinked. She hadn't even given a thought as to the security of the college's paintings. It was unthinkable that anyone would try to steal them.

'So, there you go,' Barry said. 'Thanks, Frederica.'

Frederica grinned, gave a general wave goodbye, and strolled towards Becket Arch. She had to get back to her canvas.

And she wondered whether Lorcan would be at the Ruskin.

Since that wonderful, magical afternoon, she'd seen so very little of him. It was beginning to worry her. After he'd walked with her back to the house, they'd been forced to say goodbye in plain view of her parents. So although she'd longed to kiss him, she hadn't been able to, and the agony of being forced just to watch him get into the car and drive away was still with her. Why hadn't he called her? It wouldn't have been so hard for them to bump into each other 'accidentally' at the Ruskin. She frowned as she headed into the centre of town, thinking back to that glorious day. Had she done something wrong — something to put him off? After they'd dressed, they'd walked in silence back to Rainbow House. Neither, it seemed, had quite known what to say to the other, both still shell-shocked by the sweet passion they'd just shared. Now, after several days of separation, she was beginning to feel slightly panicked.

What if it had meant nothing more to him than a pleasant afternoon's roll in the grass? What if her innocence had turned him off? Or scared him off?

As she walked up the High Street, she tried to convince herself that everything was all right. But somehow she couldn't quite manage it.

* * *

Back at St Bede's, Barry took his sightseers back to the lodge and said goodbye. The cast trooped down to a burger bar and discussed what they'd seen that morning, and how best to incorporate it into their acting scenes. Eventually the group split up, by now everyone taking it for granted that Annis and Reeve were 'an item'. Since nobody could possibly blame her for getting away from under Mrs Clemence when given the chance, she supposed it was inevitable.

Now, as she finished the last of her coffee, she leaned back in her chair and looked across at him. 'Did you have to flirt with that Fine Art student this morning?' she asked crossly.

'I didn't!'

'You did. Not that she noticed.'

'No. I realised that.'

'Hurt your feelings, did it?'

'Not my feelings. Just my ego.'

'Used to having women fall at your feet like flies?' she asked sweetly.

'At least four of them, twice a day,' he agreed promptly.

'Shame.'

'Hm. I must be losing my touch.'

'Hah!' she snorted, with such gusto that he grinned broadly at her.

'That's more like it. I was wondering where all your venom had gone.'

Annis snarled something unladylike, got up and marched out. Hastily Reeve followed her, but Annis had already disappeared into the crowds. Cursing, Reeve hopped on the bus to Squitchey Lane, and once he'd reached home, he stripped naked and headed for the hot tub. He was getting tired of putting up with her moods. Tired of her suspicious nature and jealousy. Tired of having her around and nothing happening between them. As Annis would say — hah! He leaned back in the bubbling water, a gentle smile playing about his lips. She would crack. Sooner or later.

When Annis walked in half an hour later, she too headed straight for her room and the shower, wanting to wash her hair. Dressed only in a robe, she sat in front of the dressing-table mirror and used the hairdryer to style her flowing locks. She wondered what time the nightclubs opened, for she was determined to go out tonight and have a good time, come what may — far away from Reeve Morgan and his infuriating smile.

She froze as she heard a sound coming from the room next door. Reeve was probably still in town, chatting up a pretty tourist. Burglars perhaps? She tiptoed towards the sound of human activity, pushing open the door gingerly.

Reeve was lying naked in the hot tub. And in that instant she admitted that, all along, she'd known there were no burglars — she'd just needed an excuse to snoop. To invade his territory. To be right where she was, dressed only in a robe, watching him, this man dressed in nothing at all.

Reeve heard a slight sound and his head shot up, dark-blue eyes opening in surprise. He saw her at once, her freshly washed hair gleaming blue-black against the white material of her robe. Her eyes glinted, orange-flecked, like a tiger spotting a particularly luscious deer.

'Annis,' he said softly. And patted the surface of the water. 'Care to join me?' he grinned.

Annis smiled sweetly. And shrugged off the robe. It slithered to the ground at her feet, and she had the immense pleasure of seeing his smile fade and a dark wash of colour spread across his face. He swallowed hard.

She was like a goddess standing there, one foot slightly in front of the other. Her skin was alabaster, in stark contrast to her hair, the colour of ravens' wings, and the matching, mysterious, feminine triangle of hair at the juncture of her thighs. Her breasts were high, the indentation of her waist pronounced, the smooth curve of her hips lending her a classic hourglass figure. She let him look at what he'd been missing for just a few seconds longer, then smiled.

'Thank you. I think I will,' she purred. And walking forward she stepped slowly down into the warm bubbling water. Reeve shot upright, both to make room for her and because he was suddenly breathless. He dragged in a badly needed gulp of air as they stared silently at one another.

Reeve's eyes widened as she lay back in the tub, her long legs stretched in front of her and just brushing against his as the water bubbled about her nipples, turning them cherry-red.

There, she thought with satisfaction. That's removed the all-knowing male grin from his face!

Reeve swallowed hard, his lips, in spite of the humidity in the air, feeling suddenly dry. 'I . . . uh . . . I . . .' he muttered, and then, when she arched one dark brow mockingly, abruptly shut up. So she wanted to play games? Slowly he allowed one foot to stroke her calf. Her eyebrow rose even higher, disappearing into her hairline. Then her own foot moved, and her toes were suddenly massaging the tender spot at the back of his knee. His leg jerked in helpless reaction and again he swallowed hard. One-upmanship was it? Well, two could play at that game. His foot moved higher, raised on the bubbling stream of water, until his big toe was level with one cherry-coloured nipple.

His eyes met hers. Annis smiled. Just you dare . . .

He dared. She gasped as her nipple tingled at the contact. She closed her eyes in pleasure, just for a moment, then opened them again. There was no mocking smile on his face. Just an intense look that had her body coiling like a spring.

She moved her foot, forcing his legs apart, moving forward, pressing her toes against his inner thigh now, then moving up, gently but firmly, until the sole of her foot was pressed against his hard, pulsating shaft. Reeve groaned and jerked in the water. His face had a tight, pinched look; a dark-blue flame burned within his eyes. Slowly, carefully, Annis caressed him with her foot, her shoulders moving up and down against the rim of the tub as she leaned forward and back with the movement.

Reeve closed his eyes and leaned his head back, every atom of his being concentrated on her sensual foot, the hardening of his body, the helpless reaction of his desire. When he could stand it no longer he surged forward, leaning over her, his mouth fastening on hers in a fierce kiss. Then her legs were hooked around his, her heels digging into the indent just above his buttocks. She lifted herself from the slippery surface of the bottom of the tub and gasped as he was suddenly inside her, hard, fast, demanding, igniting her own love-greedy response. She threw back her head, groaning his name, holding on to his wet shoulders, kissing his temple, his nose, his cheek, his closed eyelids, anywhere she could reach as she thrashed beneath him.

He pressed her gently against the side of the tub, thrusting into her harder, deeper, ever faster, the water splashing over the sides and running along the tiny square tiles of the floor. She clung to him, lost in the tempest, her body pulsating and exploding as the tension of the last few weeks finally eased in the cleansing, generous act of lovemaking. Reeve shouted her name and shuddered, and she clung to him, hugging him close, brushing the damp curly hair from his forehead as he collapsed against her, all his devastating male strength spent, his breathing ragged and hoarse.

Silence slowly returned to the room, only the bubbling of the water invading the peace. Annis leaned her head back and stared up at the ceiling, her sense of self returning with a vengeance.

Well. What good had that done her? She was now officially another notch on Reeve Morgan's belt. Her lips twisted ruefully.

She slowly pushed him away, fighting the tenderness that made her want to go on holding him. He opened dazed, sapphire-blue eyes, and smiled softly.

'Annis,' he murmured. 'I—'

'Don't worry,' Annis said briskly, getting out of the tub to put on her robe. When she turned, she was already doing the belt up firmly. 'These things happen when you're away touring,' she said, saying it before he could. 'We're big boys and girls, after all. We can enjoy ourselves for now, but once we get back to London, we probably won't bump into each other again.'

Reeve frowned. 'Annis . . .'

'I think I'll go out tonight,' she mused, heading for the door, her heart tight in her breast, her voice as light and breezy as the air. 'I'll ask John and Gordon if they've found a place that plays jazz.'

And then she was gone.

Reeve collapsed back into the hot tub and shook his head. How many times in the past had he made it clear to a woman that their affair was strictly for fun? How often had he made sure that she knew he didn't want or expect commitment? And now that a beautiful woman had just said as much to him, he knew he should be relieved. Be thankful that he was being offered wonderful sex without any strings attached.

So why did he feel as though she'd just hit him with a sledgehammer?

CHAPTER 14

Lorcan stepped through the main door of St Bede's and into St Agatha quad. He glanced inside the lodge, briefly checking that no one was paying any undue attention to him, then walked past the impressive clock, through the arch, and to the main door of Walton. Once inside, he stood indecisively in the cool, silent hall. He had no idea which was her room.

A group of business-suited men walked down the stairs, heading for a seminar in Webster's lecture theatre. As he moved to one side to let them pass, he noticed the door opposite him had a name card on it.

Quickly Lorcan toured the downstairs doors, with no luck. Undeterred, he walked up a wide staircase to the second floor. There, six doors down, he came across what he was looking for.

He found himself hesitating. Ever since that afternoon under the chestnut tree, he'd been fighting a losing battle to keep away from her. He'd spent nights tossing and turning, alternately feeling like the biggest scoundrel on earth, and the next, the luckiest man alive. It couldn't go on. They had to talk. Get things sorted. One way or the other.

He raised a hand to the door and knocked, firmly and determinedly. Nothing happened. He almost laughed out loud. To have nerved himself to come and see her, at last — only to find that she wasn't even in.

He shook his head again and wandered slowly down the wooden-floored corridor to the double window at the end. He leaned wearily on the windowsill and looked out over the Oxford skyline, picking out the domes of the Sheldonian Theatre and the Radcliffe Camera. But he could think only of Frederica.

He shook his head and turned his back on the view, staring down the dark corridor, his mind going back to that wonderful afternoon. A virgin. He'd never once suspected her innocence. He'd seen her as a lovely, free-thinking student. And knowing her to be a crooked artist, he'd been utterly blind to the more intimate side of her.

She was still only a kid. No! Not now. Not since he'd made love to her. She was a woman now. His woman. But, no! She wasn't his woman. He grimaced at the pain of denial the stark thought set off, ricocheting around his mind like a loose bullet. He loved her.

No.

Yes.

He shook his head, walking down the corridor, hesitating once more outside her room. His legs felt weak, as if he were falling prey to some kind of lingering illness. Without quite knowing why, he put his hand out to the door handle and pushed down.

He almost gasped when the door opened. 'Damn it, Frederica, you're too trusting,' he murmured, as the door slowly opened out to reveal a typical student room.

A single bed lay tight up against one wall and looked neat and tidy. But in his mind's eye he could see her lying on it, her hair spread out against the pillow, her skin flushed with sleep, her long lashes feathered against her cheek as she slept. He took a step inside, then another, and closed the door after him. Even accepting that students didn't usually bother with locked doors, he'd have thought that she would be more careful. But even though he felt that he had right on his side, it didn't stop him feeling like an interloper as he looked around.

Prints by Salvador Dalí and Jean-Honoré Fragonard adorned the walls. A messy desk, covered in papers, sat underneath the single window. But, instantly attracting his eye and easily dominating the room, was a covered canvas on an easel.

He had no way of knowing it, but he'd just missed Frederica, who had retrieved her canvas from the Ruskin and was now in the library, photocopying other works of Forbes-Wright from the reference books.

Lorcan stared at the white sheet covering the canvas for some time before slowly walking towards it. Every step dragged. His heart thudded sickeningly in his chest.

He didn't really want to know. Didn't really care.

Richard Braine had called him last night, confirming that 'nothing was known' about Frederica Delacroix, but asking him to have a good nose around. Well, Lorcan thought, his lips twisting bitterly, he was certainly doing that, wasn't he?

Always before, he'd been keen to track down the scavengers who haunted his world like ugly vultures, bringing greed and deceit to something that should be beautiful and pure. But now he felt sick to his stomach, although it didn't stop him from taking a deep breath and slowly lifting the sheet from the canvas.

The painting was emerging so fast it was breathtaking.

He could now make out the definite treeline, and a small pond. The square building and waterwheel. A flicker of recognition shivered over him, found a home, and lodged. He dragged in a deep breath. It was the water mill at Cross Keys!

For an instant, relief, delightful in its profundity, swept over him. He'd got it wrong. She was painting a scene from her own home! Nothing wrong with that . . .

And then, suddenly, the relief was gone. The mill being outlined and taking shape on the canvas was nothing like the mill he remembered seeing just before making love to her.

Where was the out-of-place conservatory, the new windows? Perhaps it's a deliberately romanticised painting, a desperate voice suggested, coming from the region of his heart and utterly bypassing his head. But he couldn't forget her other paintings — *Post-Millennium Home*, the combine harvester, the depictions of satellite dishes and dustbins and cars. She believed in painting things as they were, but this scene could have been painted over a hundred years ago.

He moved closer, studying it. The swans on the water were as yet bare lines, but the style reminded him of someone. One of the early Victorians. Who?

He shook his head and studied the work she'd done so far. The brushstrokes were vastly different from those he'd noted on her other pieces. Finer, more delicate, more in keeping with someone like . . . Forbes-Wright. For a long while he studied the emerging painting on the canvas, trying to project in his mind's eye what the finished piece would look like. An old mill house, trees, sky, lake and swans.

Then he turned and left. A grim, deeply horrible sense of betrayal was taking the place of pain in his heart. A part of him knew it was irrational, senseless. But he took that faked canvas like a personal insult, like an injury aimed right at him. Dammit, did he mean nothing to her? Nothing at all? She'd given him her virginity, but what about her trust? Her confidence? Her honesty? She must know how he felt about forgeries — he'd given two lectures already on the subject.

If he'd gone to the library he would have run into Frederica and found her with piles of photocopies of Forbes-Wright's work. But he didn't. He turned instead to the big Oxfordshire County Library opposite Bonn Square. There he spent the afternoon looking up the early Victorian artists. And found, in one big book chock-full of prints, a painting attributed to Forbes-Wright. *The Old Mill and Swans*.

Looking down at the glossy reproduction of the painting he'd seen emerging on the canvas in Frederica's room, Lorcan felt a hard, cold knot form in the pit of his stomach. This time there could be no doubt — the evidence stared back at him with harsh cruelty. There was no excuse for stealing another painter's work. None. Not even for Frederica Delacroix.

Not even for the woman he loved.

* * *

Frederica was just changing to go into dinner when a Classics student on the ground floor knocked on her door and yelled that she had a phone call. She skipped quickly down the stairs to the public telephone and lifted the receiver. 'Hello?'

'Hello, Freddy,' her father's voice sounded purposefully cheerful. 'How are you? I thought you'd be home by now.'

'No, I'm staying up for a little longer. I've got things to do.' As if he didn't know, the old faker!

'Oh. Ah. Right. About that, Freddy . . .' James Delacroix cleared his throat portentously. 'I think, you know, that it wasn't such a good idea after all.'

'What?' Frederica squeaked, scandalised. 'After all the hard work I've done? And the money I've spent on it. Are you mad? I only need another week or so and it'll be finished.' After sweating blood over it and tiptoeing around the greatest fake-buster in the country, surely he didn't expect her to chuck it all in, just like that? No way, Jose!

Then she felt a small shudder of foreboding slip down her spine as she realised that something must be wrong. Badly wrong. It wasn't like her father to chop and change his mind.

'Daddy,' she said quietly, her voice falling to a mere whisper. 'Daddy, is something wrong?'

James sighed heavily. 'Well, Freddy, I've heard on the unofficial grapevine that certain people have been . . . interested in us recently. Making discreet enquiries, as it were.'

It took Frederica a few moments to interpret all this careful wording. When she did, she almost yelped. 'The police, you mean?' she squeaked.

'Freddy, please! Not over the telephone!' her father admonished.

Frederica cast a furtive look around, but Walton Hall was deserted. 'Oh, Dad, you can't be serious!' she gasped. 'Why . . . How . . . ?' Suddenly all words left her. All thought left her. Because something dark and dangerous was creeping up on her, slithering into her subconscious like a carnivorous monster. Lorcan Greene, fake-buster. Lorcan Greene, suddenly and without warning, appearing in Oxford. Lorcan Greene, jet-setting millionaire playboy, taking out an unknown little Fine Art student. Lorcan Greene, policeman's friend and expert witness.

She found herself leaning hard against the wall, the phone shaking in her hand. No, it couldn't be. It simply *couldn't*!

'Freddy?' a worried voice called her name over the phone.

No, how could he possibly know what she was doing? He was not omnipotent. And why should the police be asking around about her in the first place?

'Freddy. Are you still there?'

She closed her eyes, a great miserable gulf of pain washing over her. Had it all been a con then? Had he somehow found out about her project? Had all their time together, their closeness, their laughter, their sharing of thoughts, their very lovemaking been nothing but a sham?

'No!' she groaned. 'Oh no, no, no . . .'

'Freddy! Are you all right?' Her father's voice, raised in uncharacteristic panic, roused her from the black hole she was sinking into, and she lifted the receiver once more to her ear. It felt absurdly heavy, as if it weighed pounds and pounds . . .

'Daddy, are you sure about this?' she asked, her voice small and weak.

James Delacroix sighed. 'I've been making some discreet enquiries of my own, and there are definitely rumours circulating about some kind of art fraud case being investigated in Oxford. The man in charge is a DI Braine. He was the policeman involved in that forged painting case at the Greene Gallery.'

Lorcan! Frederica caught her breath, stopping the wail of pain and denial that clogged her throat and literally hurt her. She coughed back the tears.

'But this new case can't be about us,' she said, struggling to get some sort of perspective. 'I mean, how could it be? We're not criminals — we don't have any criminal contacts. Surely they can't be after us!' Instinct told her that this just didn't make sense. It wasn't logical. But then, what did logic matter? In her heart of hearts, she knew that it was no mistake. That she wasn't being melodramatic. Lorcan was investigating her. All that attention he'd paid to her paintings — it wasn't because he really liked them. He was just studying her style. Memorising her methods. So that, if she hadn't thoroughly studied the techniques of master forger Tom Keating, she might have left some tell-tale personal touches that he would pick up on in her finished Forbes-Wright copy. And, expert that he was, he must then have expected to be called on to go over it all in court. If he thought she was going to sell the painting on — and why else would the Art Fraud Squad be involved otherwise — then, all this time, he'd just been biding his time, waiting to help put her in prison. Just like he had all the other forgers.

The darkness washed over her again. She sagged against the wall, the pain so great she thought she might pass out.

She shook her head. Took a ragged breath.

'I think you should just come home now,' James Delacroix was saying, his voice soft and full of loving understanding. 'Just forget about the favour I asked you to do and come home.'

Frederica's eyes snapped open. *And let him get away with it?* a voice hissed in her mind. *'Never!'* she yelled. Yes, that was better. Anger was so much easier to cope with than agony.

'Frederica!' her father said warningly. 'Let's not get silly over this.'

'No, let's not,' she said, her voice hardening like iron. 'We're doing nothing wrong. Nothing even remotely illegal. He'll be helpless to do anything about it,' she added, with a ragged, consuming satisfaction. 'I'm going to finish what I started, so there's no point getting yourself in the doghouse with Mum. And as soon as I've done it you can hang it up, and then we'll forget all about this.'

'But, Freddy . . .'

'Don't worry, Dad,' she said softly. 'I'll be careful. Talk to you later.' And before he could argue any further, she hung up. Oh yes. She'd be careful. From now on, it was Mr Lorcan Greene who'd have to watch out!

* * *

Lorcan, back in Five Mile Drive, reached for the telephone and dialled the London number of the Art Fraud Squad. He was put through to Richard Braine in a matter of moments.

'Hello, Richard. Yes. I've seen the canvas. No, it's not quite half-finished yet. Yes, I've identified it, and the artist. Got a pen?' Then he gave his friend all the details, aware of feeling nothing but calm. In fact, too much calm. Sometime soon, he knew he was going to pay for doing this.

'The thing is,' he finished, 'I haven't traced who has the original now. You'll have to put a team on it and find the owners.'

Detective Richard Braine promised he would and hung up a very happy man. Lorcan Greene hung up a very unhappy one.

Lorcan poured himself a stiff whisky and soda. When the telephone rang a few minutes later, he was already half-way through it, and slumped wearily on the sofa.

He reached for the phone and froze, as the sound of her voice, soft and sweet and innocently trusting, filled his ears. 'Hello . . . darling.'

Lorcan sat up stiffly, the drink sloshing over his hand. The promised pain had suddenly arrived. 'Frederica,' he said huskily.

'I was wondering if you would be free sometime soon?'

'Of course,' he swallowed hard. 'I . . . we need to talk.'

'Yes,' Frederica said softly. 'How about lunch, in my room? Tomorrow?'

Lorcan closed his eyes, picturing her tiny room. The waiting bed. He'd be mad to be there, alone with her. Mad, mad, mad. 'Yes, all right,' he agreed hoarsely.

Frederica sighed softly and hung up.

When she put down the receiver, the expression on her face was as cold as arctic ice.

CHAPTER 15

Ray Verney checked into his room at the Raleigh Hotel and signed his name with a somewhat nervous flourish. Although he'd masterminded several felonious scoops before, he'd never contemplated something quite like this. But big rewards always required bigger risks. Still, he comforted himself, if everything went according to plan, nobody would even know anything was amiss, let alone be on the lookout for one Mr Raymond Verney, organiser of murder-mystery weekends.

He walked to his window and found a pretty view overlooking the Martyr's Memorial and the golden stone facade of St John's College. But he quickly drew the curtains on such splendour, and the bright sunshine with it. The second week of June had begun as the last had finished off: hot and sultry.

It was Friday tomorrow, the first day of the conference, and Ray nervously checked that the door was locked before unpacking his clothes. The suitcase was made of grey synthetic leather, and once empty looked just like any other suitcase. But when he depressed its brass knobs and turned them anti-clockwise, the bottom of the case flicked open quietly to reveal the hidden compartment underneath.

The item Ray reverently pulled out of the bottom of the case was a loose, dirty-looking scroll. Even though he knew differently, it felt old and genuine. He unrolled it on the bed and stared down at the bewigged portrait of Alfred Gore, St Bede's one-time principal. It seemed to bear all the expertise and beauty of the great artist William Hogarth. It was even signed.

But it had actually been painted by a man called Clive Billings, and Ray's client had paid over twenty thousand pounds for it.

Ray stared at the fake for a long, long while, checking that it had suffered no mishaps in transit. It hadn't. He carefully put it back, locked the empty case and stashed it in his wardrobe.

Tomorrow he had to play the role of his life, but today he might as well enjoy himself, do a bit of sightseeing. But first, he'd take a taxi over to Headington and check up on his cast. Tomorrow morning was showtime!

* * *

At nine o'clock promptly the delegates, who'd been arriving in dribs and drabs all morning, gathered together in the JCR in Webster. The noise level was a tolerable murmur. The college butler circulated with tea trays, containing toast and little individual pots of marmalade and conserves. The tea was excellent. The china good quality Spode. It didn't take the veteran conference-goers long to realise that this was a vastly different experience from the usual fare. Big hotels were so charmless, so predictable. But this was utterly different. A grand piano, which was often played to good effect by the music students, stood in splendid isolation in one corner. The sofas were well-worn and extremely comfortable. Sunlight picked out the dust motes that danced in velvet-curtained windows. All of this helped add an air of unexpected contentment and expectation to the whole assembly.

By ten o'clock the noise level was much louder, and Ray watched his cast with quiet and unobtrusive approval. They were circulating nicely, and although it had been advertised that there would be a murder mystery over the weekend, so far, he was sure, nobody suspected the members of the newly formed Oxford Spires Publishing Company to be anything other than what they purported to be.

Reeve, over in one corner with the real editor of a large publishing house, smiled at the older woman winningly. 'Of course, I started off in admin, just so I could get on board with Oxford Spires,' he said. 'But my sights were always set on editing. We've just signed up a new author — he writes medieval murder mysteries. Anyway, I found him, helped him along, put him right when he started to get too technical, you know the kind of thing? But then, when we got to the contract stage, John Hendrix assigned himself as his editor.' He allowed venom and disgust to creep into his voice.

The editor of the publishing house found herself bridling on his behalf. 'No? After you'd guided him through the first manuscript?'

Reeve gave a hard, tight smile, and nodded towards John Lore, the first 'murder' victim. 'Yeah, that's him there, in the blue jacket and grey slacks. Little creep!' His face twisted in disgust and futile animosity. It made the older woman feel quite . . . shivery, for a moment.

'But didn't your author want to stay with you?' she asked.

'Of course he did. But I'm still only an editor, and John . . . well, he's a senior editor and he's already been with the firm a few years. He doesn't like any competition.'

The woman cast John Lore a fulminating look. 'Those kind of people make me sick.' She lowered her voice, beginning to enjoy herself; she'd forgotten how gossipy conferences could be. 'Publishing needs all the good people it can get.'

Reeve nodded, and leaned just a little closer. As he did so, Annis, talking to a lowly PR man, glanced across and quickly looked away again. Even though she knew what he was doing, building up his role, it still hurt to see him flirting with another woman. Which was as good a warning to keep away from him as any.

Thrilled by the attention, the older woman leaned a little closer to Reeve, putting a hand on his arm. What wonderful dark-blue eyes he had.

'Between you and me,' Reeve said softly, 'he's been trying to get me fired for the last few weeks.'

'No!'

'Yes. You know, dripping poison into the MD's ear. That's him over there,' he pointed out Ray Verney. 'So far, I think, Ray's not being fooled, but I don't know how long I can rely on that.' He shot the innocuous John Lore another hate-filled glance. 'The little creep's really got it in for me.'

The editor shook her head and sighed. 'There's so much backbiting going on nowadays.'

Reeve nodded, murmured a few more pleasantries and moved on, knowing that the word would soon spread that the good-looking guy with the Oxford company was holding on to his job only by his fingertips. He knew that the rest of the cast, scattered throughout the room, were doing the same as he was — sowing the seeds for their own characters.

Julie had bearded the youngest woman in the room, and he could tell she was 'confiding' in her that she was in love with a married man, and giving out hints that it was one of the men in her company. Of course, the woman she was talking to instantly thought she must mean Reeve, and Julie was having a hard time convincing her that it wasn't him.

Annis, overhearing this, ignored the twin prongs of jealousy and despair. It was yet another timely reminder — as if she needed one — that falling in love with a drop-dead handsome actor was hardly the smartest thing she'd ever done.

At eleven o'clock the door opened and a silver-haired man walked in. He was in his sixties, with a tall, lean body that moved with exquisite precision. He had ex-military and important personage stamped all over him. 'Good morning, ladies and gentlemen,' he said, bringing an instant hush to the room. 'I'm Lord Roland St John James, the principal here.' He went on to give a short but pithy welcome speech, followed by a round of applause from his hearers.

By a big open sash window, Norman Rix was telling the owner of a small publishing house about his stint in the police force, and hinting that he had to leave under a bit of a cloud. He now worked for Oxford Spires Publishing Company as a consultant for their police-procedural novels. A pity, Norman thought mischievously, that Oxford Spires didn't really exist!

The principal, known to all his friends simply as Sin-Jun, found himself next to a roly-poly teddy bear of a man, and shook hands yet again. 'Lord St John James,' Ray Verney said jovially. 'I'm Raymond Verney.' He dropped his voice. 'The organiser of the murder-mystery weekend?'

Sin-Jun smiled. 'Oh, quite. Are your people here now?'

Ray smiled. 'They are. Setting up their characters, I hope.'

Sin-Jun nodded. 'I must say, nobody is instantly recognisable as an actor.'

Ray smiled. 'I should hope not,' he said, then added casually, 'About the removal of this painting . . . ?'

Sin-Jun nodded, remembering that the bursar had arranged for one of the paintings in Hall to be removed at a propitious moment, just to help the whodunit along. 'Whatever's wanted, just say. We'll be glad to help,' he said airily.

Ray beamed. It was like taking candy from a baby.

In the middle of the room, Gerry suddenly squealed. It was a discreet, ladylike squeal, but it caught the attention of everyone in the immediate vicinity, and some of those beyond.

'Annis, love, that necklace of yours!' Gerry crowed, reaching forward and ostentatiously holding the 'diamond' pendant in her hand. 'It's a real rock!' The women in the group around them instantly looked across at the two actresses in genuine interest, while Annis laughed, a little falsely. 'Oh, it's got a flaw in it. I wouldn't have been able to afford it otherwise,' she said modestly, but uneasily.

Reeve leaned against a wall and took in her performance with hungry eyes. She'd been elusive ever since she'd all but told him that their affair was strictly short-term only. He couldn't tell whether she was already getting bored with him or whether there was something else. He hoped, fervently, that it was something else.

'I don't care,' Gerry gasped, avarice, jealousy and greed artfully displayed on her face. 'I'd kill for a diamond that size. It must be . . .' she named a vastly exaggerated carat.

Annis firmly pulled the pendant away from Gerry's grip. 'Oh no, nothing like that.' She made a great show of tucking the diamond pendant under her blouse. Gerry shrugged and moved away, but cast several obvious glances back at her.

The room erupted into conversation again. Quite a few of the delegates had by now pegged Annis as one of the actors, and they began to speculate. When would the necklace be stolen? And who would be murdered?

The sun was shining, the atmosphere was marvellous, and the St Bede's murder-mystery weekend had got off to a flying start.

Over by the door, Ray Verney took a deep, happy breath and told himself to relax.

Annis, busily denying the size of the diamond to a gently probing editor, caught Reeve's eye and hastily looked away.

Reeve's lips thinned. She looked as if she wanted nothing to do with him. It was driving him crazy. He couldn't let it go on. Sooner or later, Miss Annis Whittington was going to have to deal with him, face to face, all cards on the table.

And what if she really is bored with you, Reeve? A little voice popped up in the back of his head. What if she meant just what she said — that all she wants is a little fun, and then *adios amigo.* What will you do then?

CHAPTER 16

Frederica stepped back and viewed the room. Her desk was cleared of all paperwork and had been laid with a pretty Indian silk scarf of deep blues, greens and creams. On it were two plain white plates, a pair of crystal glasses, a vase of sweet william and a bottle of wine in an ice bucket. She'd ordered in from a local restaurant and nesting under silver warming dishes was a crab salad with a rich and creamy raspberry mousse packed in ice for dessert. Deep green napkins waited at the side of each plate. She nodded, satisfied at the pretty picture she'd created. A scene set for seduction. A scene set for ambush. Perfect.

She looked around the rest of the room, lingering on the covered canvas, an expression of pain and satisfaction warring on her face. Sometimes she hated it. As if it was easier to blame it for the mess she was in, rather than him.

The painting itself was almost finished now. Forbes-Wright had been famous for the feverish quickness with which he painted, and she'd had to work at the same breakneck speed in order to produce the same effect. Of course, she'd practised the new, faster style on several untreated canvases first, just to make sure she could do it. Those she had carefully burned afterwards.

She knew, in her heart of hearts, that the forgery she'd done had been a masterpiece of its kind. Now she wondered whether she'd been inspired to make it so perfect, or had simply been driven by a need for revenge. The damned painting, after all, was all he cared about. Not her. The pain of it had her turning away and brushing the thought aside. There was no room for self-pity now.

She deliberately left the covered canvas where he could hardly fail to see it, which was, after all, the whole point. She wanted to see just how far he would go. What would he say about it, exactly? Perhaps he'd even ignore it altogether — pretend it wasn't there. Now wouldn't that be amusing?

She checked her appearance carefully in the mirror. It had taken her hours before she'd achieved the look she was aiming for. She had on a plain white blouse, but it was tied in a knot to leave her midriff bare, and unbuttoned at the neck to reveal the valley of her breasts. To go with it, she'd donned a very brief pair of turquoise shorts, which revealed her long, slim, pale legs in all their shapely glory, and hinted discreetly at the rounded cheeks of her buttocks. Her feet were bare. Her face had not a scrap of make-up on it. She'd left her hair loose, and careful styling had left it an artful, waving mass, tumbling over her shoulders, swinging across her back whenever she moved. Her freckles had caught the sun, making their march across her nose unmistakable. She looked as young as she could possibly look. And as provocative and sexy.

Good. She wanted to confuse him. To torment him. To see if he would feel guilty at taking her innocence under false pretences. She'd lain awake at night, like someone on the rack, wondering if he even felt the slightest tinge of conscience about that afternoon when he'd made love to her. Or was it all just in the line of duty?

He'd seemed genuinely surprised by her untouched state. Did it worry him now? Somehow she doubted it. Oh yes, she doubted it very much. But, just in case she was wrong, she wanted to see the truth for herself.

She glanced at her watch. Nearly twelve-thirty. She jumped, her heart pounding, as a discreet knock sounded against her door. Now that he was here she felt weakened, scared and nervous.

And hideously excited. To see him again, his handsome face, his cool, sophisticated aura, to hear his voice. She raised her chin. A grimace of remembered pain and anger briefly twisted her lips, then was gone. When she opened the door, she opened her eyes very wide and smiled at her visitor.

'Lorcan! Are those for me?' In his hand he held a large bunch of sweet-smelling white and yellow roses. 'They're lovely. Thank you!' She walked across the small room to a glass vase standing on the windowsill, making sure he got a good view of her bare legs and rounded bottom. When she looked back over her shoulder, she was sure his eyes had darkened.

Lorcan said nothing as she put the flowers in the vase, watching her young, playful form in thoughtful silence. Where was the sophisticated vision he'd taken out to dinner that first night? Where was the summer nymph he'd met on the riverbank, in front of the old mill?

Frederica saw a bleak look cross his face and felt an odd combination of satisfaction and pain. So the man did have a heart after all. Somehow it both upset and annoyed her.

'Well, I hope you like seafood,' she smiled, hastily revealing the succulent crab meat on its bed of lettuce. 'Would you like to pour the wine?'

Lorcan forced a smile on to his face. He walked towards her, covering the yards in a few measured steps, and couldn't help but flick the covered canvas a puzzled glance. Why the hell hadn't she hidden it? Frederica saw the direction of his eyes and hid a smile. Later, she'd give him the chance to take a look at it. He must be eaten alive with curiosity. And when he'd seen it, what would he do then?

Her heart stalled as she suddenly realised that her whole future depended on that one question. Now that he was here, filling the empty space around her, she could no longer hide behind her pain; behind this desire for revenge that was nothing more than a distraction, a way of trying to convince her heart that it was in no peril at all. But it was.

If he did nothing after looking at that canvas — didn't warn her, didn't get angry with her, didn't say something, anything, then her life was all but over. She knew, even as she thought it, that it sounded incredibly melodramatic. She waited for a little voice of reason to pipe up and tell her that of course her life wouldn't be over. She was still young and beautiful and would find someone else. And so she might. But she'd never find someone that she could love again. Not like she loved this man.

A life without love. Or a life with the man she loved. Those were the stakes in this game she was playing. And, for an instant, it was too much. She felt her head swim, felt herself sway, and took a deep, desperate breath. She forced herself to move, to say something.

'I hope you like white wine?' she heard her voice ask calmly, as if from far away.

Lorcan competently opened the bottle of wine and poured it into the glasses. 'This is fine,' he assured her. Then he utterly undermined her by the simple act of walking around and holding her chair out for her. Frederica, her heart pounding all over again, took her seat, every nerve and fibre of her being aware of his arms, so close to her, as he pushed the chair forward. Of the soft sigh of his breath against her head as he leaned over her. She wanted, suddenly and overwhelmingly, for him to touch her. Anywhere. Just the touch of his hand on her shoulder. The brush of his fingertips against her forearm. Any contact at all.

They were so far apart. In that moment, each of them was playing their own game, each aiming for a different goal — they were universes apart, and she knew it. She fought a rising tide of panic yet again, dragged in a painful breath, and waited for him to sit down opposite her.

He was dressed in an ice-blue shirt under a cream jacket, with cream linen slacks. He looked cool, unapproachable, and so incredibly handsome that it took every atom of resistance not to reach out to him. It no longer mattered that he was a betrayer, a seducer, a hunter. All that mattered was that today, she was going to turn the tables. The hunter was about to become the hunted. Not out of revenge or hurt feelings, but because it was the only chance she had left. He was so set on what he was doing — catching a forger — that he couldn't see what really mattered. If only she could shock him from the path he was following, she might, just might, have the opportunity to show him that she loved him, and for him to demonstrate that he had feelings for her too. He must have. She couldn't believe that a man could make love to her as he had done and feel nothing.

And if she was wrong . . . No. Don't go there, she warned herself, as a great chasm of pain and darkness opened and then closed before her. With an all-too-human instinct for self-preservation, she pushed the possibility away, and smiled.

Her eyes were soft and guileless as she reached for her glass. She waited until he'd lifted his own wine, then said softly, 'What shall we drink to?'

Lorcan's eyes flicked to hers, a strange expression crossing his face. He knew, as sure as he knew his own name, that something was wrong. That canvas, for a start, shouldn't be where it was. He hadn't missed her sudden pallor either. And he didn't miss the strange, dark look in her eyes now. He could only hope it meant that she was having second thoughts about the forgery. That she meant to show him the painting. To confess what she'd done and ask him to help her. But even as he hoped and prayed that that was the case, he couldn't quite bring himself to believe it.

'To us, Frederica,' he said at last. I think we need it, he added silently and sadly to himself.

Us? Frederica thought bleakly. There is no us. Not yet. I thought there was, for just a briefly magical, stupid moment. 'To us,' she echoed softly.

The crab was delicious, cooked to perfection and melting in the mouth, but she hardly tasted it. Instead she watched him like a hawk out of doe-soft velvety dark eyes. 'I kept expecting to see you at the Ruskin,' she opened the battle with a tender salvo. She allowed, just for an instant, all the real hurt and bewilderment she'd felt to show through, before bravely covering it with a smile. 'But I expect you were busy?'

Lorcan felt his stomach muscles clench. She looked so vulnerable. She sounded so vulnerable. 'I'm sorry,' he said softly. 'I had to go back to London for a few days. I meant to call you, but then I realised you'd have to talk down in the hall, with who knows listening in. So I thought it best to wait until we were alone.'

Frederica smiled softly. What a wonderfully good liar he was. 'Of course, you're right. And I keep forgetting that you have a gallery to run,' she added softly. 'I can't expect such a busy man just to drop everything for me.'

Again, Lorcan felt a savage fist clench inside him. He already felt like a prize scoundrel — and she was turning the knife in him with every word she spoke.

'It's not that,' he said, and meant it. But how could he tell her that he'd kept away from her just because he was afraid of the very thing that was happening now? He wanted to reach across the table to her, tell her to burn the damned canvas which stood behind them, to trust him, to give herself over to him. He'd protect her. Take care of her. Give her everything she could ever want — fame as an artist, love from a man who adored her. Wealth, anything.

Damn it, he was being a fool. Why didn't he just put his neck on the block and hand her an axe? He smiled, leaning back in his chair, his eyes wary as he watched her. 'It's just that . . . you took me a little by surprise that afternoon. You should have told me that I was the first.'

Frederica felt herself blush. She couldn't help it, and it wasn't part of the plan, but suddenly she felt mortified. Aghast, she felt a huge tear slide down one cheek.

Oh damn! She was supposed to be seducing him, torturing him, not breaking down and crying like a ninny!

Lorcan lurched out of his chair, his face pale. 'Frederica, don't!' he cried, coming round the table, dragging her to her feet as she struggled and tried to turn her head away.

He caught her pointed chin in one hand and turned her to face him. 'Don't cry, sweetheart,' he said softly. 'Please don't. I'm sorry. I didn't mean to be so clumsy.' He held her to him, felt her cheek press against his chest, felt the warm salt of her tears seep through the material and dampen his skin. He closed his eyes. This was agony. So much worse than he'd ever have thought. 'I love you.'

The words snapped Frederica's eyes open, cutting off every sensation like an anaesthetic. 'What?' she gulped. For a moment, a happiness so profound it was almost too much ignited inside her like a flare. Then, just as suddenly, it went out. Because it was too good to be true.

Lorcan took a shaky breath. Had he really said that? But she was straining back in his arms now, looking at him with shocked, almost black eyes, and he realised that, yes, he really had said it. And meant it.

'I said,' he repeated, 'that I love you.'

Frederica felt her legs give way beneath her. Even as she asked herself what game he was playing now, even as she warned herself this was — had to be — yet another trick, he was taking her weight, lifting her, carrying her easily to the bed.

'Are you really so surprised?' he asked softly, kneeling down beside the bed as he lowered her gently on to it. One finger curled around a stray lock of curly auburn hair that clung to her damp cheek. For a long moment their eyes held.

I don't believe you, Frederica thought bleakly. But I want to. Oh, how I want to!

Lorcan shook his head. 'Oh, Frederica, what a mess I'm in.' He laughed harshly. If someone had told him just a month ago that he'd fall head over heels in love with a much younger woman, an art forger and a virgin, he'd have laughed himself sick at the absurdity of it. Yet now, here he was.

He took a huge breath. It was now or never. 'Frederica,' he said softly. 'What's on the canvas under that sheet?'

Tell me, he urged her. Oh, my darling, just confide in me and I'll tell Richard that I've made a mistake. Confide in me, and I'll see you never have to forge another work of art in your life. Trust me and I'll forgive you anything.

Frederica swallowed hard. First he says he loves you, she thought bleakly. The next he wants to see the painting. How much more proof do you need? He'd do anything, say anything. She was beaten before she'd even started.

There was only one last card she could play. One last desperate gamble.

'Why don't you go and look?' she offered. And, as he went to rise, she added softly, 'Or you can make love to me.'

Lorcan's green eyes darkened. Something — some brief, excruciating pain — seemed to flash across his face, as he understood.

'But I can't do both, can I Frederica?' he whispered hoarsely.

Frederica shook her head. 'No,' she said sadly, 'you can't do both.'

* * *

Over in Hall, Reeve's angrily flushed face contorted in venom. 'Why don't you just face it, Hendrix,' he hissed, 'you don't understand the book the way I do.'

Their immediate neighbours, who'd been chatting happily over their lunch of cold chicken salad, slowly fell quiet as Reeve and John played out their big argument scene.

'I know more about editing, proper, responsible editing,' John hissed right back, 'than you could ever possibly hope to learn. It might come as a big shock to you, Reeve, but your pretty-boy looks won't get you anywhere in this business. In this business you need brains.'

Reeve half-rose from his chair, pushing it back, the sound of the chair scraping across the floorboards as teeth-tingling as chalk across a blackboard, and leaned across the table dramatically. 'Don't think I don't know what you're up to, you little—'

'Boys, boys,' Ray interrupted, casting their avidly agog audience an apologetic look. 'Please, don't make a scene,' he begged them, with unintended irony. 'Now is not the time to talk about this.'

Reeve shot Ray a fulminating look. 'Are you trying to tell me this little sod hasn't been trying to get me fired?'

'You don't need any help from me,' John shot back. 'Incompetence has a way of catching up with you in the end.'

'Oh yeah?' Reeve sneered. 'And how incompetent was it to sign up the author of the Brother Felix Stowe murder mysteries then?'

The atmosphere was now electric. Even though all the conference-goers were aware that it was an act, the two were so good that you could almost cut the tension with a knife.

John shot to his feet. 'That was just a fluke!' he yelled, a vein throbbing in his jaw. 'You stumbled on to him!'

'Stumbled, hah!' Reeve was shouting now. 'Admit it, I hooked a big money-spinner and you didn't.'

'That remains to be seen!' John snapped, the two actors eyeing each other balefully.

Reeve allowed his face to fall into an astonished mask. 'Are you trying to sabotage the book, John?' he asked, as if amazed at his discovery. 'Is that why you're insisting on all those unnecessary rewrites? To ensure that it flops?'

'Don't be so bloody stupid,' John snarled, but flushed guiltily. 'I could kill you sometimes, you troublemaking little creep.'

'Darlings, don't be so melodramatic,' Gerry drawled, right on cue. 'Calm down and eat your tomatoes like good little boys.'

Julie laughed, again right on cue. Annis turned to her neighbour. 'I think I prefer the modern whodunits, don't you?' she asked loudly, conversationally, like any other good-mannered woman trying to defuse an ugly scene.

Reeve and John reluctantly sat down. The show over, people began to eat again. And confidently expected to find either Reeve or John 'bumped off' before the day was out.

* * *

Frederica gasped, her fingers clenching painfully in Lorcan's wheat-coloured hair as he sucked hard and passionately on her engorged nipple. She pushed her head back against the pillow in painful pleasure as his teeth nibbled her delicate flesh.

His hands found the waistband of her shorts and fever-ishly pushed them down, his palms cupping her buttocks, all sense of civilised man gone now as he surrendered to her and the overriding need of the moment. Somehow, it seemed to him now, it had always been inevitable. This fall into love.

He groaned as her fingers scratched a path down his spine, her nails raking him, her soft, inarticulate cries filling his ears. He reached for his belt, fumbling with it, freeing himself as her long, slender legs looped around him, impris-oning him, demanding, urgent, her action as mindless as his.

Lorcan gasped, tried desperately one last time to draw away from her, but when she opened those dark, dark eyes, her lips parted for his kiss and she sighed, he was lost. Finally, irrevocably lost. He closed his eyes and buried himself within her, groaning as her tight inner muscles encircled him. He threw his head back, his jaw clenched tight in exquisite ecstasy. Amazed, Frederica watched him, fresh tears starting in her eyes as she realised that, whatever else he was, he was hers.

At least for this moment of agony that was also ecstasy. She clung to him, holding him close, crying out as he plunged into her again and again, his lithe, hard body not hurting her, always just . . . pushing her a little higher, nearer to that apex that submerged the mind like molten lava. Her heels dug into him, her breasts were hard points pressed against his chest. She felt his body leap, and he cried out her name, shuddered, and collapsed on top of her.

Frederica, surfacing slowly, heard only the echo of her own name as she cried out his.

Eventually she opened her eyes. Reality, in the shape of a crack in the ceiling, brought her crashing back to her senses.

So, she had forced him to choose between her and the canvas. And he'd chosen her. This time. But what about next time?

She moved, sliding out from beneath him, and pulled on a long, simple dress that covered her from neck to shin. That covered the skin he'd so lovingly kissed. She shivered, feeling colder, not warmer, with the covering. She looked down at him, lying naked on her bed. Gone were the cool, classy clothes. His hair was ruffled and his skin had the silken sheen of sweat. He had a hand over his eyes, as if he couldn't quite face the world yet.

She wanted to kill him. And love him for ever.

'I'll be back in a little bit,' she whispered softly, and when he looked at her questioningly, murmured vaguely, 'the bathroom.'

She went out of the door, and even walked a few steps down the corridor, before slowing to a stop.

She felt as if her heart was breaking as she tiptoed back to the door she'd purposefully left just a little ajar.

For she already knew what she'd see. The moment she'd left the room, he'd have leaped off the bed, walked to the canvas and pulled back the sheet.

She took a breath, preparing herself for the ultimate proof of his betrayal. His lies. His sweet, wonderful, marvellous lies. But when she peeped through the crack the sheet was still on the canvas, and he was still lying gloriously naked in her bed, his hand over his eyes. Could it really be that he loved her after all?

She didn't know it, of course, but Lorcan had no need to look at the canvas. He'd seen it already. Instead he lay, satiated, throbbing with the aftermath of their lovemaking, staring at the darkness of his closed lids, wondering just what he was supposed to do now. And knowing that there was only one possible answer.

CHAPTER 17

As Frederica stood in the corridor, spying on him through the crack in the door, Lorcan slowly got up, his naked body bathed in the afternoon sunlight streaming through the windows. She licked lips gone suddenly dry, her heart aching with tenderness as she watched him drag back on the clothes that he had discarded in such a hurry. The transformation from impassioned lover to cool, sophisticated gallery owner seemed less acute now. As if, miraculously, the man was merging into one entity. But was the entity her lover or her enemy?

He ran his hand through his hair in a gesture that had become heart-achingly familiar to her by now and walked, not towards the painting, but towards the window. Frederica's heart hammered. What was he waiting for? Why didn't he check out the bait she had set for him so tantalisingly? She lingered there for what seemed like an eternity, or at least a lifetime, but he only continued to stare out of the window at the tops of the famous silver birches, his hands thrust deeply into his trouser pockets as he scanned the Oxford skyline. He looked weary, and yet tense at the same time.

Frederica's heart continued to thump heavily. What did it mean? Why wasn't he looking at the canvas? Eventually she pushed open the door and walked in, warning herself not to get too far ahead. Not to hope too soon.

At the sound of her footsteps on the wooden floorboards, he turned and looked at her. His hazel eyes ran over her, drinking in every detail. The glorious hair hopelessly tangled now. The concealing dress. The blank, puzzled look in her lovely eyes. He sighed. 'Would you like to come back to my place for a drink? There's something I'd like to show you,' he offered quietly, both of them shying away from talking about what had just happened.

Because she didn't know what else to do, she nodded wearily. 'All right.'

They closed the door on the painting and the untidy bed, and walked out into the glorious afternoon. Lorcan helped her into the car and drove the Aston Martin out on to the Woodstock Road. Sitting beside him, so close to him she could feel his body heat, Frederica felt dazed. She was wearing nothing but the dress and a pair of sandals. Everything about her felt battered. Her senses, her heart, her soul, even her body. But her body, at least, was content.

She supposed she should feel wickedly wanton, sitting in a sports car beside a handsome man, wearing no underwear. She supposed she should feel grown up and liberated. But she didn't. She sighed and looked out of the window at the beautiful laburnums that were cascading yellow bunches of flowers over garden walls. She felt sick at heart and scared of the future. She loved a man who might still be planning on sending her to prison. The fact that she had done nothing wrong and wouldn't actually be arrested seemed utterly irrelevant. Lorcan heard the massive sigh she gave and glanced across at her. Her face was a picture of misery.

'Frederica,' he said, 'what the hell are we doing?'

She laughed. It was a bleak, blank kind of laugh. It matched perfectly the way she felt. 'I don't know. I was hoping you might.'

Wisely, perhaps, he said nothing more until he'd negotiated the big roundabout and pulled up outside a white villa in Five Mile Drive. Leading her inside, Lorcan pushed open a door to reveal a large lounge. Acres of plush carpet gave way to cream chairs and sofas. Cool mint-green curtains picked up the same colours on the cushions.

'Do you want a drink? A glass of wine? Or tea?'

'Tea would be fine,' she said quietly. Listen to them. A pair of friendly, polite, civilised strangers. But she didn't feel particularly friendly just then. And Lorcan hadn't been anywhere near civilised in his lovemaking. But at least they could be polite, she thought, and fought back a wild desire to laugh like a lunatic.

When he came back with a loaded tray, she watched him place it on the table, pour out two cups, and offer her the sugar lumps. The sense of unreality heightened. Ever since the phone call from her father, she'd felt as if she'd taken a step outside the real world into some other kind of existence. Now, this feeling of otherworldliness was almost suffocating. It felt just like a nightmare. A sense of being somewhere utterly alien. Except that this time, there was to be no waking up.

Lorcan handed her the teacup, noticing that his own hand was shaking. When she took it from him, her hand was no steadier.

He leaned back in his chair and took a deep breath. Time to get everything out in the open. Time to take back control of his life. He wasn't used to being as out of control as this, and he didn't like it. He'd demand to know what she was doing, make her give it up, drag her into his life and keep her there no matter what it took.

'Frederica,' he said, and then the telephone rang.

She jumped and it seemed to jolt her back into gear. The cotton-wool feeling in her head disappeared. Suddenly, she was alert and aware, and thinking clearly.

'You'd better answer that,' she said softly, and got up from the sofa to give him a little privacy. She gravitated naturally towards the window as Lorcan snatched up the receiver.

'Lorcan! Richard here. I was expecting to get the answering machine. I just wanted you to know — our stool pigeon has disappeared.'

'What?' Lorcan said, hardly listening.

Of all the times to call! He fought back the unreasonable anger and shot a quick, agonised look over his shoulder. She was standing with her back to him, staring out over the gardens.

'Gone,' Richard repeated obligingly. 'As in scarpered. Word has it that he's left the city. Something he's never done before. And I don't know why.'

Lorcan sighed. 'Perhaps he was telling you lies?' he said, as quietly as he could without whispering, but over by the window, Frederica's ears pricked up.

'What do you mean?' Richard asked sharply.

Lorcan took the cordless phone through to the kitchen. Frederica waited for just a few seconds, then softly moved towards the doorway, being careful to hug the wall and keep out of sight.

'I mean,' Lorcan said softly, 'perhaps your little bird was having you on.'

'Why would he do that? Have you found out something?'

'I mean,' Lorcan said, keeping his voice even and calm, 'perhaps he lied to you to cover up something else. To focus your attention on Oxford.' He glanced at the half-open door, not knowing that Frederica was lurking behind it. 'While his friends pulled a fast one somewhere else.'

Frederica bit her lip. Fast one? Focus on Oxford? He was talking to the police! He had to be. Right here and now, after he'd just made love to her! She slapped her hand to her mouth to stifle the small sound she made. Pain washed over her, and she forced it back. She'd wanted definite, solid proof, hadn't she? An end from all this wavering uncertainty? Well, she had it now. In spades.

'I don't think so,' Richard Braine said, his voice becoming wary now. 'Skeeter's always been on the level before.'

'There's always a first time for someone like him to play both ends against the middle,' Lorcan pointed out briskly. 'How do you know someone hasn't paid him to feed you misinformation?' As he spoke, he mentally winced. Now he was committed. He'd changed sides utterly, like a turncoat in the midst of battle. But, really, the decision had been made the moment Frederica had asked him to choose between her and that damned painting. There was no way now that he could feed her to the lions.

'Lorcan,' Richard said quietly. 'You have found something out, haven't you?'

Lorcan cast another look at the open doorway. Picturing the curve of her slender back as she stood at the window. Remembering her soft sighs against his ear. Her breasts crushed to his chest. He took a deep breath. 'You're right. I found out that I've been on the wrong track. That student I was telling you about . . . she's clean.'

There. He'd done it. What did his honour mean to him if it meant losing her? What good were having principles and convictions if they crucified the woman you loved?

By the door, Frederica was glad she still had her hand over her mouth, for she felt a cry of happiness rising from her throat. It was so overwhelming, so acute, that for a moment she thought she was going to pass out. He was defending her. Lying for her. For a man like Lorcan, it meant the world.

'What do you mean? I thought you said it was . . .' Over the line Lorcan heard a rustle of paper, and he could almost picture his friend pulling towards him a print of *The Old Mill and Swans*. 'A painting by Forbes-Wright?'

'I was wrong,' Lorcan said flatly. 'Her tutor, knowing that she was interested in depicting modern living in a contemporary way, had set her the task of comparing a well-known painting of a dwelling of the last century and repainting it as it is now. I found some notes of hers at the Ruskin. Living right next to the mill at Cross Keys, the Forbes-Wright was an obvious choice.' It sounded good. It even sounded plausible. So much so that Frederica, listening to him, felt like applauding. She wanted to throw her arms around him, promise him she'd love him for ever and ever. But something kept her rooted to the spot.

Richard Braine wasn't an easy man to convince, however. 'I thought you said she was making an exact copy?'

Lorcan closed his eyes, hating to do it, but then shook his head. 'She was. That's what threw me, at first. But I've just seen the canvas — she's overpainted all that clever preparation in her own style. The damned mill's even got a conservatory on it now.'

There was silence on the end of the line for so long that Lorcan felt sweat pop up on his forehead. He gripped the receiver hard. He knew Richard of old — if he couldn't put him off, nothing would shake him. The man was a terrier when it came to getting his teeth into a case.

'So that old canvas and all the Victorian-style paints . . ?'

'She's a perfectionist,' Lorcan said quickly. 'I'd already learned that. She's the Ruskin's star pupil, although they're being very careful not to say as much. Everyone expects her to get a First.'

'I see,' Richard said, but his voice was ominously flat.

'Which is why this stool pigeon of yours disappearing makes me wonder if we haven't been set up,' Lorcan added craftily, tossing the distraction into the conversation like a master fisherman. 'You say he's never pulled a stunt like this before?'

'No,' Richard admitted.

'So, isn't it possible that he was paid to give you false information? And, knowing that you're soon going to realise it, he's gone into hiding. It makes more sense than some second-year student turning rogue.' He swallowed hard, his heart pounding.

Behind the door, Frederica's heart did the same.

But could she really trust him? Even now? That old worm, suspicion, wriggled deep inside her. He knew that she'd heard him answer the phone. He'd gone out into the kitchen, fairly screaming the fact out loud that it was an important phone call. And he was clever enough to guess that she might be listening in. What if he was just laying the groundwork to set up a false sense of security on her part?

Was she being paranoid? Or was she just being realistic?

Once again she was back in the realms of a nightmare. Was he a heartless seducer, a cunning, ruthless hunter? Or did he mean it when he said he loved her?

'Hmm, you might be right,' Richard Braine agreed cautiously.

Lorcan disguised a sigh of relief, and said casually, 'Well, I'll still keep my eyes open down here. Just in case.'

'Good idea,' Richard said dryly. Then, just as Lorcan was about to hang up: 'Is she very beautiful, Lorcan?'

Lorcan went cold. He stared at the wall opposite him. Then he said quietly, 'Yes, she is.' And hung up.

Frederica moved quickly back to the window. When Lorcan returned and put the phone back in its place, she was standing exactly where he'd left her.

'Frederica,' he said softly. His breath caught as she turned to look at him. His heart melted as those dark velvety eyes met his. And he knew it would always be this way. He walked towards her, his arms coming out to hold her. Frederica panicked.

'You said you had something you wanted to show me?' she reminded him, taking a hasty step back. She needed to think. She needed time to recover, to try to make sense of all that had happened. If she let him hold her now, she'd be lost all over again.

'What? Oh . . . yes.' Lorcan tried to ignore the pain he felt as she moved determinedly away from him. Pretended it didn't matter. Reassured himself that, in time, he'd win her over. After all, he'd just given up a very important part of his life for her. He knew without having to ask that Detective Inspector Richard Braine would never again ask him to help the police. He knew that he'd never again be able to meet his own reflection in the mirror without knowing, and acknowledging, that he had sacrificed a great part of himself for the sake of a woman who might not even love him. But it didn't matter.

He loved her. Such was the power of love. He smiled, suddenly glad that, no matter how things turned out, he hadn't cheated himself. Hadn't betrayed her. He knew, in a flash of illumination, that he'd never, ever regret what he'd just done.

Frederica saw an astonishing look cross his face, and wondered what had caused it. Before she knew what she was doing, she'd taken an instinctive step towards him. Something wonderful had just happened. She knew it. She felt it. But then she checked herself.

She still didn't dare trust him.

'What I wanted to show you is over here,' he said calmly, and walked to one corner of the room, where a plain-looking frame faced the wall. 'I got it the other day, in a junk shop in Botley. What do you think?'

He turned it around and showed her the vibrant, colour-ful, cartoon-like print of a Roy Liechtenstein. 'What do you think this was doing in Botley of all places?'

Frederica shook her head, but for once failed to be inter-ested in a piece of art. She turned away from it, not even bothering to check whether it was one of the earlier prints. Lorcan put it back and said casually, 'Of course, his work is very easily faked. Any competent cartoonist could have a reasonable go at faking a Liechtenstein.'

Now, Frederica thought. Now was the time to turn round and tell him that she was copying the Forbes-Wright, and more importantly, why.

Now, Lorcan thought. She's going to tell me now. But even as Frederica turned, even as she opened her mouth, even as she began to speak, something insisted she remain silent.

Had that phone call been a setup between him and his policeman friend? He'd invited her back to his house — he could have asked his buddy on the Art Fraud Squad to call at three o'clock on the dot. She didn't want to believe it. She didn't even really think it was true. But she didn't know. And until she did, she'd just have to stick it out. Until the painting was finished, until she showed it to him in all its glory, in all its fine detail, and waited to see what he'd do. Would he call the police in, or tell her to destroy it? Until then, she was in limbo: that place between heaven and hell, not knowing which was to be her final destination. Her only consolation was that it wouldn't be long. The painting was all but finished. She could hang on just that little while longer. She had to.

And so she smiled merrily at him, took a step towards him, and held out her hand. 'Want to go punting on the river?' she asked brightly.

Lorcan swallowed hard. Felt something deaden and crumple inside of him. Then he nodded. 'If that's what you want,' he agreed, his voice as bleak as a winter wind.

CHAPTER 18

Detective Inspector Richard Braine didn't look happy as he boarded the train to Oxford. In his pocket he had a search warrant for Frederica Delacroix's room in St Bede's, and another one for her work area at the Ruskin School of Art. He stared at the passing scenery morosely. He wanted his suspicions to be wrong. Dead wrong. What he most definitely didn't want was to find out that Lorcan Greene, a man he'd always trusted, had lied to him.

* * *

At four-thirty on the dot, the conference-goers at St Bede's began to assemble for afternoon tea, the impressive college butler and several scouts beginning to circulate with delicious meringues and trays of dainty cucumber sandwiches and pots of tea.

Carl Struthers, the owner of a large and successful non-fiction publishing company, was a thin, dark, intense-looking man, who rarely smiled. He had only one ruling passion, and it wasn't publishing. His eyes flickered around the room restlessly, and he glanced, more than once, at his watch.

'Do you have to salivate whenever she walks by?' Gerry hissed loudly at her 'husband' John Hendrix.

'Oh, don't start . . .' John said wearily. And as the conference-goers quietened down to watch the next instalment, Reeve moved slowly across the room, careful not to interfere with John, Gerry and Julie's big husband-wife-mistress love triangle.

'Looks like things are going well,' Reeve murmured to Annis, as Gerry scornfully asked her errant spouse why he had to rub her nose in it by bringing his mistress to Oxford?

Reeve gently took Annis's hand. 'Come on. We're not needed for this scene.' He put a hand on her elbow and began to move towards the door.

'No!' Annis hissed desperately, but Reeve was firm.

'Come on, I want to talk to you.' His grip on her elbow became more insistent, and, knowing she couldn't make a scene, steered her quietly and unobtrusively out of the door.

Once inside Webster's main hall, however, she yanked her arm free. 'Now look here . . .' she began mutinously.

'No, you look! Oh, let's take a walk,' he said exasperatedly. 'I've found a walled garden that looks pretty deserted to me.'

Annis felt her heart pound, and knew that the last thing she needed was to be alone with him. Pity it wasn't the last thing she wanted, too! As they stepped into Wallace Quad and headed towards Becket Arch, she shot him a quick, anxious look. What exactly was all this leading up to?

He led her diagonally across the lawns to where a square walled garden shimmered in the afternoon haze. A single wrought-iron gate allowed access. On it was a white plaque. *PRIVATE Fellows' Garden — No Students Allowed.*

'We can't go in there,' Annis whispered.

'Why not?'

'We're not fellows,' she muttered, but he was already opening the iron gate, which creaked protestingly. Inside, they stood and looked around, admiring the tall hollyhocks, lushly blooming borders and the neat square cut of lawn.

'Over here,' Reeve said, pointing to one shady corner, where he sprawled on the grass. Dressed only in a lightweight dark-green shirt and black slacks, he looked dark and dangerous. He patted the grass next to him. 'Come on. I won't bite. Not unless you want me to.'

Annis snarled. 'You just try it!' she warned him, then collapsed bonelessly to the ground beside him.

'Good faint,' he said admiringly. 'Learn it on stage?'

'For a small TV bit part, actually,' she corrected. Looking up at him, her amber eyes glowed sleepily in the mellow afternoon heat. 'I was one of those housemaids who find a body, scream and pass out.' She stretched luxuriously. She was wearing a simple blue cotton summer dress, her long legs bare and her loose black hair spread across the grass.

'How nice for you,' Reeve agreed. 'Now, I want to know what that crack you made in the hot tub was supposed to mean,' he added blandly. Annis shot upright. Her eyes narrowed.

Talk about being ambushed! 'What do you mean?' she asked warily.

'I mean,' he said, meeting her eyes boldly, 'do you really just see me as a roll in the hay for the duration of our visit to Oxford? Or were you just blowing bubbles?'

He'd had time to think since she'd caught him so unawares that time, just after leaving the tub, and for a sophisticated woman who just wanted a casual fling, she was behaving very oddly indeed. Avoiding him. Keeping him at arm's length. Looking as nervous as a cat on a hot tin roof. Hardly the picture of a carefree woman out for a bit of harmless fun — which had given him at least some hope. He tried to ignore the cold clammy feeling that washed over him as he realised how easily this could all backfire on him if he'd read her wrong.

'Now just a minute,' Annis huffed. 'I meant every damned word I said.' She angled her chin up. Just who did he think he was?

'You don't have feelings me then?' he asked quietly.

Her heart stalled. 'Hah!' she forced herself to snort scornfully. 'Fancy yourself, don't you?'

'You don't want to see me again when we leave Oxford?'

She licked painfully dry lips, and managed a magnificently nonchalant shrug. 'I don't suppose that it will matter, one way or the other.'

'So what happened the other afternoon meant nothing?' he persisted, struggling to control his elation, because he was beginning to see right through her.

Annis blushed. 'Oh . . . that.' She turned to tweak a blade of grass. 'It was nice of course,' she murmured.

'Nice?' Reeve protested, and Annis grinned. She couldn't help it. Now that *had* hit home, hadn't it? She turned to him, mischief glimmering among the gold flecks in her eyes. 'That's rather a shame,' Reeve said, and saw her smile falter. 'Because that afternoon with you meant a hell of a lot to me.'

Annis frowned. 'It did?' Careful, she thought. He's an actor, remember. He can do 'sincere' standing on his head.

'Yes. And if it's all the same to you, I'd rather like to keep on seeing you when we get back to London.'

'You would?'

'Yes. So, what do you say?'

'About what?'

Reeve growled. The sound rumbled from his throat like the warning from a wild animal before it leaped upon its helpless prey.

'Annis, it's time to quit stalling. Admit all that talk in the tub was just so much hot air — and come here!'

A bee, drowsy and full of pollen, backed out of a foxglove, buzzed loudly around his dark curly head before heading for a Californian poppy. Annis watched it, then, slowly, looked up into his dark-blue eyes.

'All right,' she said. She could take a gamble as well as the next girl, when she had to. 'So I was feeling a bit defensive. But look at it from my point of view. You're the great super-stud, so-handsome-he-hurts-your-teeth Reeve Morgan. You'd just seduced me in the hot tub.'

'*I* seduced *you*?' he exclaimed. 'I like that! *You* were the one who dropped your robe and waltzed down into the tub — like Cleopatra with attitude. And it was *your* foot, I seem to remember, that had trouble keeping itself to itself!'

Annis waved a hand vaguely in the air. 'Whatever,' she said dismissively. 'The fact was, I felt as though I was just another notch on your belt. So the last thing I wanted to hear was all the usual stuff men dish out at times like that. About how commitment is overrated, et cetera . . .' Her eyes looked troubled and just a little hurt.

Reeve felt all sense of levity drain away. 'So you thought you'd get it in first, hmm?' he queried. And in a way, it made sense. 'But if you'd just kept that lovely mouth of yours shut for a few seconds longer,' he continued, ignoring the way her eyes flashed and her chin jutted out, 'you'd have heard me tell you that, unbelievable as it may seem, I've fallen head over heels in love with you.'

Annis felt the ground beneath her shift. She felt the elbow on which she was leaning give way, half-tipping her back on to the grass. She straightened her arm again. She'd gone very pale. 'Head . . .?' she whispered.

'Over heels,' Reeve finished helpfully. 'So you see, if it's all the same to you . . .'

Annis squealed and launched herself at him, pressing him back against the grass, knocking the breath out of him.

'Stop!' Reeve laughed, but then her mouth was on his, her legs tangling with his, her hands finding their way inside his shirt and her fingertips roaming over his chest — and suddenly he didn't want her to stop after all.

* * *

When the train from Paddington pulled in at a few minutes past five, Frederica was sitting in a silent and deserted Ruskin, staring at her canvas *Post-Millennium Home*. She'd walked down from Magdalen Bridge on her own, having said goodbye to Lorcan after a quiet and emotional hour on the river. He'd seemed distant. Mad that his ploy hadn't worked? Or really hurt that she hadn't trusted him? She sighed and continued to stare at her painting for a long, long time.

Which was why she wasn't in her room when Richard Braine tapped on her door. Receiving no answer, he tried the handle, found it open and stepped inside. He went straight to the canvas on the easel and yanked the sheet away.

An almost completed painting looked back at him. It was exquisite — one of the best forgeries he'd ever come across.

The mill had no conservatory.

'Oh, Lorcan,' Richard said sadly. 'You idiot!'

* * *

Back in the JCR at St Bede's, Gerry stormed off, threatening a divorce and slamming the door behind her. Julie burst into tears. John tried to comfort her. The rest of the conference delegates, forgetting it was supposed to be an interactive game, burst into spontaneous applause. Ray Verney filtered out with the rest of the group, watching Carl Struthers linger behind to inspect one of the paintings — a brace of pheasants, painted by a competent enough but uncollectable artist. He frowned.

He didn't like having Struthers around. Not when he was this close to making the switch. Sighing, and fighting back a tingling sense of fear and anticipation, Ray made his way to the bursar's office and knocked.

The bursar, a grey-haired and distinguished man, looked up with watery blue eyes that blinked at Ray from behind tortoiseshell-framed glasses.

'Hello, Mr Verney isn't it? How's the whodunit coming along?'

Ray beamed. 'Splendidly. That's why I'm here. You remember you agreed to help our plot along by removing one of the paintings from Hall for us and keeping it in your safe?' he prompted, looking around the room vaguely. The safe was a concealed one, but Ray had no trouble guessing that it was housed in the fake cupboard set flush against one wall.

'Oh yes!' The bursar rose. 'So it's time is it?'

Ray could hardly believe it was all working out so easily, but within minutes they'd collected the principal and were trooping into Hall.

It didn't take long to carefully remove the painting by Hogarth from the wall. Ray, being so close to it now, was practically trembling, but that didn't stop him from helping them to carry it back to the bursar's office. The bursar, something of an antiquarian, very competently set about removing it from its frame so that it would fit into the safe. It was, of course, to reside there during the course of the play — something insisted upon by the insurers.

Ray let himself be steered tactfully out by the principal, beamed at him, thanked him profusely yet again for helping out their little production in this way, and trotted off, the image of the gorgeous Hogarth still imprinted on the back of his greedy eyes.

Soon, now. Soon.

CHAPTER 19

Dinner in Hall went well. Next day, at lunch, the bursar would exclaim in horror over the missing painting, pointing out its 'theft'. Those who had failed to notice it missing over dinner tonight would be kicking themselves.

Ray, eating his avocado starter, glanced nervously at Carl Struthers. To Ray, it was obvious how much the reclusive, antisocial millionaire coveted the Hogarth. He'd done nothing but stare at it every time they'd been in Hall. Luckily, though, no one else seemed to have noticed his preoccupation with it.

Ray leaned back in his chair and wondered if he should change his plans and make the switch tonight. But no. He'd already decided when and how to do it. Changing plans at the last minute was always dangerous. He could wait.

* * *

When Lorcan pulled up in front of his house the sun was just developing a reddish tint. A blackbird sang in a cherry tree, its melodious song filling the evening air. But he was in no mood for anything beautiful. He was reaching for his key when something moved behind him. He spun round, the key pointing outwards, ready to attack any drug-crazed mugger or his associates.

Richard Braine grinned, took a backward step, and held up both his hands. 'Don't shoot,' he drawled.

Lorcan frowned. 'Dammit it, Richard, what the hell are you doing here? And why are you skulking about in the bushes?' Now that the initial adrenaline rush had subsided, he felt a cold, unpleasant sensation snake up his back. He ushered his friend into the lounge. 'Want a drink?'

'Scotch, if you have it.'

'I always have good Scotch,' Lorcan agreed cheerfully, wondering what the DI was doing here. He poured them both a drink, and when they were sitting in matching comfortable armchairs, facing each other like two wary gladiators in the ring, he said quietly, 'So, what brings you to the city of dreaming spires, Richard?'

'You do. Or rather, you and Miss Frederica Delacroix do.'

Lorcan took another sip of whisky. Not a flicker of emotion, alarm, or even interest, crossed his face. 'Oh?'

Richard smiled. 'I had a search warrant for her place at the Ruskin. I thought I'd come and take a look.' Was it his imagination, or did the gallery owner seem to relax just a little? 'And, of course, I had another one for her room at St Bede's,' he added, as if as an afterthought.

Lorcan took another sip of the Scotch and leaned his head further back against the chair, the epitome of a man at ease. 'And . . . ?'

'And I found an exact replica of Forbes-Wright's *The Old Mill and Swans* in her room at St Bede's,' Richard said, waiting patiently, like a cat at a mouse hole.

For a long while Lorcan said nothing, his mind racing. Was the policeman bluffing? No, somehow he didn't think so. He had to find a way of getting back in Richard's confidence. He had to think, dammit.

And Lorcan Greene could think very fast and very well. He could do most things very well, in fact. 'I see . . .' he said slowly. 'Then she's done two copies,' he mused, watching his old friend carefully, trying to gauge his reaction. 'The one I found, which she's painting over in her own style. And another.' He paused, then went on a fishing expedition. 'Did you find the one in her own style at the Ruskin?'

Richard frowned. A tiny pulse jerked in his jaw, and Lorcan was on to it in a moment. A hesitation. A hint of . . . confusion. 'No,' Richard finally said. 'When I found the copy in her room, I didn't go on to the Ruskin,' he admitted slowly. 'There didn't seem to be much point.'

Part of his mind warned him to tread carefully. Frederica Delacroix was a stunner. And a man like Lorcan — when he fell, he'd fall hard. But the other part of him, the part of him that valued Lorcan Greene's friendship, wanted desperately to give him the benefit of the doubt.

'Fine Art students aren't allowed to paint in their rooms,' Lorcan said, allowing his voice to sound surprised now. Even as he lied, as he cheated, as he manipulated his old friend with a treachery he wouldn't have thought possible, his heart was aching. Not for Richard. Not even for himself — for what he had become, for what he was doing. But for Frederica. Dammit it, Richard Braine was not a man to mess with. If they weren't careful, the only time he'd get to see Frederica again would be during the visiting hours of whatever woman's prison she was sent to.

'Well, Miss Delacroix seems to be breaking all the rules,' Richard pointed out softly.

And she's not the only one, is she, Lorcan? Richard thought wryly. But then, Richard himself hadn't gone to the Ruskin. Suppose she really did have a modern version of *The Old Mill and Swans* there? That would account for Lorcan's telephone call giving her the all-clear.

'So it didn't occur to you that she might have another painting in her room?' Richard probed.

Lorcan took another sip of his drink. Steady, he told himself. Steady. 'Why should it?'

Then Lorcan felt himself break out into a cold sweat as he suddenly realised something. If Richard talked to

Frederica's tutor he'd find out in an instant that Frederica had never been set an assignment like the one Lorcan had described. Then both he and Frederica would be well and truly up the creek. He had to distract him somehow . . . 'This painting in her room,' he said. 'How near is it to being completed?'

'Very near, I should say,' Richard said, a reluctant tone of respect creeping into his voice now. 'She's done a fine job.'

Lorcan obviously had something in mind, and Richard was very interested to know what it was.

'I'll have to see it,' Lorcan said.

'Fine. You'd better pick a time when she's out of her room though. I doubt she'd volunteer to show it to you.'

Lorcan laughed. He couldn't help it. If only Richard knew . . .

Richard looked at him oddly. 'You all right, Lorcan? You don't seem to be yourself, somehow.'

Lorcan swallowed the last of his Scotch. 'I'm fine,' he said flatly. 'So, what's the drill? You and I both know that painting a copy in itself isn't a criminal offence.'

'Right. We'll have to wait and see where she takes it. She's got permission to stay up only until Monday. Then she has to leave the college. Hopefully she'll take it straight to whoever commissioned her to paint it,' Richard mused.

Lorcan nodded. It made good sense. 'So you'll follow her, and see who her client is.'

'Right.'

'She hands the painting over and you arrest her?'

'If we can identify her client as a known dealer in fake art, yes,' Richard corrected cautiously. 'If her contact is an unknown, it might be best to let Miss Delacroix go about her business unmolested until we can track the final destination of her copy, and thus prove criminal intent.'

Lorcan felt himself relax a little. So far, Richard was letting him in on the deal. Which meant, nominally at least, he was still regarded as being on the team. He should feel like a treacherous turncoat, but he didn't. The only thing that mattered was Frederica. That he keep her safe. That he keep her his.

Lorcan nodded. 'So, have you had any luck in tracing the original owners of *The Old Mill and Swans*?' he asked.

Richard shook his head. 'Not yet. We're a bit under-staffed at the moment, but I've got Collins on it.'

Lorcan nodded and rose slowly, feeling stiff and oddly battered. 'Have you had dinner yet?'

Richard shook his head. 'No.' He too got up and glanced at his watch. 'And I should be getting back to London.'

'Let me treat you. The Raleigh's always good. Or there's Browns.'

Richard grinned. 'Go on then. You've twisted my arm.'

The two men smiled, neither one trusting the other, as they left the house and walked towards the waiting Aston Martin.

CHAPTER 20

Saturday morning dawned bright and early. In her room, Frederica worked feverishly on the painting. She had to get it finished by the end of the weekend, and nothing was going to stop her. Then she could get on with the rest of her life.

If she still had one.

* * *

In his room at the Raleigh, Ray Verney awoke and got ready to meet the delegates for the scheduled breakfast at his hotel, due to start at nine o'clock. It was a feature of the conference that they got to dine in one of Oxford's top hotels during the weekend, and since breakfast was the cheapest meal of the day, Ray had opted for that.

He hoped Carl Struthers was feeling in a more patient mood than he had been recently. Ray had spent most of last night resisting Struthers' demands that they do the swap there and then. But Ray had been adamant. It was far better to do the switch during the normal course of the day, when the bursar would be less inclined to make special arrangements for the guarding of the safe.

Ray swung out of bed and began to dress, his fingers fumbling with the buttons. This evening was the best time to strike, while everyone else was in Hall having dinner. He could easily pretend to nip off to the loo during the meal, and then make the switch.

And if something went wrong . . . Ray licked lips gone dry. No. Best not to think like that.

* * *

Lorcan Greene didn't wake up at all on Saturday morning, for the simple reason that he hadn't fallen asleep to begin with. He watched the early rising of the sun, his mind crystallising into one obvious, determined course of action. He had to take that canvas of Frederica's and destroy it. Then there would be no evidence with which Richard Braine could convict her. There would be no sale of a faked painting to a gullible art collector. And he would be rid of the spectre of it once and for all.

And Frederica . . . ? Frederica would just have to face up to what she'd done and the fact that she wasn't going to get paid her big fat juicy fee. And if she was mad at him? Tough!

* * *

At twelve-thirty the delegates, fresh from a workshop by a guest author in Webster's theatre, trooped happily into the Hall. There the bursar was in good form. Even before they'd started to queue at the hatches for lunch — which was always self-service — he was there, wringing his hands, looking ostentatiously distraught.

'Ladies and gentlemen,' the bursar announced, enjoying himself enormously. 'I'm afraid we've had something of an 'incident' this morning.' The group of fifty or so hungry delegates promptly forgot their rumbling stomachs.

'Really, something most dreadful has happened. As you can see . . .' he led the group to the open archways that led into Hall, '. . . one of our paintings has been stolen!' He threw his arms dramatically wide as he gestured to the empty space.

'A bit overblown,' Reeve muttered to Annis out of the corner of his mouth.

'I know. But he's an academic not an actor. Give the man a little leeway.'

John Lore walked forward, aggressively looking up at the gap on the wall. 'There was a glass case covering this one, wasn't there?' he challenged. There hadn't been, of course, and some of the more observant delegates knew as much. So when the bursar nodded and said emphatically, 'Yes, indeed,' they very quickly caught on that this was part of the act.

'The police are here now,' the bursar said his final line, and retired to High Table, where Sin-Jun and some other fellows teased him about his acting abilities.

Gordon stepped forward into the limelight. 'Ladies and gentlemen, I'm Inspector Gordon Nye. As the bursar has stated, a very valuable painting has indeed been stolen. It was housed in a narrow glass case affixed to this wall, and wired to an alarm. Unfortunately, a panel was cut in the front of the glass without touching or removing the whole thing, and the painting itself was cut and removed from the frame. When the fellows came in to breakfast this morning it was to find the glass case and frame still on the wall, but the painting, by William Hogarth, gone.'

'Where's the frame and case then?' one of the delegates piped up.

'Ah, erm, well they've been taken into evidence, naturally,' Gordon explained, not entirely convincingly.

He let them chat excitedly among themselves for a few moments longer, and then added ominously, 'So I'm afraid I'm going to have to ask that none of you leave Oxford for the time being.'

'But surely, Inspector,' Reeve shot out, with just the right mixture of surprise and hurt indignation, 'you don't suspect one of us?'

'Well, sir, I don't imagine the principal or one of the fellows took it, do you?'

'But that's preposterous!' Gerry spluttered. 'What about the scouts? What about the kitchen staff? They'd have more opportunity than any of us.' Annis and Reeve grinned at each other as mayhem broke out. But it was happy mayhem, with the delegates piecing together the timing and offering up suspects — all of them, funnily enough, being members of the Oxford Spires Publishing Company. Annis, Reeve and the others vigorously defended themselves. Eventually Gordon restored order. There was no need, after all, for everyone to go hungry, he pointed out with good common sense. He suggested that they collect their meals and then, after lunch, he'd start questioning everyone individually.

The bemused and amused kitchen staff, who obviously hadn't taken the slurs on their character to heart, dished out the meals to the excited, chattering delegates.

'I think it was really sporting of the bursar to get in on the act,' the woman Reeve had been flirting with on the first morning noted to her fellow delegates.

'Yes. They're very good. There really was a painting there you know.' And so it went on over lunch, everyone discussing how it could have been done, everyone agreeing how clever the thief had been to cut out the glass, and so on.

Gordon announced that he had constables searching everyone's rooms for glass-cutting equipment, which caused a considerable stir. Of course, they knew that no one really was going through their things, but just the thought of it raised hackles and sent pleasurable goose-bumps rising on their flesh. One and all agreed it was by far the best mystery weekend they'd ever attended.

Ray looked at the gap on the wall and smiled. He caught Carl Struthers' gimlet eye, and the smiled faltered. Damn him. He was going to blow the whole thing if he wasn't careful.

Reeve slipped off his shoe and ran his bare foot over Annis's calf. Annis choked on a tender piece of turkey.

Outside, the temperature was rising. It was going to be another scorching day.

In more ways than one.

CHAPTER 21

Frederica put down the paint brush and stepped away from the easel. Just another hour's work and it would be done. She'd found the process of making the copy fascinating, but there had been no creative buzz. No sense of achievement. She wanted desperately to start on another painting of her own. Perhaps another harsh, colourful, powerful canvas, like the one Lorcan had admired so much.

She carefully propped a sheet over the troublesome painting so that it didn't touch the drying surface and set her brushes in a jar of turpentine which stood on the shelf above. She washed her hands and had just reached up to free her hair from its ponytail when she heard the knock on her door.

She jumped, then walked warily across the room and cautiously opened the door. Lorcan pushed past her, a hard look on his face. Frederica swallowed painfully, then carefully shut the door behind her. When she turned to face him, he was standing in front of the canvas, staring at the covering sheet but making no effort to remove it. Then he swung round, fixing her with a cold look which pinned her to the spot.

'The police were here yesterday. Detective Inspector Richard Braine,' he said flatly.

Frederica blinked. Whatever she'd been expecting him to say, it wasn't that. 'What? Here at St Bede's?'

'No. I mean here,' Lorcan pointed down at the floor. 'In this room.'

'In my room?' Frederica squeaked. 'He had no right . . .'

'I daresay he had every right,' Lorcan corrected harshly. 'If I know Richard, and I do, he had a search warrant in his pocket and everything was above board.'

Frederica, her knees suddenly weak, sank down on to the side of the bed. 'I don't understand,' she murmured, her pale face making her dark velvety eyes look enormous. 'Why is he doing this? Why are you doing this?' she gritted. And, finally, her sense of grievance at last bubbling over, wailed forlornly, 'I've done nothing wrong!'

Lorcan gaped at her. Nothing wrong? Was she insane?

He turned and ripped the sheet off the easel. 'Nothing wrong? What do you call this then?' he asked savagely. His face was as pale as her own now. He was obviously a man at the end of his tether, and the fact that she was the one to take him there both appalled her and, deep down, thrilled her. Then both emotions fled. It was just him and her against the world. Or so it seemed. For a long moment, Frederica hesitated. Should she tell him the truth now? Or wait? She was sick of waiting. Sick of the mistrust that ate at her soul. Love was about a lot of things, but especially trust. She took a deep breath.

'I call that a favour,' she said softly.

Lorcan's eyes narrowed. 'A favour?'

Frederica nodded. 'Yes. I painted it for a . . . friend.' Although she was willing to put her own head on the block, and trust that Lorcan wasn't going to chop it off, she couldn't bear to drag her father into this. At least, not without consulting him first.

'What friend?' he asked suspiciously.

Frederica shook her head. 'Does it matter?'

Lorcan closed his eyes briefly and prayed for strength. 'Frederica,' he said, his voice ominously calm, 'you have one of the best art fraud detectives there is breathing down your neck. And if he has his way, you're probably going to spend the next three to five years of your life in Holloway. So yes, I'd say that it mattered.'

Frederica licked her dry lips and looked down miserably at the hands in her lap. He was warning her. He'd even told her about the police plans. Surely that was enough. What more proof did she need?

'I'm not going to sell the painting on, Lorcan,' she said softly, looking up at him, her face naked in its honesty. 'We never intended to. So you see, there's nothing the police can do to us. Whatever it was you and the police thought was happening in Oxford, whatever criminal activity brought you down here, it has nothing to do with me. It never has.'

Lorcan took a series of slow, deep breaths. She sounded so earnest. But it was not her truthfulness that concerned him now. Jealousy, sharp as a dragon's tooth, began to nibble away at him. 'Who's "we", Frederica?' he demanded. 'Who put you up to this? And what rubbish did he feed you? Of course he's going to sell it on!' he snarled. 'Why else do you think he got you to paint it in the first place?'

In his mind he could just picture some charming con artist seducing her into this mess.

Frederica shook her head. 'You don't understand,' she insisted stubbornly. 'You've got it all wrong. It's nothing like that, I swear. I promise.'

'Frederica, you've been conned, sweetheart,' Lorcan said grimly, not liking the look of stubborn defiance in her eyes one little bit. Whoever this scoundrel was, he had a hold on her that was driving him crazy. Why was she being so damned loyal? 'Whoever this man is, he means to make money out of the fake,' he gritted. 'And if anything goes wrong, it won't just be him that pays for it. You will too.'

Frederica burst into tears. She couldn't help it, because suddenly, and without a shadow of a doubt, she knew that he meant every word he was saying. He thought she was innocent. He loved her. He was willing to fight her corner.

Days and restless nights of suffering were suddenly washed away in a glorious tidal wave of relief.

Lorcan groaned and gathered her into his arms, holding her tight, rocking her back and forth as she cried as if her heart was breaking instead of mending.

'You d-d-don't understand,' she hiccupped, trying to pull away, to look him in his wonderfully handsome, loving face. 'It isn't l-l-like you th-think. I . . .'

'No, you don't understand,' Lorcan insisted, one hand cupped behind her skull, caressing her. 'You've got to let me take the painting.'

He felt her stiffen. 'Take it?' she asked, her tears drying up instantly. 'Take it where? Why?' she demanded.

'To burn it,' Lorcan said. 'I've got all I need to do it back at the house.'

Frederica wiped the tears off her cheeks, her eyes scanning his face restlessly, searching for signs of deceit. 'Can I come with you?' she asked quietly, her eyes intent and full of fear. If he really wanted to burn the painting, he'd have no objection, would he?

Lorcan frowned. Was she afraid of this man, whoever he was? 'Of course you can come,' he agreed.

'And watch you burn it?' she added persistently.

Lorcan nodded. 'Yes. We'll burn it together,' he agreed eagerly. 'And then we'll be rid of the damned thing.'

Frederica laughed. For one awful moment back there, she'd thought . . . Oh, but she was wrong. Wrong, wrong, wrong!

'All right,' she agreed, getting up.

Lorcan let out a long, wilting sigh of relief and pulled her close. His mouth fastened on hers, hard, strong, hungry.

Frederica melted against him, gloriously happy, her heart singing, her blood pounding. 'Oh, Lorcan,' she murmured, when he finally lifted his head.

His green eyes glinted. 'Come on, let's—' A knock at the door made them both freeze. Lorcan slowly turned his head towards it. 'You'd better see who it is.'

Frederica nodded, and walked to the door. She half-expected to see the now infamous DI Braine standing there, but it was one of the scouts. 'Hello, luv,' she said cheerfully. 'This was in the lodge for you. I thought I'd bring it up, since I was headed this way.' She handed her a letter, casting the handsome man standing behind her a curious, smiling look.

'Thank you, Edie,' Frederica murmured, and closed the door behind her.

She looked down at the envelope and recognised the writing at once. It was her father's. In the left-hand corner he'd written the single word 'urgent'. Frederica opened it, unaware that Lorcan was watching her, his sudden jubilation draining out of him as the old dragon's tooth, jealousy, took a savage bite out of him. Was the letter from the creep who'd dragged her into this? Somehow, he was sure it was. Frederica read her father's letter quickly. It was brief and to the point.

Her mother had been pressing him about the missing Forbes-Wright. He'd told her it was still being cleaned. Should he now admit to selling it, or had Frederica been serious about finishing the painting? He needed to know. Either way, he'd informed their insurance company that the painting had been sold. It was a typical letter from her father — honest and fair. She'd have to ring him up and tell him that yes, he'd have to confess to her mother and take his medicine. She looked up, about to show the letter to Lorcan. To tell him that there was no conman, no deceiver out to make money from her. Just her father, needing a favour. But there was a strange, tight, angry look on his face. A worried look.

'You're not going to do it, are you?' Lorcan said flatly. 'You're not going to let me burn it.'

'No,' Frederica said, with resolve. She couldn't let him do it, especially when she knew she was doing nothing wrong. 'Lorcan . . .' She held a hand out to him, but he was already moving past her.

'Leave it, Frederica,' he said, his voice more weary than she'd ever heard it. 'Just leave it.' He left the door open behind him as he walked away.

165

Frederica rushed forward, about to call him back, and then hesitated. No. She had a much better idea. She'd take the damned painting home. Let Richard Braine's detectives follow her. Then they would all know that she had nothing to hide.

Then she laughed hollowly. She'd been so busy testing Lorcan for loyalty and honesty and trust that she'd forgotten that he had every right to test her.

There'd be no chance of happiness for either of them until they'd proved their love to each other, once and for all.

* * *

The afternoon passed pleasantly for the delegates. Some checked out Oxford's pretty botanical gardens. Others opted for a punting expedition from Magdalen Bridge on the River Cherwell. Some die-hards went Saturday-afternoon shopping.

Reeve and Annis caught the bus back to Squitchey Lane. As they got off and walked hand in hand along the pavement towards their love nest, Annis sighed happily. 'You know, I'm always going to remember Oxford,' she ventured fondly. 'As a place in which to fall in love, we could have done worse, couldn't we?'

Reeve pushed open the gate and dug into his jeans for a key. 'I'd say so.'

Inside, they headed for the conservatory, where the scent of orange blossom hung headily in the moist, hot air. Reeve opened the windows and glass doors as Annis flopped down into a sun lounger. 'Get me a long, tall glass of lemonade, lover, loaded with ice cubes. Please,' she drawled lazily.

Reeve looked down at her, his lips twisted into an amused curve. 'And what did your last servant die of?'

'Sexual exhaustion,' she purred. Reeve felt his breath catch. The minx knew what it did to him when she said stuff like that!

'In that case,' he drawled, 'lemonade coming up.' When he returned a few minutes later with two tall iced glasses full

166

to the brim, he glanced at her. 'Madam's lem . . .' Annis was naked. Lying on the sun lounger, one knee slightly bent, she was leaning back, her black hair splayed against the cheerful red-and-yellow lounger, her breasts already beading with sweat in the humidity. His hand shook, and drops of ice-cold lemonade splashed on to her navel. Her eyes snapped open, and she shuddered.

'Clumsy,' she said, shaking one finger at him. 'For that, you have to be punished. Come here.'

Reeve put down the glasses, his heart leaping about all over the place, and dropped to one knee. 'Don't tell me,' he said huskily. 'Fifty lashes?'

'Something like that,' Annis murmured, her arms looping over his shoulders. 'Why are you wearing so many clothes?'

Reeve shook his head. 'No idea,' he gulped.

'Well, get them off. Uh-uh,' she waved a finger under his nose as he fumbled feverishly with the top buttons of his shirt. 'Slowly. I want to watch.' Her amber eyes glowed as she leaned back, curving one arm behind her head and settling in for the show. Reeve slowly stood up. He eased his feet out of the sandals he was wearing, then slowly unbuttoned the cuffs of the shirt. He pulled the shirt free from his jeans and slowly, from the bottom up, began to unbutton it. Annis's breath caught, making her breasts rise and fall erratically. Reeve's eyes darkened.

Annis was like mercury, he thought dizzily. One moment a spitting cat, the next . . . a sleepy-eyed seductress. Life with her would be a wild rollercoaster ride. Especially if either one of them, or both, made it big in their chosen careers. He knew, too, that he would never be bored. Never get a moment's peace. Never know what she was going to do next. And that was a wonderful prospect. He slipped the shirt from his shoulders, exposing tanned, lightly muscled flesh.

Annis let her mouth fall open, and held out her hand vaguely for the glass.

Reeve, eyes glinting, gave it to her. She took a sip, her eyes never leaving his. 'Lose the jeans, Reeve,' she said huskily. Reeve lost them. For a long moment they froze as they were — Annis, reclining naked on the lounger. Reeve, naked and erect, standing over her. Then Annis slowly got up. Her hair fell over her shoulders as she moved towards him. She reached up and put one hand against his chest, then slowly lowered her head, pulling one hard male nipple into her mouth.

Reeve threw his head back, throat taut, as he stared up at the glass ceiling and the blue cloudless sky above him, before slowly, carefully, pushing her back on to the lounger.

Annis sighed, closing her eyes as his dark head lowered over hers. She arched her back as he repaid the compliment, his tongue licking first one nipple then the other in loving tenderness. She reached up one hand, running it though his dark curls, pushing him down, lower, lower, letting her legs fall apart, and soon her gasps and cries echoed out, filling the conservatory with sound.

* * *

Ray arrived at St Bede's an hour early for dinner, coming in by one of the postern gates on Walton Street. If anyone had seen him, and later, for any reason, happened to remember it, he had the perfect excuse. For tonight was the most dramatic scene in his murder mystery. Tonight, when the delegates entered Hall, it would be to find John Lore slumped theatrically across one of the tables, his head 'bashed in' by a heavy silver candlestick. Naturally, 'the police' would then have the body removed, while everyone — civilised society being what it was — enjoyed a fabulous dinner. With such shenanigans to supervise, he had the ideal excuse for moving around.

Just as he was passing the college clock he recognised the bursar leaving Webster's main doors and heading straight for the lodge. Ray instantly made his decision. He had the lockpick in his briefcase, along with the copy of the Hogarth. There was not a soul in Wallace Quad. He strolled casually across the gravel towards Webster and walked inside.

He felt sick. His skin was sweating, a slick mixture of hot and cold. There was no one in sight as he approached the bursar's office. He slipped on a pair of vinyl gloves and tried the door. It was of course locked. Which meant that there was no one inside. He cast one last glance around, then dropped carefully to one knee and extracted the lockpick from his case. He inserted it, added just the right amount of pressure, turned and . . . *click*.

Ray stood up and looked around again. Nothing and no one. He stepped inside and closed the door quietly behind him within the space of a second or two. For a moment he just stood, looking around the office, taking deep calming breaths. Then he went straight to the cupboard. It too was locked — Ray's trusty lockpick went into action once again. He recognised the heavy, old-fashioned safe instantly, and grinned. It would be no problem.

After three minutes, he was down to the last number. After four, he'd found the combination. He pulled open the safe door, his heart thudding so loudly he felt nauseous. There, among the ledgers, iron petty-cash boxes and papers, the carefully wrapped scroll was instantly recognisable. Ray slowly removed it, his hands shaking just a little as he unwrapped the white linen. He had the Hogarth in his hands. Literally. He yearned to unroll it, to feast his eyes on it, but he knew better. There was no time for that now. He removed the copy from his briefcase and made the exchange.

Having shut the safe and twirled the dial, Ray walked to the door for the final gamble. The last risk. He eased the door open a crack and looked out. Clear. His heart skipping nervously, he pushed the door open and stepped outside. And, with the original painting of Alfred Gore by William Hogarth in his briefcase, Ray Verney walked across Wallace Quad towards Hall, slipping the vinyl gloves into a bin on the way out. Now he would have to sit through the 'murder' scene at dinner with the painting in the case beside him, but he knew his nerves would hold out. They had to.

CHAPTER 22

Sunday, the final day of the conference. In her room, Frederica put the last brush stroke to *The Old Mill and Swans*, not caring if she never saw it again. It was nearly ten o'clock when she left the college to collect a rental car. Outside, a man watched her, then followed.

The city dozed in a typical Sunday morning torpor, as its many clocks and church bells tolled for worship. It was a glorious day, in a glorious city, but Frederica, for once, failed to notice. Instead, she glanced at her watch. If she wanted to, she could be home in time for Sunday lunch. The sooner she was away from here, the better.

Oh, Lorcan, what a mess we made of things, she thought bitterly, as she turned into the premises of the garage.

Behind her, the man following her extracted a mobile phone and made a short call.

Frederica paid for the car, returned to St Bede's, and carefully manoeuvred it into the small car park. She was watched by more than one interested party. Parked in Walton Street on a double-yellow line, a silver Aston Martin was attracting many admiring glances.

Lorcan was just walking through Becket Arch when he saw a familiar red head disappear through Webster's main

170

doors. He paused in the shadow of the arch, a tired blonde Adonis in his blue shirt, navy trousers and jacket.

His eyes roamed around casually. No policemen. They must be parked elsewhere, waiting for her to come out.

Lorcan straightened up, wincing as he watched her emerge, the sheet-covered canvas glaring whitely in the morning sun. Dammit, why didn't she just carry a great big sign saying, 'Here I am, the Forger — Come and Get Me'! The woman's recklessness was enough to make his blood freeze.

He followed her as she disappeared into the car park, watching as Frederica very carefully placed her burden in the back of the spacious vehicle.

* * *

Behind Lorcan, a gang of conference delegates headed for the chapel, curious to experience Oxford college worship for themselves. Inside, Annis was already in place, waiting to enact her big dramatic scene about sitting in a pew which didn't have a radiator next to it.

* * *

Frederica, suddenly remembering she'd left her jar of brushes behind, sprinted back to her room. Lorcan tried the door of the estate car, relieved that she hadn't locked it behind her.

He looked around, very carefully scanning non-college windows, but could see no tell-tale movement. He carefully extracted the canvas, shut the car door behind him, and headed for one of the postern gates that led into the alley.

He quickly checked both ends, and once he was certain that it was deserted, sprinted towards Walton Street. Carefully placing the canvas on to the back seat of his sports car, he covered it with a black and red checked picnic cloth. Then he gunned the engine and roared off just as Frederica returned to the car park. Her footsteps faltered. Where in the hell was the painting?

* * *

In the chapel, everyone rose for the opening hymn, wondering about the significance of Annis's half-hysterical choice of seat. The chaplain's service was simple, reverent and touching, leaving everyone feeling uplifted and relaxed.

Everyone, that is, except Ray. He had his briefcase beside him, and instead of it being innocently empty now, it still contained the Hogarth. As he sang 'Abide with Me' his eyes bored into the back of Carl Struthers' neck, in the pew in front. Ray could cheerfully have strangled him. Right now, the painting could be in his suitcase in the wardrobe back at the Raleigh, as safe as houses. But no. Struthers had rung him this morning demanding to see the painting. Demanding to inspect it. Threatening to withdraw his offer to buy it if Ray refused. Damn him! First he'd insisted on joining the conference, now he was throwing his weight about.

The service came to an end and people began to leave.

'I don't know why you made all that fuss,' Reeve said loudly, glaring at Annis. 'You're a real spoilt brat, you know that?'

Annis glowered back at him. 'I just don't like radiators, that's all,' she snapped, both of them ramming home the clue for the benefit of the late arrivals, who hadn't been there in time to catch it.

Reeve shook his head. 'What's up, Annis dearest? Nerves a bit on edge, hmm? Perhaps you know something about dear John that nobody else does?'

'Oh shut up,' Annis snapped, taking a step back and unintentionally bumping into Ray. Ray, caught half-rising from the pew, found himself knocked forwards, the briefcase falling out of his hand and down on to the hard-tiled floor with a dull thud.

'You're the one John was gunning for, not me,' Annis snapped, desperately ignoring Ray's fumbling. Reeve's eyes glinted as he realised the problem, but they were in no danger of losing their audience! By now everyone was watching them. The conclusion to the murder mystery was tonight, and everyone was determined to get the identity of the murderer right. It had become a matter of principle to everyone, especially the publishers who specialised in books on crime.

Ray watched, aghast, as the locks of the briefcase caught on the side of the pew and snapped open. Annis half-looked down, aware that she'd been clumsy, trying desperately to think of a way to cover it up. Reeve's voice rose magnificently. 'Hah! I know a few things about the dearly departed John that would make your hair curl. And I have a good idea who killed him!' he announced dramatically. All eyes flew to his face.

Ray scrabbled for the briefcase. As he did so, some of the papers became dislodged, revealing the scroll. Out of the corner of her eye, Annis saw it. One end had come undone and unfurled a little, giving her a glimpse of dark, deep oils.

Ray shut the briefcase with a snap and stood up. His face was flushed. He glanced around quickly — luckily, everyone was too busy concentrating on the performance by the two actors to pay any attention to him. But as he turned, he caught Annis's eye, just as she was looking up from the floor. He felt a hard, cold snake of fear lance through him.

If he'd seen the rolled-up painting, so had she!

'Oh that's so much rubbish, Reeve darling,' she purred. 'If you know who killed him, why don't you just tell the police? The inspector is just outside, after all.'

Reeve sneered. 'Don't worry, I will. But first, I just want to check something out,' he said, before leaving, shouldering his way through the thrilled delegates, a look of fury and determination on his handsome face.

Annis shrugged elegantly, smiled at her watching audience, shot Ray a thoughtful look, and left.

Outside, she headed for the lodge and waited for Reeve to catch up with her. She wondered, vaguely, what Ray was doing with a painting in his briefcase. Something to do with the play, probably. Perhaps he'd thought up a last-minute change?

'Hello, you murderous female, you,' a warm voice whispered in her ear, and she jumped and looked around.

'You idiot!' she spluttered at Reeve. 'Don't creep up on me like that. I might extract a dagger from my sleeve and stab you.'

'You? You'd probably miss, you clumsy so-and-so. Don't think I didn't notice you knocking our esteemed director for six.'

Annis laughed. 'I know. Wasn't it awful? Thanks for helping me cover it. Do you think they noticed?'

'I think the men were far too busy watching your flushed cheeks and flashing eyes to notice anything,' Reeve drawled. 'So what did Ray have to say? Did he haul you over the coals or applaud us for our impressive improvisation?'

They had an hour before lunch, and without thinking about it, headed for the Fellows' Garden, which they now thought of as their own, secret sanctuary.

'He didn't say anything, as a matter of fact,' Annis murmured thoughtfully. 'He just stared at me as if he'd seen a ghost.'

They sat down on the warm grass, in the shade of the magnificent silver birches. 'I wonder why he was so shaken?' Reeve said, leaning back on one elbow.

Annis smiled lovingly down at him. 'I've no idea. But when his briefcase fell open, I saw a rolled-up painting. A bit strange, don't you think?'

Reeve opened his eyes and looked at her. Then he frowned. Suddenly he remembered the feeling he'd had when he and Annis had gone to rehearsals in London that day and discovered Ray arguing with someone in the bedroom. He had the same feeling of unease now. The sensation of something being not quite right. And now this. The more he thought about it, the more he didn't like it.

'You know,' he said thoughtfully, 'that painting the college was good enough to take down from Hall is a really valuable picture. You heard what that Fine Art student said.'

Annis scowled. The last thing she wanted to talk about was a girl as pretty as that student. 'I suppose,' she shrugged indifferently. 'But what are you saying? That it somehow found its way into Ray's briefcase?' she laughed. 'That's stretching your imagination a bit too far, isn't it?'

'I suppose so.' Reeve shrugged. 'But, Annis, I don't like this,' he added slowly. 'Something's not quite right.'

'Not quite right . . . ?' she repeated softly, letting two of her fingers walk up his calf.

Reeve swallowed hard. 'Minx,' he muttered thickly. 'Concentrate on the task in hand. You can ravish me later.'

'Promises, promises,' Annis murmured with a grin. And for the next half an hour, neither of them gave the painting in Ray's briefcase another thought.

* * *

Ray was at that moment knocking on Carl Struthers' door. It was opened almost at once.

'You have it?' Struthers demanded the moment Ray stepped through the door.

'Yes, I have it,' Ray snapped back, slinging the briefcase on to the bed and opening it. He extracted the painting and rolled it out on the bed. A look of pure rapture crossed Struthers' face that Ray, for some reason, found distinctly disgusting. Perhaps it was the naked greed that accompanied the look.

'It's magnificent,' Struthers breathed, stroking the painting sensuously, as if it were a cat. 'Wonderful!'

'Glad you like it,' Ray snarled. 'But if you want to take possession now, I have to have the money. Cash, like we agreed.'

Carl straightened. He had a thin face, topped with dark hair and greedy eyes. His thin mouth sneered. 'I'm hardly likely to carry that amount of money around with me.'

Ray nodded, having expected nothing else, and rolled the canvas up again. 'Then we meet in London, as planned.'

'Yes,' Carl said, his eyes burning with the hot flame of obsession. Soon the painting would be all his. 'Things have gone perfectly,' he muttered.

Ray grunted. 'They *were* going perfectly,' he corrected.

Carl Struthers stiffened. 'What do you mean?' his voice cracked like a whip. 'The painting's ours, isn't it?'

'Oh yes, it's ours,' Ray said flatly. 'But your stupidity in having me bring it back here could have cost us dearly. In the chapel, the briefcase was knocked out of my hand. It snapped open,' Ray said, his voice spilling out in a rush. 'Someone saw the scroll.'

'Who?' Struthers hissed like a lizard. 'Who saw it?'

For a moment, Ray had no intention of telling him. Then he saw the look in the avid art collector's eye and gulped. 'Annis Whittington,' he squeaked. 'The pretty actress with the black hair and beautiful eyes. She saw it. But I'm sure she's already forgotten all about it,' he wheedled hopefully.

Carl Struthers said nothing, and Ray, hugging the brief-case to him, all but ran out of the room. It wasn't in his nature to feel ashamed of himself, but as he headed back to the Raleigh to stow the painting, he began to feel worried. Very worried. But, surely, not even Carl Struthers would do anything stupid at this stage?

Back in his room, Carl Struthers stared blankly at a wall. Then his mind filled again with the vision of the Hogarth. So perfect. So utterly exquisite. Nothing must stop him gaining possession of it. Absolutely nothing! And no one.

CHAPTER 23

When Frederica left St Bede's for Lorcan's house, she was livid, and driving far too fast. The two policemen who were following her in a grey car pulled off on to the side of the road at a discreet distance and watched as she marched up to the front door of an impressive white villa. She pushed her finger on the bell and held it there aggressively, fuming.

'Better phone this in to the boss,' the driver of the car said to his companion.

'You think her contact's right here in Oxford then?' the other policeman asked, surprised.

'Could be.'

Detective Inspector Richard Braine, contacted at home just before sitting down to his traditional Sunday roast, ignored his long-suffering wife's indignant look and took the phone call. He recognised the address at once, told his men that it was not the drop-off point, and to keep following Miss Delacroix. Next he rang Lorcan's number. The telephone rang and rang, but the man did not seem to be at home.

Frustrated, Frederica returned to her car and sat there, thinking. Behind her, the policemen waited patiently. He obviously wasn't burning the canvas here then. For she had no doubt whatsoever that it was Lorcan who'd taken *The Old*

Mill and Swans. Could he have gone back to London? She supposed his gallery would have a basement, a room where he could safely burn the painting, far away from prying eyes.

Or perhaps even now he was taking it to the Art Fraud Squad? 'No,' she said aloud. Enough of that. Apart from anything else, the police needed to catch her in possession of the canvas in order to bring charges. The last thing Lorcan would do, if he was still working for the police, would be to steal the painting.

Suddenly, Frederica began to laugh. 'Oh, Lorcan, you crazy, gallant, wonderful fool.' She shook her head, wiping away tears of relief. It was over at last then. Not in the way she'd planned, but then, what did it matter? She could let him have his way this time. She turned on the engine and then thought, where am I going? She'd intended to go home, but now . . . Lorcan would return here, to Oxford, when he was done, of that she was sure. If for no other reason than to confront her and tell her what he'd done. And her room at St Bede's was still officially hers until Monday morning.

She nodded, turned the car round, and headed back to college. She didn't know it, but she had two very puzzled policemen to keep her company on the short journey back.

* * *

In the JCR, Reeve and Norman Rix were doing their big scene, hissing in whispers that no one, no matter how they strained their ears, could quite catch. At one point, Reeve put out a hand and physically restrained Norman from leaving.

Norman shook his head vehemently. As arranged, all the 'employees' of the Oxford Spires Publishing Company stood in one group, and when both Reeve and Norman pointedly looked their way, to the frustration of the delegates, none of them could tell who the two men were looking at. Right on cue, Julie said defensively, 'I know everyone thinks I killed John because he made me have an abortion, but I think there's more than one killer,' she pouted. 'I mean, it stands to reason it would take more than one person to steal the painting. I think those two,' she looked at Reeve and Norman, 'are in this together, and are planning to frame me for it.' And she burst into hysterical tears.

Gerry turned away in scorned wife-turned-widow disgust. Annis patted her arm gently, but looked worried. The delegates conferred. Just after dinner, before the conference finally broke up, the inspector was due to give the final denouement. Before then, everyone had been invited to write down who they thought had killed John, and why. None of them had any idea, as yet, that they were due to be treated to the magnificent spectacle of Reeve being poisoned with the wine!

* * *

Frederica returned to her room, and, with time hanging heavy on her hands, pulled out a paperback, as she waited restlessly for Lorcan to return. She refused to think, even for a moment, that she might never see him again. He was not the kind of man to get out when the going got tough. No. He just got tougher. Half the time she kept an ear cocked, expecting a knock on the door and a burly policeman with a warrant for her arrest.

The afternoon wore on, and there was no knock, but no Lorcan either.

* * *

In the basement of the Greene Gallery in London, Lorcan's eyes glowed orange in the reflected blaze of the burning canvas. Frederica's weeks and weeks of careful planning, sketching and painting went up in flames in a remarkably short time. With the smoke curling up to the ceiling, Lorcan felt the tension slipping away at last. Now Frederica was safe. And the only thing she had to worry about was him.

He would keep her on the straight and narrow if he had to chain her to the bedpost. The thought made his body ache . . .

* * *

By two-thirty, everyone from the conference had already made their way to the park for the scheduled cricket match between the delegates and St Bede's, even the women whose interest in cricket was zero.

The bursar's team, consisting of a few graduates who were still up and several dons, won the toss and elected to bat first for St Bede's. The delegates had assembled a fair team from their own ranks, and soon the very English sound of a cricket match filled the somnolent afternoon air. Several tourists and local families out enjoying the sunshine soon discovered the match and sat on the grass, swelling the audience, clapping politely in all the right places.

'I know nothing about cricket,' one woman confessed to her companion, 'but I could watch it all day if they all looked like him.' She nodded towards Reeve.

The other woman turned to look at Reeve, who was standing nearby ready to field. 'I know what you mean.'

Annis, who was sitting within eavesdropping distance, felt the dual thrill of ownership and jealousy lance through her, and she smiled softly, settling down on the grass, hands tucked behind her head.

They'd be back in London tomorrow. She wondered if he'd ask her to move in with him. It would be nice to get out of her depressing little bedsit. It would be even nicer to have a real life again. Since Reeve had come into it, she was beginning to realise how empty it had been before.

Parked in the shade of a big horse chestnut tree out on the road, a dark-blue Mercedes with darkened windows waited silently. Its number plates had been smeared with mud, making them impossible to read. Inside, Carl Struthers watched the cricket match through the park railings, his fingers drumming impatiently on the edge of the steering wheel. It was baking hot in the car, but he didn't seem to notice. In his mind's eye, he could see again the dark-haired actress, walking hand in hand with her handsome companion, entering the park gates as if she hadn't a care in the world.

His lips thinned. How dare she interfere with his plans. How dare she? Visions of the painting of Alfred Gore swam through his mind. He pictured nights and nights of sitting in the hidden private room which housed his collection, drooling over it in pleasure. Nothing would stop him from doing that. Nothing.

Any threat simply had to be removed. His fingers tightened on the steering wheel. Sweat poured, unnoticed, from his forehead. The afternoon wore on.

* * *

Lorcan poured water into the ashes in the can, watching it dissolve into a grey slush. He then carefully emptied it down the drain. He hadn't dared do this in Oxford. With Richard around, it was best to take no chances.

As the last of the evidence disappeared down the drain, Lorcan let out a huge sigh of relief. It was not quite four o'clock when he got into the Aston Martin and took the now familiar route back to Oxford.

* * *

Reeve made a mad dash, jumped into the air, and squarely caught the cricket ball. The batsman groaned as he was caught out, but left the field in good grace as the umpire indicated that it was time for the teams to change places. Reeve, who had gone to a public school that appreciated cricket, was a fair bowler, and as he began to play, interest in the game markedly perked up.

Outside, in the car, Carl Struthers sweated and waited, his eyes glimmering with dark, obsessive hatred.

On the grass, Annis turned on to her stomach and watched, with amber eyes that glowed, as her lover played cricket.

At the end of their innings, the delegates were winning by a comfortable margin. As the players shook hands with traditional sportsmanship, the spectators began to disperse, and everyone slowly made their way to the park gates and back to their rooms in time to bathe and change for dinner. Annis stayed where she was, and as Reeve walked over to her, she sat up and watched him with a secretive smile.

'Quite the sportsman, aren't we?' she drawled.

Reeve grinned. 'I'm a bit out of practice.'

'Poor baby,' Annis purred, holding out her hand. Reeve helped her up, and casually slung his arm across her shoulders as they walked to the gates, laughing. There, they met a mother with a double-buggy pushchair, taking pretty identical twins through the gates. Annis moved to one side and Reeve to the other to let her through, Annis emerging on to the pavement first.

'Are we going to go back to Squitchey Lane before dinner?' she asked over her shoulder, stepping out on to the deserted road. Reeve, who was still grinning down at the pretty twins, nodded and looked up. 'I think so. We've got a few hours before the final scene.'

'Oh yes, I'm looking forward to poisoning you!' she called cheekily, heading across the road. Somewhere to her left a quiet engine suddenly purred into life.

Carl Struthers moved slowly away from the kerb, lining the woman up in front of him, and then, with a sudden jerk on the accelerator and a jubilant grin on his face, roared towards her. Reeve heard the change in engine pitch at the same time as Annis did. Annis's head swung around, her black hair creating a perfect fan around her head as she swivelled. All she saw was a dark-blue shape bearing down on her at terrific speed.

Carl saw a white oval face and big, shocked eyes. He laughed. She was as good as dead.

Reeve shouted, but even as his agonised voice filled the air with her name, he was already moving. There was a short stretch of grass that led down on to the road, but he didn't even touch it as he leaped over it, landing with a jarring sensation that rattled his teeth. But even then he kept going, moving, diving forward towards Annis, who stood frozen in the road.

Although it had been less than a second it seemed like an eternity. Annis's brain frantically assimilated all sorts of useless data, taking up precious time, as she stood rooted to the spot. She could make out the insignia of the car and thought, dazedly, It's a Mercedes. Her favourite car. It was so close, she could see the tiny chip marks on the front bumper. And then something hit her, propelling her forward with brutal force. She felt the air of the car rush by her legs as she flew forward, and then the heat from the exhaust.

As she hit the tarmac with a painful thump, she heard the squeal of brakes, then the sudden gunning of the motor as the car that had missed her by inches sped away. She was aware of pain then, and a crushing weight upon her, and found herself lying in the middle of the road, Reeve on top of her, holding her tight.

Annis, dazed, felt herself being hauled to her feet. She turned a white, shocked face to find Reeve's face as white as her own. His sapphire-blue eyes were wide with shock and horror. 'Annis, I thought I'd lost you,' he said, his magnificent actor's voice for once dull and devoid of all expression except blank horror.

Suddenly he hugged her close, rocking her back and forth in his arms. 'Annis, for pity's sake, don't ever do that to me again,' he choked out.

Annis closed her eyes. She had nearly died! She hugged him back fiercely, ignoring the bleeding scratches on her arms and legs. 'I won't,' she promised him. 'I won't. Oh, Reeve, I love you so.' Reeve shuddered and continued to hold her, knowing he'd never let her go again.

CHAPTER 24

Reeve carried in a mug of coffee laced liberally with brandy, and brought it to the settee. 'Here, drink this,' he urged her, handing her the steaming brew.

They'd taken a taxi back to Squitchey Lane, and Reeve had insisted on carrying her inside, before going into the kitchen for a hot drink and a bowl of warm water and antiseptic. He tenderly cleaned her grazes, while Annis watched, wincing painfully.

'Don't tell me you're one of those cry babies who can't stand a dab of ointment on a cut without yelling blue murder?' he teased.

Annis stuck her tongue out at him.

'I'll call Ray and tell him you can't do the poisoning scene,' Reeve added, as he reached for the sticking plasters.

'You'll do no such thing,' Annis squeaked and Reeve laughed.

'You've got to be feeling better,' he said. And she was. The brandy had helped chase away some of the coldness of shock.

'I'm fine,' she said. 'At least, fine enough to kill you off.'

Reeve grinned. 'I might have known. You've been looking forward to that from the moment we met, haven't you?' He leaned forward to kiss her tenderly.

Annis smiled as he pulled away, relishing the taste of him on her lips. 'You bet,' she purred. 'Besides, it's the final scene of the play. Of course I want to do it.'

'I still think that nearly getting run over and killed is a reasonable excuse for crying off a performance,' he added, determined to get in the last word. He sat on the floor beside her, his back to the sofa, and stared unseeingly at the fireplace. With his dark curly head so close, Annis couldn't resist the temptation to play with one black curl, and wrapped it around her index finger. Reeve closed his eyes briefly at her touch, then opened them again. In his mind, he replayed the scene of twenty minutes earlier.

'You know,' he said softly, 'that car. It was parked up. I'm sure it was. And how many people normally shoot away from the kerb like that?'

Annis tensed. 'What are you saying?' she asked, her voice suddenly harsh with tension.

Reeve looked up at her and took her hand in his. 'I don't think that what just happened was an accident, Annis. The moment you stepped out into the road, the driver went straight for you, like a guided missile.'

Annis swallowed hard. 'But . . . why would anyone want to kill me? It has to be a mistake. Maybe he lost control of the wheel?' she asked hopefully.

But Reeve shook his head. 'No. Ever since we started this Oxford gig, I've had a niggling feeling at the back of my mind that something isn't quite right. It all started that time we found Ray arguing with someone at rehearsals. Remember?'

Annis nodded miserably. 'You think it's got something to do with Ray?' For a while they both thought of good old roly-poly Ray Verney. It seemed so . . . unlikely.

'Let's think. If someone wanted you out of the way, it was for a good reason,' Reeve said, fighting off the rage that he felt. If he ever got his hands on that damned driver . . .

Annis took a shaky breath. 'OK,' she agreed bravely. 'What have I done, seen, said or what do I know that would upset someone?'

Reeve propped his chin on one of his cupped hands. 'It has to be something recent too, or he would have tried before. Come on, darling, think. Did Ray say anything that made you wonder, at the time? Anything suspicious?'

Annis shook her head. 'The only thing I can think of was when I nearly knocked him flat this morning in the chapel. And you're not going to tell me that made him so enraged he was suddenly overcome with a murderous desire for revenge!'

Reeve suddenly shot upright. 'You said you saw a rolled-up old painting in his briefcase.' He got up and began to pace, his dark-blue eyes glimmering. 'Have you realised,' he mused out loud, 'how this whole murder-mystery weekend — which Ray wrote, produced and organised — all revolves around a missing painting?'

'But that's fiction, Reeve,' Annis chided, though a cold feeling trickled down her back.

'Yes, I know,' he agreed. 'But what's happened because of that fiction? Think painting, Annis. What happened because of us? Because of Ray?'

Annis frowned. 'Nothing. Except that the college was good enough to remove one of their paintings to give the illusion to the conference delegates that it really had gone missing. But, Reeve, it hasn't really gone. The bursar's just moved it somewhere — to his office, probably.'

'And what's the significance of that?' Reeve pounced, his hands shooting out to grip the tops of her arms gently. 'The Hall has to be fitted up with a good alarm system — the insurance company would have insisted on it. But the bursar's office . . .'

Annis suddenly had a brainwave of her own. 'A copy! Reeve, he would have to substitute a copy for the original! That way nobody would even suspect that a switch had been made. The thing I saw in his briefcase must be the copy! He was going to make the switch, and thought I saw it, and . . .'

Her jubilation fled. Someone had tried to kill her. A man she knew, and liked. Suddenly all her strength left her. Reeve moved to the settee and put his arms around her, kissing her neck, nuzzling against her ear. 'I know,' he said softly. 'I know.' For a long, long while, he kissed her, gently, softly, lovingly, restoring her strength and pouring comfort into her through his lips.

Finally Annis leaned back and opened her eyes. 'So. What do we do about it?' she asked, her voice weary with exhaustion.

'We go to the police,' Reeve said flatly.

'I think we should go to the principal first,' she corrected him. 'After all, it's his college, his painting, and, let's face it, we could just be wrong. And nobody would thank us for creating a needless scandal,' she laughed grimly.

Reeve ran a hand through his hair. 'I don't know,' he said cautiously. 'I don't like the thought of you being in danger for a moment longer than you need to be. The police could protect you.'

Annis felt her heart thrill at the protectiveness he was displaying. But she firmly pushed him away and sat up. 'We need to go about this logically,' she said, making his eyes glitter.

Logic? Annis Whittington talking about logic? But he smiled and got up, taking one of her hands into his. 'OK, what do you suggest?'

'Before we do anything else, we need to see the painting in the bursar's office, if indeed that's where it is. We need to find out if it is a copy, or the original. If Ray hasn't made the switch yet, who'd believe us?'

Reeve smiled. 'Good plan, sweetheart. But do you think you could tell an original from a forgery? I know I couldn't.'

Annis scowled, then they both had the same idea at exactly the same time. 'That pretty redhead!' Reeve said.

'That know-it-all student,' Annis drawled, but with a twinkle in her eye. 'Come on, let's go.'

* * *

Lorcan arrived back at Five Mile Drive and poured himself a stiff drink, his mind, as always, returning to Frederica.

* * *

Frederica shot up off the bed as a sharp and urgent hammering on her door split the quiet afternoon air. It was nearly a quarter to six, and she'd been expecting him back long before this.

She quickly trotted to the door and threw it open. 'Lorcan, where have you . . .' Her words trailed off at the sight of the two dark-haired strangers on her doorstep.

'Hello,' Annis said brightly. 'I don't suppose you remember us, but we're with the group of actors who are putting on the murder mystery here?'

Frederica blinked. 'Oh. Yes, yes of course. You asked about the Hogarth.'

Reeve nodded. 'That's right. I know this is going to sound . . . well . . .' he shot Annis a half-worried, half-amused look, 'kind of hysterical, if not downright unbelievable. But . . . well . . . we were wondering if you could help us.'

'The thing is,' Annis broke in, 'we think that someone has made a copy of the Hogarth and switched it for the real one, while it was in the bursar's office or wherever he was keeping it.'

Frederica's eyes widened. 'I think you'd best come in and start from the beginning,' she said, opening the door and inviting them inside. And as she listened to their story, Frederica began to feel sick with excitement and fear. Because she knew something these two actors didn't. She knew the police had had a tip-off that 'something big' was going down at Oxford. And if stealing a Hogarth from St Bede's wasn't big, then what the hell was?

When they'd finished, Frederica was thinking furiously. 'You don't believe us, do you?' Reeve asked flatly.

Frederica shook her head. 'No. I mean, yes, I do believe you . . .' She shot up. 'We've got to go and see the principal — at once.'

Reeve gave Annis the thumbs-up sign, and together they followed Frederica to Sin-Jun's office, where Frederica, as a member of the college, felt obliged to be the one to tell the tale. But once she began to talk, the story didn't sound quite as far-fetched as it might, and when she had finally finished, the principal looked so grim that there was little doubt that he believed them.

'I think we'd better get the bursar and have a look at this painting of ours,' he said at once, and rose from behind his impressive desk.

The bursar also had rooms in the college, and once the principal grimly filled him in, they all hurried to his office in Webster. Frederica, trailing at the end of the procession, wondered if she was up to this. Could she tell a fake from the real thing? Painting a fake was one thing, but detecting one was something else altogether!

The bursar opened the safe, watching as Sin-Jun extracted the canvas of Alfred Gore and unrolled it on the table.

'Well, Miss Delacroix?' the principal asked quietly, stepping aside to let her get a good look.

Frederica studied it. It certainly looked like a Hogarth original. But then, it would, wouldn't it? She reverently carried it to where the bright June sunlight streamed through the windows, and inspected the painted head again. There, on the eye . . . She leaned closer, touched the oils. Was the bottom layer just a fraction too liquid? The brushstrokes definitely looked like those of Hogarth. But were they? She felt a frisson of . . . something . . . atavistic . . . climb up her spine.

It just didn't feel right. She turned to look at her principal. 'Sir,' she said softly, 'I don't think this is the original.'

'But you're not sure?'

'No, sir,' Frederica said honestly, knowing how important it was to be honest. 'But I know a man who will be able to tell you.'

Sin-Jun nodded. 'The visiting fellow at the Ruskin? The one the police sent down here because of this . . . tip-off?'

Frederica nodded. 'I can ask him to come over. Nobody knows more about forgeries than Lorcan Greene,' she assured them.

Sin-Jun nodded. 'Very well. But don't tell him why,' he added hastily. 'I don't think it would be . . . prudent to speak of such matters on the public telephone.'

As she dialled, the principal turned to the two actors. 'Since you are in danger, Miss Whittington, I think it best if you give this Mr Verney no reason for further worry.'

Reeve's eyes narrowed. 'Meaning what, exactly?'

'Meaning, you have a final scene to do at dinner tonight, isn't that correct? Then I think you should carry on as if you suspect nothing. As if you know nothing.'

Reeve nodded. It made sense. He glanced at Annis. 'You up to it?' he asked anxiously, but Annis grinned back.

'Of course. Besides, we'll be surrounded by the others, as well as all the delegates. He's hardly likely to do anything silly with all those witnesses around is he?'

And so Reeve and Annis left to prepare for their final scene, not knowing that it was not Ray Verney they had to worry about.

Over the telephone, Frederica could hear Lorcan's number begin to ring.

And in his room, Carl Struthers neatly tied his bow tie, and smiled at his reflection in the mirror.

So, he had missed this afternoon. There was always the next time.

CHAPTER 25

Annis and Reeve cautiously entered the Hall, which was full of excited chatter and the clink of cutlery against porcelain. Tonight, dinner was to be served by the scouts.

Annis, wearing a sleeveless black dress, took a deep breath, felt Reeve squeeze her hand in a quick gesture of support, and then swept across to join the others at Oxford Spire Publishing Company.

'You look ravishing,' Norman Rix said at once. Annis opened her mouth to answer him, then looked up as Ray Verney took his seat almost opposite her, and the words died in her throat.

Ray beamed at everyone. 'All set for the big scene and denouement?'

'You bet,' Gerry said, taking a sip of the wine a scout had just poured out. 'Hey, great plonk.'

Annis forced herself to relax. Not easy, but she knew the principal was right. Ray mustn't suspect anything. She must give him no reason to panic. Beside her, she felt Reeve too make a determined effort to smile and to keep his eyes from straying to Ray.

The first course was served: melon boat. As she reached for her spoon, Julie noticed the plaster on Annis's elbow.

'Hey, what did you do to yourself?' she murmured, flicking Annis's arm lightly. 'Hurt yourself?' Ray, catching it, looked up quickly. Reeve caught the movement, and saw the strangest look cross Ray's face.

'Oh that,' Annis laughed. 'Clumsy so-and-so that I am, I took a header on the pavement outside Reeve's place. Scraped my knees too,' she added lightly. 'They don't half sting!'

Beside her, one part of Reeve was admiring her courage and acting ability, but another part of him was focused grimly on Ray Verney. The funny thing was, he didn't look guilty. Or put out. Or even nervous.

He looked scared.

Perhaps he knew they were on to him. And yet . . . Reeve took a sip of his wine. No, there was something not right here. Everything in him was telling him that Ray was not behaving like a man who had tried and failed to kill someone. In fact, when Julie had mentioned the word 'accident' he'd looked surprised. And worried. For a man who'd just supposedly tried to run her down . . .

'I've got that information you wanted, Reeve,' Norman Rix said, so loudly that it must have been his second time saying it.

Guiltily, Reeve realised he'd missed his cue. He turned to Norman. 'Oh? Was I right?'

Annis, hearing her own cue, reached down into her bag. 'You know, I think I'll take some aspirin,' she murmured, but loudly enough for everyone at her table to hear her. She had noticed, but hadn't really taken in, that Gerry had said her piece and snaffled a gulp of Reeve's wine, as in the script.

'Yes, you were right,' Norman Rix said loudly. 'But I don't see what you hope to gain by it. What does it prove?'

By now, several delegates, who were just being served the main course by beaming scouts, looked across at them, patently interested.

'Geraldine, can I borrow your glass of water?' Annis said loudly. Luckily, she'd remembered to empty her own glass of water before Norman Rix's cue.

'Course,' Gerry disinterestedly nudged her water glass a little further over.

'Thanks,' Annis said, reaching across, and making sure her palm went straight over the top of Reeve's glass.

Ray pretended not to notice, but he scowled thoughtfully at Annis's elbow with its sticking plaster. She said she'd fallen. Perhaps she had. Perhaps he'd just mistaken the murderous look in Carl Struthers' eyes that morning? He took a gulp of his wine, and couldn't help but look across the room, over to Struthers' table.

Reeve noticed him give someone behind him a strange, fulminating look, and felt his heart miss a beat. Again he had that strange feeling that there was something else going on that he didn't know about. He fought the urge to look over his shoulder, even as he felt a prickling in his spine, as if he was being watched. Or Annis, sitting next to him, was being watched . . . He wondered whether that art expert Frederica Delacroix put so much store in had arrived yet. And if he had, whether he agreed with her opinion that the painting had already been switched with a copy.

* * *

In the bursar's office, Sin-Jun, the bursar himself and Frederica all seemed to hold their breath. Lorcan, responding at once to the controlled urgency in her voice, had come to St Bede's straight away.

Sin-Jun himself had met him at the lodge and brought him to the office, explaining on the way the story the two actors and one of his Fine Art students had related to him.

Lorcan had been stunned at first. Numbly he'd confirmed that he was indeed working for the police, and that a certain Inspector Richard Braine of the Art Fraud Squad really had been tipped off that some big art forgery was going to be perpetrated in Oxford this summer. None of which made Sin-Jun feel any better. When they'd walked into the office, Frederica's eyes had gone straight to Lorcan's face. He

looked pale, angry and . . . hopeful, all at once. She understood how he felt. Somehow, uncovering the real plot, right
here at St Bede's, in some strange way vindicated them.

'This is it?' Lorcan had said, making straight for the
painting and taking it into the strong sunlight. And then, for
ten minutes, he had simply looked at it, covering every tiny
inch with intense, sharp-eyed scrutiny. He hadn't spoken so
much as a single word in all that time. Now, the tension in
the room was reaching breaking point. And when Lorcan
slowly looked up, the others held their breath.

Lorcan looked first at Frederica, then at Sin-Jun. 'Lord
Roland,' he said flatly, 'this painting is a forgery. A very good
forgery, but I think X-rays and radiocarbon dating will prove
it beyond any shadow of a doubt.'

Sin-Jun blinked once and slowly nodded. 'I see. This
Inspector Braine . . . would you be so good as to call him?'

Lorcan nodded and reached for the telephone. Luckily,
Richard was still at home. 'Richard,' Lorcan said, after the
inspector's long-suffering wife had handed the phone over to
him, 'Lorcan here. I have something for you . . .'

* * *

Upstairs, Reeve clutched his throat, holding his breath so that
his face turned dark red. He half-stood, making just enough
noise to stop every other diner in the Hall in mid-chew. He
clutched the tablecloth dramatically. Julie screamed, her high-
pitched, terror-filled yodel making chills run up the spines of
nearly everyone there. Reeve slowly folded up, toppled side-
ways off his chair, and lay in a theatrical heap on the floor.
Gordon shot up. 'Nobody move!' he bellowed ominously.

He got up and felt the pulse. 'Dead,' he said dramatically. 'Poisoned.'

The conference delegates buzzed with conversation. The
scouts smiled and prepared to serve the pudding.

* * *

194

Downstairs, in the bursar's office, Lorcan beckoned Frederica to the door. 'If you don't mind, Lord Roland,' he murmured politely, 'Richard will be here in about an hour. In the meantime, I'd like to have a word with Miss Delacroix?'

Sin-Jun waved a hand. 'Of course.' He walked to the forgery and stood examining it, shaking his head in disbelief.

Outside, Lorcan took Frederica's hand and pulled her away from the office. 'Come on, let's go to your room. I want to talk to you,' he commanded. They said nothing until they were in the sanctuary and privacy of her room. Then he turned, looking at her, his hands stuffed deeply into his pockets.

The evening was heavy with the promise of a thunderstorm, and Frederica felt the silence like a physical thing. She took a step or two closer to him, wanting to hold him, but not sure yet that she could.

'Do you know this Ray Verney character those actors talked about?' he asked finally. But there was no accusation in his voice. No doubt. He was just asking, to get it over with.

Frederica shook her head. 'Never heard of him,' she said honestly.

'You know I've burned your own forgery, don't you?' he said, his eyes scanning hers for any sign of pain or reaction.

Frederica nodded. 'I guessed as much.'

Lorcan's tense shoulders slowly relaxed. He ran a hand through his hair and sighed. 'I don't get it,' he said softly. 'If this Hogarth scam was what Richard was after all the time, what the hell were you doing painting a copy of the Forbes-Wright?'

Frederica smiled. 'I told you. I was doing a favour. For my father,' she added, as he began to frown.

Lorcan blinked at her, then swallowed hard. 'Your father? What's he got to do with this?'

Frederica smiled. He looked so . . . confused. She was sure it was a new experience for him, and although she felt a twinge of sympathy, she also felt a twinge of satisfaction. It did men good, once in a while, not to have things all their own way. 'As you'll no doubt soon find out,' she said softly, taking another few steps towards him, 'we owned the original Forbes-Wright. It was in our collection all the time. Then Daddy had to sell it to pay for a big roof repair. But he didn't tell my mother. So he asked me to make a copy. That was all. It sounds weird, but if you knew my mum and dad . . .' she shrugged. 'Anyway, he wanted the copy to hang on our wall in place of the original.' She smiled and held out her hands in a gesture of helplessness. 'There was nothing more sinister to it than that. There never was.'

Lorcan stared at her. A darkness began to gather on his face, like a thundercloud, building first in his eyes.

'But when I learned who you were,' she added hastily, 'and that you were . . . well . . . after me,' Frederica hurried on, not at all sure she liked the gleaming, glittering look that was coming to life in his eyes, 'I was so mad and . . . and hurt.'

Lorcan took a step towards her. 'Are you telling me,' he said softly, his voice ominously low, 'that you put us through all this,' he hissed, 'because . . .'

'Because I thought you'd seduced me, and made love to me, and told me you loved me just so that you could help the police arrest me,' Frederica put in harshly. 'Yes, I suppose I am.'

Lorcan, whose hands had been clenching and unclenching, suddenly froze. His face had gone dreadfully pale. He shook his head. 'Oh, hell, Frederica,' he said quietly, appalled. 'You thought that?'

Frederica smiled weakly. 'What else could I think?'

He shook his head, then slowly sank down on to her bed. He dropped his hands between his knees and leaned down, staring at the carpet. Again he shook his head. He closed his eyes, a picture of misery that pierced her to the heart. With a small cry, Frederica ran to him, dropping to her knees in front of him. She reached up, pushing back the wheat-coloured locks of hair that fell across his temples, looking up into his hazel eyes that had his heart in them.

'But I don't think so now, Lorcan. I know you love me,' she whispered. 'And I love you.' She reached up and kissed him, her arms coming around him, holding him close as he slowly, slowly, pulled her on to the bed beside him.

* * *

Upstairs, Gordon pointed his quivering finger at Annis. 'So you see, Miss Thorndyke, it could only have been you! As I said earlier, no glass-cutting equipment was found in any of the rooms, and only you wore a diamond big enough to cut the glass case around the painting. And only you could have put the poison into Mr Reeve Scott's wine glass.'

Annis tossed back her mane of dark hair and let a sneer cross her face. Around them, the delegates burst into spontaneous applause as Gordon marched her out of Hall.

'Pity we couldn't have stayed for the pudding,' Gordon said prosaically as they were going down the stairs. 'I wonder if Reeve will have the gall to revive himself and tuck into the sherry trifle?'

'Probably, if I know him,' Annis laughed. 'Look, Gordon, I've just got to go and see someone.'

Gordon nodded. 'I think I'll go back up. Tell them you're on your way to clink. I don't see why I have to forgo the trifle as well.' And with a cheery wink, he left her.

Annis smiled, but the moment he'd turned his back, she rushed across Wallace Quad and towards the bursar's office. There she found the police had just arrived. For the next half an hour she answered question after question about Ray Verney, telling them what she knew. Which, all in all, wasn't much.

As Annis was being interviewed by the police, Carl Struthers slipped out of the dining hall and drove to Squitchey Lane. The sound of breaking glass made a dog bark, but nobody came out to see what had excited him. Once inside the house, all Carl had to do was to pick his spot and wait.

He took off his dark red silk tie and twisted it around both hands, drawing it tight. It made a very chic garrotte.

* * *

Lorcan and Frederica stepped into the bursar's office, which was now crammed with people. DI Richard Braine looked at Lorcan, and then at the dewy-eyed, swollen-lipped beauty beside him and smiled. Nobody could be happier than Richard that things were working out so well for them.

'Right then,' Richard said softly. 'I think it's time we arrested our man of the moment, Mr Verney. Johnson, nip over to the Raleigh and see if the original painting isn't stowed away under a mattress or in the wardrobe. Miss Whittington, we won't need you any more at this stage,' he turned towards Annis, 'but tomorrow, we'll ask you to make and sign a formal statement. Do you have somewhere to stay tonight?'

Annis nodded. 'Yes, a place in the north of the city.' She suspected Reeve had stayed upstairs to keep an eye on Ray, and hoped he wouldn't be long coming home. She couldn't wait to compare notes.

A policeman very kindly offered to give her a ride to the house.

CHAPTER 26

Annis got out of the police car, thanked the driver and walked up the path towards the house. Inside, Carl Struthers moved to the window, the tie in his hand tightening convulsively. He had no idea of the events unfurling back at St Bede's. Of Ray Verney's arrest, or the collapse of the scam. And if he'd known that, even at that very moment, the original Hogarth was being retrieved from Ray Verney's room at the Raleigh, he'd have been furious.

But as he listened to Annis using her key to unlock the front door he felt remarkably calm and cool. This time, there would be no mistake. This time, he wouldn't fail. And if it was that dark-haired lover of hers instead, he'd just have to take him down first.

* * *

Back at St Bede's, Lorcan and Frederica quickly answered Richard's few remaining questions, and when Lorcan finally explained about the mix-up over the Forbes-Wright, Richard burst into laughter. He couldn't help it. It was just so funny. After a moment or two, first Frederica and then Lorcan had to join in.

* * *

Reeve looked up at the moon as he stepped through St Bede's big wooden doors and on to the pavement. Although he'd always remember Oxford as the place where he'd fallen in love, he wouldn't be sorry to leave.

He turned, watching as a police car pulled out and headed towards Kidlington and the Thames Valley Police Headquarters. In the back, Ray Verney, sitting next to Richard Braine, caught his eye only briefly. Then he was gone.

Reeve watched the car disappear out of sight and then raised his hand quickly as a taxi cruised past. As he leaned back in his seat, Reeve dragged in a sigh of relief. At last, it was all over. He'd thought tonight was never going to end. Now all he wanted to do was get back to Annis.

* * *

Annis switched on the hall light and stepped inside, shutting the door behind her. She hummed a tune under her breath as she put the keys in an ashtray on the hall table and walked through to the kitchen. There she put on the kettle, reached up for some cups, sugar and instant coffee, then moved towards the fridge.

But as she turned, the hairs on the back of her neck stood on end. A dark shape, seen out of the corner of her eye, had her swinging around. A man, a perfect stranger, stood in the kitchen doorway staring at her. No, not a stranger, she thought, in the next instant. I've seen him before. At St Bede's. A conference delegate.

'Who . . . ?' Annis said weakly.

* * *

In the back of the police car, Ray Verney stared out of the window at the passing scenery. It would be his last glimpse of freedom for quite some time, that much he already knew.

'Carl Struthers,' he said suddenly, making Richard jump. For he'd just remembered something else. Struthers hadn't been in Hall when he'd been arrested. He'd left some time earlier. Not long after Annis Whittington had made her grand exit in fact . . . Something cold and ugly snaked down his spine. 'Oh hell,' he said, going white. 'That girl, Annis Whittington. I think . . . I think she's in danger.'

As Ray was telling Richard Braine all about his client, and giving the policeman an alibi for the time of the attempted hit-and-run, Reeve's taxi was headed at a stately thirty miles per hour up the Woodstock Road, well within the city's speed limit. Reeve, leaning back and letting the tension drain out of him, wondered if Annis would be agreeable to him giving her a massage. He'd bought some scented oil just yesterday. He smiled dreamily.

* * *

Annis backed away from the doorway, putting the kitchen table between them as Carl Struthers ominously closed the door behind him. It was then that Annis noticed the tie, taut and deadly, stretched between his two hands. She didn't know who he was, but she knew, in an instant of sickening clarity, that Ray Verney was not in this thing alone.

And as the fanatical art collector walked slowly towards her, backing her further and further away from the door and any possible escape route, she also knew that it hadn't been Ray behind the wheel of that Mercedes this afternoon. And she opened her mouth to scream.

* * *

Richard ordered a squad car to Squitchey Lane immediately. Then he looked across at Ray Verney. His eyes glittered in the passing streetlamps and his voice was cold, hard and flat when he spoke. 'I hope for your sake that they're on time,' he said simply.

Ray Verney swallowed hard. He hoped so too.

* * *

Reeve got out of the taxi and turned, digging into his pockets for change. The next instant a woman's scream rent the calm Oxford night air. It was the scream of a trained actress — a woman accustomed to using her voice as a tool, who understood projection of sound, breathing techniques and lung power. The scream filled the air with its terrified pitch, penetrating through the walls of the house, making even the taxi driver jump.

'Bloody hell, what's that?' he muttered.

But Reeve already knew what it was. It was Annis. And she was in trouble! He sprinted up the drive as the taxi driver scrabbled for his own cab radio to ask his office to call the cops. He gave the address and then slowly, reluctantly, got out of his cab. Reeve had already disappeared inside.

In the kitchen, the sound of her scream made Carl Struthers flinch. 'Shut up, you interfering . . .' he growled, moving quickly around the table.

Annis, thinking furiously, made a feint to her left, saw him move to intercept, then ran swiftly to her right, heading for the kitchen drawer where she knew an array of sharp knives waited. She sobbed as she scrabbled at the drawer handle, got it open and reached inside for a knife.

And suddenly she saw a red flash in front of her eyes, felt herself being pressed hard and painfully against the kitchen unit as Carl Struthers slammed into her from behind. Then she felt a cool silky strip of material tighten around her neck. Her body went cold. She gasped, then choked, as the air was suddenly, horrifyingly, cruelly cut off.

She felt her head begin to pound. And then, over the roaring of the blood in her ears, she heard an outraged yell. Carl Struthers jerked around, his grip on his victim loosening in surprise. Annis managed to drag in a small but life-saving gulp of air as Reeve launched himself across the room.

Reeve took Carl in a flying rugby tackle, knocking the publisher away from her as they both crash-landed against a washing machine. Reeve grunted in pain as his shoulder connected painfully with a knob. Carl let out a blood-curdling yell and swung a fist.

Annis looked up, eyes streaming with tears of fright and pain, just in time to see Reeve duck below the punch, get up on his knees and land a punch of his own squarely on Struthers' jaw. Struthers went down, bashing his head on the way, slackening enough for Reeve to straddle the man's chest and pin his arms to the floor — as far as he was concerned, this bastard was going nowhere.

'Annis, call the police *now*,' Reeve demanded. Seeing her frozen to spot, still in shock, he tried more softly to coax her into action, praying the man underneath him would remain woozy for a few minutes longer. 'Annis, sweetheart, come on, you can do this. I need you to do this for me, darling . . .'

Annis finally began to move, slowly at first, and then more swiftly as she began to register the danger they might both be in if Reeve couldn't keep him restrained. She pulled herself to her feet and made for the phone, but before she could pick up the receiver blue lights were flashing outside the window. Reeve gave an audible sigh of relief, and mentally thanked his quick-thinking taxi driver. Within seconds, the room was full of blue-uniformed men. One of them reached for Reeve, dragging him up with hard hands under his armpits.

Annis tried to protest, but her voice was nothing more than a hoarse croak. But she needn't have worried. The other policeman had gone straight for Carl Struthers and was now holding on to him as Struthers struggled and swore furiously.

Reeve shrugged off the hold on him and flew straight to Annis, who was kneeling on the floor, wide-eyed, shaking and battered. She held out her arms as he raced to her, dropping on to his knees in a skidding thud on the slick kitchen tiles, and gathered her close. She sobbed into his chest as the two policeman handcuffed and took the struggling art collector away. Reeve held her for a long, long time.

* * *

Monday morning brought heavy thunder and rain.

At Squitchey Lane, it wasn't the remembrance of the night's terrors that came back first to Annis Whittington, but the gentle, tender, wonderful lovemaking she and Reeve had shared into the early hours of the morning. She stretched, enjoying the somnolent, boneless feeling a woman has when she's just spent a night with the lover of her dreams.

'Good morning,' Reeve said cheerfully, pushing the door open and walking in with a tray of freshly squeezed orange juice, steaming hot coffee and a bowl of porridge.

'Porridge?' Annis said, sitting up. 'I was expecting smoked salmon and French toast at the very least.'

Reeve grinned as he put the tray on her lap. 'I thought porridge would be easier to get down,' he said casually, and kissed her tender throat. Annis swallowed back the desire to cry. His thoughtfulness cut her to the quick. It was so rare in a man.

'Well,' she said, leaning back against the headboard and raising one of her dark eyebrows in query, 'just what does a lady say to the man who saved her life?'

Reeve stretched out on the bed beside her and grinned. 'She says yes,' he responded softly.

Annis's other eyebrow shot up. 'Yes?' she echoed. 'Yes to what? You've already had your wicked way with me — most of the night, as I seem to remember.'

Reeve grinned. 'True.'

'So,' she persisted, 'what must I say yes to?'

'A question, of course,' he said, bending down to kiss her knee through the quilt.

Annis smiled. 'Ah. Well now, it depends on what the question is,' she said reasonably, 'doesn't it?'

Reeve looked up at her. His dark curls were damp, as if he'd showered before making breakfast. His oh so handsome face was sober. His dark-blue eyes were like sapphires, sparkling and precious to her.

'Will you marry me?' he asked softly.

Annis blinked. 'What?'

'Will you marry me?'

'Yes.'

'See,' he said. 'I told you you'd say yes.'

* * *

Lorcan Greene turned off the windscreen wipers as they finally drove out of the storm.

'Mum and Dad are expecting us,' Frederica said, as she wound down her window. 'I called them just before we left.'

Lorcan nodded. 'Good. I want to have a word with your father,' he said ominously.

Frederica turned her head towards him. Her hair was back in its usual ponytail, and the sunlight was sparking little flames off it. Her freckles stood out like so many tiny beauty spots, begging to be kissed individually, and he had to drag his eyes from her or run them into a ditch. As they approached Cross Keys, Lorcan reached out and took her hand in his. 'Feeling OK?' he asked.

Frederica laughed. 'Why shouldn't I be?' Last night they'd slept together the whole night through in her narrow college bed, Frederica curled up against his chest like a little ginger cat. It had been the first time she'd ever slept with the sound of a man's heartbeat pulsing in her ears, and knew it was how she wanted to sleep for ever after.

They turned down the drive and pulled up outside Rainbow House. As he turned off the Aston Martin's purring engine, he turned to look at her. 'Well, here we are,' he said softly.

Frederica sighed. 'I suppose we'd better face the music. Dad will be disappointed we don't have the painting with us.'

Lorcan smiled mysteriously and got out of the car. He walked round and opened the door for her, helping her out.

'Your father,' he said, pulling her to her feet, 'will have other things to worry about.'

'Oh?' Frederica asked curiously. 'Like what, for instance?'

'Like whether or not he'll have to sell off another painting in order to pay for his daughter's wedding,' Lorcan said. 'Not that he will. I thought we'd go for something quiet and simple. At the church here, of course,' he added, turning to look at Cross Keys parish church tower, nestling in a dell of red horse chestnut trees. 'A few guests — no more than thirty or so, I should think,' he carried on, his voice soft and thoughtful. 'I've got a friend who'd design and make your wedding dress . . .'

Frederica leaned weakly against the Aston Martin.

'And for a honeymoon . . . Tahiti? Step in Gauguin's footsteps?' He turned, smiling at the stunned look on her face. 'Well, after all this, you didn't think I was going to let you get away from me, did you?' he asked, his voice not quite teasing, not quite threatening. But nearly.

Frederica felt her heart thump. He was so damned arrogant. So damned sure of himself. So out of her league . . . Except that now, he wasn't out of her league at all.

'Tahiti sounds nice,' she mused. 'But since we Delacroixs are temporarily impoverished, I think we can forget tradition and you can pay for the wedding.'

Lorcan grinned. 'Done.'

'I think I have been,' Frederica said drolly, but she was already reaching up for him.

Obediently, he took her in his arms and kissed her.

He was still kissing her when Donna and James Delacroix, alerted by the sound of the car, stepped outside on to the porch.

'Well!' Donna said, for once speechless.

Frederica looked across at her parents and sighed. 'Poor old Dad. She'll kill him when he tells her he's sold *The Old Mill and Swans*,' she said ruefully.

Lorcan put his arm around her, and together they turned to walk to the house. 'Well,' Lorcan said, 'you could always paint him another copy.'

Frederica stopped dead in her tracks, her head snapping around to look up at him.

'What?' she squeaked.

He looked down at her dark velvety eyes, freckled nose and a mouth gone slack with shock.

He burst into laughter.

'Oh, Frederica,' he crowed, 'you should see your face!'

THE END

ALSO BY FAITH MARTIN

DI HILLARY GREENE SERIES

Book 1: MURDER ON THE OXFORD CANAL
Book 2: MURDER AT THE UNIVERSITY
Book 3: MURDER OF THE BRIDE
Book 4: MURDER IN THE VILLAGE
Book 5: MURDER IN THE FAMILY
Book 6: MURDER AT HOME
Book 7: MURDER IN THE MEADOW
Book 8: MURDER IN THE MANSION
Book 9: MURDER IN THE GARDEN
Book 10: MURDER BY FIRE
Book 11: MURDER AT WORK
Book 12: MURDER NEVER RETIRES
Book 13: MURDER OF A LOVER
Book 14: MURDER NEVER MISSES
Book 15: MURDER AT MIDNIGHT
Book 16: MURDER IN MIND
Book 17: HILLARY'S FINAL CASE
Book 18: HILLARY'S BACK

JENNY STARLING MYSTERIES

Book 1: THE BIRTHDAY MYSTERY
Book 2: THE WINTER MYSTERY
Book 3: THE RIVERBOAT MYSTERY
Book 4: THE CASTLE MYSTERY
Book 5: THE OXFORD MYSTERY
Book 6: THE TEATIME MYSTERY
Book 7: THE COUNTRY INN MYSTERY

MONICA NOBLE MYSTERIES

Book 1: THE VICARAGE MURDER
Book 2: THE FLOWER SHOW MURDER
Book 3: THE MANOR HOUSE MURDER

GREAT READS
THE LYING GAME
AN OXFORD REVENGE
AN OXFORD SCANDAL
AN OXFORD ENEMY
AN OXFORD SECRET
AN OXFORD FRAUD

More coming soon!

Join our mailing list to be the first to hear about
NEW FAITH MARTIN releases!

www.joffebooks.com

FREE KINDLE BOOKS

Made in the USA
Monee, IL
09 November 2020